THE SENSORIANS

TRUST

Brigitte Morse-Starkenburg

To Julia,
Thank you so much for
your fabulous review!
Much appreciated!

First published in 2020

© Copyright 2020
Brigitte Morse-Starkenburg

The right of Brigitte Morse-Starkenburg to be identified as
the author of this work has been asserted by her in
accordance with the Copyright, Designs and Patents Act
1988.

Cover art: © 2020 Miquel Gonzalez Lumigo-film

This book is a work of fiction and any resemblance to actual
persons, living or dead, is purely coincidental.

PROLOGUE

"Tom, it's me," a man whispered, not to scare his friend. He was hidden amongst some random stacks of wood on what looked like an abandoned farm yard. It was dark but the two men didn't seem to have a problem seeing each other. Tom joined the other man, a little reluctantly to an outside observer.

"You have one chance Tom. Come back with me, show your regrets and they will be lenient. They promised," the man pleaded.

"I can't. I have gone too far. I have betrayed you all. I'm over the age; they will kill me. That's the rule. They won't break it for me," Tom sounded exhausted and defeated.

"But they may for me. It's worth the chance Tom. Please. I'm sure they will consider it, but only if you come now," the man tried again.

"Consider it! That's not a guarantee! I'm scared, man." Tom wasn't convinced at all. He had broken the number one rule of the community and he feared he would have to pay for it with his life. He was tempted to give himself up and go with his friend, as he was tired of hiding and running. But he didn't trust Valentino to be lenient.

Footsteps approached. Both men recognised immediately who it was. Tom stiffened in fear.

"Markus? Did you follow me?" the other man questioned indignantly.

"I needed to know you were safe. You can't trust Tom. You know that," Markus replied self-assured.

The man stood up and inched himself forward to square up to Markus.

"I trust him with my fucking life. He's my best friend."

Markus put both his hands on the man's shoulders.

"So am I, Rick. So am I. But I don't want you dragged any further into this fucking mess. I've told Valentino everything. I don't want you going down with Tom."

Rick looked back at the space where Tom sat only seconds ago. He was gone, his scent still lingering. Rick ran after the trail, now shouting at the top of his lungs. His friend had signed and sealed his own death sentence. Rick sank to his knees and screamed Tom's name once again. There was no way he could escape them forever. Valentino wouldn't stop until he was captured and sentenced.

CHAPTER 1
Zaphire

"Aaaargh. That girl never learns! She's doing my fucking head in!" Zack growled when he stormed into my room.

"What's she done now?" I asked, more out of obligation than anything else. I was still in bed, having passed my fitness test nearly a month ago, so I didn't have to get up at the crack of dawn to attend the extra classes, unlike Zack.

"She bloody overslept. Again! How you can sleep through three wake up calls is beyond me," he exclaimed in utter frustration, flopping down on my sofa.

"Ugh, you need a shower. Get your sweaty arse off my furniture, brother!" I grumbled, which he completely ignored and carried on with his tirade.

"I've had to take her TV privileges away and her hour of outside time for two days in a row now. She'll be climbing up the walls by tomorrow. Plus I had to do a double session of exercise as I was late for mine because of her, which I could really have done without!"

"Stop whinging. How's she doing with her exams? Are they nearly done?" I tried changing the subject, now nearly fully awake and clambering out of bed to make us a cup of coffee.

"Yeah, she seems confident with them. She's only got one more to do tomorrow afternoon. Thank God, as invigilating those three hour exams are the most boring thing ever. I wish I could have farmed that job out. It's like being in isolation myself, for fuck's sake," he carried on, still in a foul mood.

"Only three more days to go now, grumpy. Then she'll be out."

I passed him a cup of steaming hot coffee.

"You look like you can do with one."

"Thanks Zaph. Yeah, three days left. Although I threatened to add another one if she overslept again. Fingers crossed that won't happen."

He took a big sip of his coffee and closed his eyes. I groaned.

"Not another day! You've already given her two extra days. She could have gotten out tomorrow!"

"I know. I know," he sighed. "Let's hope she'll behave herself then these last couple of days. I do want to see her out as much as you do."

Zack was right. I did want her out, desperately. I missed her so much, I couldn't wait to see her again.

Feel her wonderfully soft skin and smother myself with her scent, let alone getting lost in her inscrutable grey eyes. My feelings for her hadn't abated one bit despite not seeing her for nearly a month now. I hoped the same was true for Eliza, my brave, stubborn crazy girl, who I hoped to call my girlfriend soon. I still suspected Zack of secretly quite enjoying the fact that I had no access to her, when he still saw her every day. Granted, he probably wasn't Eliza's favourite person in the world right now, but they were still able to build on their relationship. He was also the only person she had contact with so it could work in his favour in the end.

"Stop stewing, sis. I'm not in her good books at all right now. Don't worry, you'll be her angel when she comes out," Zack blurted out, perfectly tuned into my feelings which I clearly hadn't cloaked at all.

Did I detect a little jealousy on his part? I wasn't sure. He had been really closed off about his feelings, even though it was obvious before that he had a thing for Eli. I shuddered, thinking of the time I'd walked into their room after they had clearly got off with each other. I'd been seething then, and still found it difficult to forgive Zack. But he had promised to keep himself in check and be professional and, if anything, Zack was a man of his word. He wouldn't try and take advantage of her again, I knew that. The problem was that I was still worried she might fall for him after all and not me. I would be devastated, but it would be her choice. A choice I couldn't bear thinking about.

I'd noticed Zack was trying hard to forget about Eli. He'd had, very unlike him, several one night stands since Eliza had been in isolation. I'd tried to talk to him about it, but so far with little success. He simply cut me off as soon as I even thought about asking anything to do with the girls he'd met. None of them Sensorians.

"Right, I'm going to have myself a shower. I suggest you do the same, stinky pig."

I'm the only person that could address him like that. Even his friends were more careful than that, never disrespectful even if they were joking. Zack's verbal dressing downs were notorious and no one wanted to be on the receiving end of one if you could help it. He could be such a dick, but an amazing friend and brother and loyal to the core. That's why everyone admired and respected him so much. He would always have your back and stand up for you if he felt you were wronged. However, if he felt you were to blame he would make you bear the consequences. Not everyone could deal with that and those individuals tried to stay well out of his way as much as possible.

Whilst I was in the shower I heard the door close, so he had taken my 'hint' this time. I took my time getting ready as it was still quite early. Markus wasn't expecting us until 10am in the meeting room for our daily update on the whereabouts and actions of Rick. About two weeks into his disappearance, we finally had some confirmed sightings and we managed to put him under observation again. He had moved location though to about a hundred miles northwards, which made things more difficult to coordinate and monitor. Frank had taken a group of Sensorians to relocate there temporarily, including Ned and Sam, which sucked. I missed them and it made it even harder to cope with not seeing Eli. I whiled away some time scrolling through my phone, catching up with what everyone had been up to, then Zack was back.

"Come on Zaph, let's go and see what our tasks are for today."

He sounded more upbeat, thank goodness. It was better for all involved, especially me. Shielding Zack's negative vibes was hard work and I was tired of it.

Most people were already in the room, making me check my phone for the time, fearing we had somehow misjudged it and had turned up late. But that wasn't the case, so I relaxed. I walked over to Laura who came towards me straight away with a concerned look on her face.

"How are you holding up, sweetheart? I could feel your sadness the moment you came in today," she whispered gently in my ear, putting both arms around me in a rare gesture of physical affection. I nearly lost my composure, but managed to breathe through it and allowed myself to embrace her hug. She had been checking in with me a lot more than usual. She knew I was struggling with Eliza's isolation.

"Keeping busy helps a lot," I simply said.

She nodded and rubbed my back briefly before she let go. Markus was about to start the meeting and I needed to focus, banning any thoughts about Eliza from my head.

"There isn't a lot to report today on Rick's whereabouts. Frank told me he suspects there's a lot going on behind the scenes, but we're not getting any access to that at the moment. We are, however, close to having enough evidence to close down one of his money supplies. The drug pushers are quite sloppy and have made mistakes which we have been able to utilise. We are about to hand over to the police and hopefully they can make the right arrests. That will slow Rick down somewhat." *That was good news at least.* "What we really need now, is someone on the inside who can find out exactly who's involved before we capture Rick. We need to be able to absolutely guarantee that we'll get to each and every one and deal with them. We cannot have a potential loose canon floating about, threatening to go off at any time, destroying our lives and community."

All of us nodded in agreement.

Questions had been asked why Markus had not just gone in and captured Rick as soon as he was located, but it wasn't sensible. It had gone far beyond just a lone man's actions. Too many people were involved and it needed proper rooting out.

"Laura, how's your investigation into our own people's state of mind going? Is there anything you have learned so far that could expose a way in for Rick?"

He stood aside to let Laura take the lead.

"Nothing major. We have some minor grievances that we have dealt with and there are a couple of things

I need to talk to you about in private."

I glanced at Zack. I knew he was behind a push to have a more lenient approach to the monthly fitness tests. He's tried and failed several times to persuade Markus to agree that you shouldn't have to improve on your fitness levels when you're on a busy job. Just maintaining the same level should be enough. Everyone agreed with Zack as it was almost impossible to achieve continuous improvement. The consequence of failing was having to attend daily extra fitness classes at 6am in the morning till the next test. It was pissing a lot of people off and hopefully Laura's investigation had given a platform to reveal the extent of annoyance it caused. Zack deliberately avoided my glances, trying not to alert Markus that he'd been behind rallying everyone to mention it. He would get into so much trouble if Markus found out he'd been stirring.

"Okay Laura, we can do that later today. Zack and Zaphire, I require you to stay after the meeting to discuss Eliza. Let me just talk to everyone about their tasks for today, then I'll be with you. Get yourselves and me some coffee and go to my office, please."

Zack and me looked at each other with a similar raised eyebrow expression which made me snigger slightly, earning me a warning stare from Markus. We made ourselves scarce quickly and headed for his office and the coffee machine.

CHAPTER 2
Eliza

I was so mind-blowingly bored, I couldn't even describe it anymore. There were no words. I knew every little inch of my cell off by heart. The little scratch on the third brick to the right of the light switch, the piercing squeak of the door when it opened, and then a lower grinding sound when it closed, a ring on the table where someone once placed a hot drink and it never quite cleaned off. I could list a hundred things and more.

I wanted to kick myself for having been given two extra days, though I still thought it was harsh of Zack, especially the first one. I'd only just been put in isolation and I hadn't realised that no talking, meant no talking, even to myself. Zack came down so hard on me, making me feel stupid and small and I felt furious with him for ages. The second extra day, I probably deserved. After about ten days I was so desperate for some company, I had tried to bribe one of the girls who'd brought me my dinner, for a little bit of conversation. She wouldn't have any of it of course and reported me immediately to Zack. I couldn't deny any of it, even if I wanted to, as CCTV was permanently on.

I don't think I had seen Zack so angry before. He

was outraged that I had tried to get one of the young girls in trouble and he made me feel deeply ashamed of myself. It had been selfish and I promised myself I would not sink that low again. I wrote a grovelling letter of apology to the girl and hoped that she would forgive me. He read it in front of me, stony eyed, which made me feel all hot and embarrassed again, but he did agree to pass it on.

Three days to go and I was literally counting down the hours. I had to make sure I didn't oversleep again as I really did not want to spend another extra day in here, Zack's warning still ringing in my ears from this morning. He would be here after lunch to invigilate my last exam. I think the exams have kept me going at least, looking forward to each and every one of them. I don't think many people could say that!

It had been hard to focus on the content of what I was studying as I kept thinking back to that horrifying moment when my father decided to strap the explosives to my leg. The reality had hit me hard, realising this man would stop at nothing to reach his goal, even sacrificing the health of his own daughter. What made me feel sick though, was the fact that I still felt so incredibly connected to him and wanted to find some sort of solution where he wouldn't end up dead. I didn't understand my own feelings and was scared to tell anyone for fear they would see it as a sign that I couldn't be trusted. The only person I possibly could tell was Zaphire, but it would put her in an awkward position, and I really didn't want to do that. However, for my own sanity, I had to open up to someone. Zack just seemed too unapproachable now, and I knew it was because he was meant to be like that, but I still found it hard to accept. I thought he would find it more difficult to shut me out completely, but he seemed to have found it quite easy to move on from whatever feelings he had for me. I had noticed several times he carried different scents on him that I didn't recognise. I assumed he was seeing other girls and there was no doubt in my mind that he had slept with them. Those scents tend to linger. The first time it had happened I must have emitted signals that I'd noticed as he stared me defiantly in the eyes and walked off without saying a thing. I don't know what I'd been expecting, but it hadn't been that.

I couldn't wait to see Zaphy again. I fantasised about our reunion daily but actually was getting more than a little apprehensive now it was imminent. What if it didn't live up to all the expectations I had created, or worse if she didn't feel the same anymore. What if in the mean time, she had found someone else to love, or had forgotten about me. What if I hadn't read Zaphire's signals right and there was nothing to explore? In my loneliness I had built up a whole relationship with her and it could be shattered in an instant. I feared the words "just be friends" or "I don't like you like that" as much as "I don't want to see you again". It would crush me. Something had been unleashed inside me that had to be taken care of. I'd never felt the burning sensation of a desire so fierce, I could not physically deny it. I wanted Zaphire more than I'd ever wanted anything else before.

A soft knock on the door followed by the clanking of the keys disturbed my musings and I jumped to my feet, standing ready to receive my lunch. They were always brought to me by the sixteen year olds who had just started being operational. This time it was a slightly chubby boy who I hadn't seen before. I'd started assigning animals to people again to entertain myself. I used to do it all the time, before I was plunged into the Sensorian way of life. This boy moved like a cute fat Guinea Pig. His nerves filled the room and I assumed it was his first ever task and he was eager not to mess it up. He glanced briefly at me, but quickly looked back at the table where he placed my food.

"You may sit down to eat," he mumbled quickly, barely audible, before scuttling out of the room again, nervously dangling the keys.

Poor boy. That performance would not have pleased his trainer, if he was being observed. At least he hadn't forgotten to give me permission to eat as had happened once, when I had to wait about twenty minutes before anyone had noticed. Luckily it had been a sandwich so at least it hadn't gone cold. I suspected the girl had been given a telling off as, when she came back to inform me I could eat, her face was tear stained. I'd felt sorry for her and narrowly stopped myself from saying something comforting. She must have felt my compassion because she did give me the tiniest of smiles and a little nod. I hoped to God that her trainer hadn't been watching her.

I sat down to eat my hot ham and cheese panini and savoured every little morsel of it. I had learned to take my time with food as it gave me something to do, though I once had taken so long it had been taken away from me before I'd finished. From then on I made it my sport to time my eating so that I was exactly done after thirty minutes, as that is when they would come back and collect it. Most days I was spot on, and today was the same. Those tiny little victories kept me sane.

Now there wasn't a lot to do apart from just going over my notes again and wait for Zack to arrive with the exam papers.

CHAPTER 3
Zaphire

Zack and I were waiting for a good fifteen minutes in Markus' office before he and Michael joined us. Michael had stepped into Frank's boots as the right hand man, after Frank had moved up north to lead the mission there. Michael was a very smart man and a master of manipulation, so you always had to have your wits about you when he was around. He would have you agree with things that you'd never even thought about or were likely to ever agree with. Frank had been more of a second father figure, whereas Michael was like a strict teacher. Highly respected in our community but also someone to be slightly wary of.

"Sit down everyone. We need to discuss what your plans are for Eliza, and where we're going from here. I asked Zaphire to be here because she will be useful for Eliza when she first comes out of isolation. I want you to help Zack ease her back in and keep control over her senses. She'll have a hard time for a few days adjusting to exposure to the outside world again and there may be a danger of sensory overload."

Both Zack and I nodded in unison, agreeing that a

meltdown was highly likely on the cards, with her only just getting to grips with her gift even before isolation.

"Do I still need to be on 24/7 with her?" Zack chipped in.

"No, not so strictly. Her exams are finished, but she still needs to be protected as Rick knows she's with us. So, though there is no need for round the clock observation, she is still your responsibility. She can't leave the compound unsupervised, under no circumstance. You need to think of a way to set up boundaries, ensuring her safety."

"Zack, do you think she will choose to stay with us?" Michael raised.

The question shocked me slightly. It hadn't even crossed my mind that she may want to leave us and go back to live with her mum, if that even was a real option. I wasn't sure if Markus would truly let her go back to her old life even if he may have presented that as a choice. The thought of what would happen if she chose not to cooperate mortified me and looking at Zack he wasn't entirely sure what she would do.

"She hasn't given me any reason to believe she's faltering in her loyalty to us. She has been relatively compliant in isolation and eager to show she's accepting her punishment. However, as I haven't had a chance to talk to her properly I'm not a hundred percent sure."

"What did you have in mind for her after she comes out?" Markus asked.

I was curious about that too. Zack had been a bit coy with sharing his ideas with me.

"She needs a few days to acclimatise and then I want her to go to Alice for a short break. She can have a good think about what she wants to do with the rest of her life. Hopefully, she'll choose us voluntarily and then we can start the next mission training with her. What time frame do you have in mind Markus?"

"I would like to see her operational in two weeks ideally. We need to get insider information sooner rather than later as I don't want Rick gathering momentum. If that were to happen, it becomes a question as to whether we should just take him in before he can do more damage rather than collecting all the intelligence to know who and what exactly is involved."

"It's tight, but I'll do my best. Zaphy will help with building up her fitness again, though I made sure she did enough exercise to keep her fairly fit, so that shouldn't be a problem. A few more self-defence lessons and boxing won't go amiss though. Can I rely on you to help build up her resilience as well?"

That question was directed at me and I nodded eagerly. I couldn't wait to work with her again. It meant I would definitely have plenty of time with her.

Michael wanted to know if Zack had any ideas as to how to get Eliza back in touch with her father and Zack explained he thought it was best if Rick was the one that made first contact. It had to look like she was having second thoughts about living with us. Zack was hoping the time with her mum would not only clarify Eliza's mind over whether to be loyal to us, but also would send a signal to Rick making him think there may be a way in for him. He hoped that Rick would try and contact her during that time.

"Rick will know exactly where she is but he'll assume she's monitored, so he isn't just going to approach her, is he?" I questioned.

"No, obviously not. But he'll find a way. Trust me," Zack answered a little prickly.

"Don't underestimate him. I got the feeling he really wants Eliza on his side, so he will be prepared to take a few risks to get his way."

"I know, I know. But how do we keep control of the

whole situation if we're not physically there? I feel uncomfortable about leaving Eliza on her own with her mother," I persisted.

"Who said she was going there on her own? I want you to go with her, Zaphire," he answered smugly.

My heart made a little leap which didn't escape the men's attention in the room. Zack quickly continued to cover my embarrassment.

"Rick would be highly suspicious if we just let her go back on her own, but we have to make him believe he has at least got an opportunity to approach her and get inside her head again, using their familial bond."

I nodded in agreement, still feeling excited by the prospect of accompanying Eliza to her mum's. Then a horrible thought entered my head.

"How safe is this for Alice? Could it encourage Rick to use her as some kind of leverage to help "persuade" Eliza to join his side?"

"That thought did cross my mind. We've been monitoring Alice from the moment Eliza came back to us and we haven't seen any suspicious movements as yet. I think he'll leave Alice out of it as he wants Eliza to join him by her own free will. He knows if he coerced her, he would never fully be able to trust her. He wants Eliza to be his full willing partner in his absurd bid to take over society. That's what I'm counting on anyway. However, as I said, we have Alice under observation, so we would be made aware of any danger she might be in and will be able to act immediately." Zack answered confidently.

"Well, it seems like you have covered every angle so far. Well done," Markus spoke appreciatively, seeking agreement from Michael, who with the tiniest movement in his eye muscle did just that. No need to speak.

I could tell Zack was chuffed, he always was driven to please Markus, from the moment we were taken into the Community when we were mere toddlers. Not that he was a goodie-two-shoes, as he was certainly no angel, but he did love to win Markus' respect and appreciation. My main motivator has always been the acceptance and love from my peers. Loyalty to and from my friends and brother is the most important factor in my happiness. I could never be like Zack, and I'm okay with that. The fact that Markus rarely praises me, doesn't bother me that much and I know he thinks I'm brilliant at what I do, which was working in the field.

I was never going to be management material, I could only just about manage living within the rules myself, let alone imposing them on other people!

Markus got up and that was our signal to leave. Laura was waiting to speak to him next. I wondered how that meeting would go down. We surely would find out soon and I was keeping my fingers crossed for more flexibility in the requirements to pass the monthly fitness test. Only a small thing, but sometimes it's the small things that can make the biggest impact on morale. I just hoped for Zack's sake that Markus wouldn't find out it was him that instigated the issue once again. Markus did not like being challenged on things he really believed in. He could be a stubborn sod sometimes. Actually, most of the time.

"What are you smiling about, sis?"

Zack put his arm around me and his warmth enveloped me. His touch was so comforting and a feeling of nostalgia engulfed me, taking me back to our childhood where it had always been Zack who had offered comfort and safety.

"Nothing much Z. Just having a little silent dig at Markus in my head," I giggled.

"Don't we all, from time to time," Zack half smiled, half sighed.

A message came in on my phone reminding me of

my huge list of chores I had to do today, none of them particularly interesting. I longed to go out investigating again. I loved catching people out in their lies and deceit, going undercover and weaving my way into people's lives. It was super rewarding to see criminals caught and punished because of the evidence you had been able to provide. If you know when people lie, it becomes a whole lot easier to know where to look for incriminating evidence. The best part of my job is to prevent crimes from happening though, even if they are small scale. I personally saved a woman from rape when I realised the sick plan forming in the attacker's head, and even foiled a plot to rob a local bank. Exciting times. However, today I just had to get on with the boring stuff.

CHAPTER 4
Eliza

I thought today would never come! The last three days were possibly the longest ever. I practically jumped out of bed this morning, even though yesterday was the last day of the 6am exercise classes (*thank God*). I was up and waiting for Zack at 5.59am. He wouldn't come for another hour at least, but I woke up and was so ready to be out of here, there was no point trying to go back to sleep. I regretted that now though, so I forced myself to lay down and close my eyes for a bit, counting down the minutes only to be up again not long after.

I felt excited, nervous, happy, scared and a multitude of other emotions swished through my body like a tornado, and like the proverbial ants in your pants, I could not stay still. I kept lying down, getting up, pacing around the room and back to lying down again, for what felt like, a hundred times at least. I wasn't sure how I was going to react when Zack would finally say the words that meant I could get out of here. I tried not to think about it too much and just let it happen. I didn't even dare to think about Zaphire. I just wouldn't let my mind go there. It was too much.

At 7.28am I heard Zack's familiar footsteps approaching and then the keys jangling. Everything seemed to be going painfully slow but finally the door opened and Zack stepped in. Annoyingly, as calm and collected as always. He stood there, I swear for a full minute, just looking at my face, still testing me. But I was strong. I waited, trying to show as little emotion as I could muster, breathing slowly and focussing on a little dark spot on the brick wall behind Zack.

"Eliza, I am now terminating your solitary confinement. Your time in here is over and you are free to speak."

He looked at me expectantly but my mind was blank and I was vaguely aware my mouth was hanging open. When I still hadn't said anything or had moved after what must have been a few minutes, his eyes turned to concern, his hand gently touching my arm. My arm jerked back involuntarily.

"Eliza?" His hand back on my arm but now a bit tighter. "Are you okay? Answer me," he insisted.

The sheer sensation of his hand around my arm, shook me back to reality, so odd the feeling of someone touching me and so intense at that. I had forgotten the magic of human touch and the feelings they elicited, magnified a hundred times over due to our gift. My body responded.

"Uh...yes Sir, yes I'm.....I'm fine," I managed to stutter. "Thank you, thank you so much." My voice more steady now, though still sounding fragile. I hadn't used my voice properly for ages and it felt odd, feeling my vocal cords tremble. I stepped forward and embraced him, surprising myself as not long ago I had just wanted to slap him. Zack allowed my hug and gently put his arms around me too for a brief moment. Then he took my arms and more or less forcefully broke us up, which I was grateful for, not wanting to embarrass myself.

"Come on, Eli. Let's go to your room. Have a shower, get some decent clothes on and then we'll have some breakfast together."

Being in my own shower, singing to my heart's content (revelling in stretching my voice), with my own shampoo and conditioner and a lovely warm fluffy towel waiting for me, was heaven. Choosing what clothes to wear a pleasurable novelty, probably soon to wear off, but I was enjoying every moment to the full. It had somewhat taken my mind off my, hopefully imminent, reunion with Zaphire.

But first, I had to deal with Zack. I felt awkward with him, not knowing exactly what our relationship was. Was he my friend? Trainer and coach? Ex (nearly) lover? My superior? It was complicated and I didn't know how to behave towards him. I had tried to read him a little but he wasn't letting me in much. On top of that, I wasn't sure how I felt about him myself. I swayed from intense hatred to pure admiration and love, and most embarrassingly, lust. However, whatever my feelings were, I knew he, and the whole Sensorian community, had my complete loyalty. That hadn't diminished one bit during my time in isolation.

"Hey, Eli. Come sit down. I made you some breakfast. It's still hot, so tuck in."

Zack sat back in his chair, waiting for me to join him, which I did.

"Oh my, this smells soooooo good!" I exclaimed whilst cramming my mouth full of the scrambled egg and bacon bits. A month of plain Shreddies every morning banned from my brain instantly. A little smile played around Zack's lips whilst he lifted his eyebrows slightly.

"Someone's forgotten their manners, somewhat," he chastised mockingly. "Slow down a little, please.

Don't want you to choke on your first day out. Zaphire would never forgive me."

"No chance," I snorted but trying to resemble some sort of decorum whilst I wolfed down the rest of my breakfast.

"Have you noticed anything in your room?" Zack asked randomly. I looked around.

"Your bed has moved? Does that mean you are trusting me to stay in my bed now?" I dared joke a little.

"Yes it has, and no, not at all. But, you don't have to be under 24/7 observation any more so you can have a bit more freedom now. I'm still in the bedroom next to you, though, and your door will be locked at night."

His smile softened his words a little. He wasn't being grumpy about it, just matter of factly.

"Hmm, afraid I might do a runner?"

I pulled a defiant face, but Zack ignored that wisely. I finished off the last crumbs on my plate and took a deep sigh before asking Zack the question I had been dying to ask since getting out.

"When can I see Zaphire?"

It came out like a whisper, but I couldn't hide the passion and desperation behind it, judging by Zack's face and the spike in the emotions he emitted. Sometimes I hated our gift.

"Get yourself together and then we can go and see her, if you want."

Hearing the words I had been waiting for for weeks made me feel both overjoyed and scared shitless.

CHAPTER 5
Zaphire

A soft knock on the door made my heart leap, but Zack gave me no time to gather my thoughts as he was already standing in my room and beside him was Eliza, looking gorgeously cute but ever so nervous. Her thumping heart and huge pupils gave away that her feelings towards me had not waned whilst in isolation. I breathed a sigh of relief and allowed some of my own emotions out too. I wanted Eliza to have no doubts about my feelings towards her.

"Hey, long time no see!" I blurted out, running into Eliza's arms and hugging her hard.

"I've missed you so much," she whispered in my ear, which made my whole body shiver.

I felt Zack's awkwardness instantly and before I had a chance to say something he mumbled his excuses and was out the door. Almost immediately I received a message to meet up with him in an hour to discuss plans and I was to bring Eliza.

"How the hell are you, crazy girl? How are you feeling? I have a thousand questions for you but first this." I don't know what came over me but before I knew it, I manoeuvred Eliza onto the sofa and planted my lips on hers and waited just a second to gauge her response. After an initial stiffening in her body, she went soft and her lips melted into mine. It looked like my unpremeditated and bold move had paid off. I gently pulled back and gazed in her eyes. "I needed that," I sighed with satisfaction.

She didn't say anything for a minute, but I let her be. I could feel she was happy, though maybe a little overwhelmed.

"Wow. Zaphy, I wasn't expecting that. I don't know what to say."

She shifted slightly uncomfortably in her seat. I gave her a bit of space, fearing I was going to cause a sensory overload. I should remember she had only been out of isolation for barely a few hours, making her vulnerable.

I noticed a little tear forming in her eyes, but I felt it stemmed from a feeling of relief, rather than sadness.

"Talk to me, Eliza. I can second guess what you're thinking by the signals you're giving but I would like to know what exactly is going through your mind. I want to hear you say it."

"I was so scared you'd moved on, or that I'd

imagined you had feelings for me. I drove myself mad with all sorts of scenarios of our reunion. I had far too much time to think about it this last month!"

A shy smile formed on her face.

My heart melted thinking of the agony she must have gone through in her cell, without much to distract her. I had truly fallen in love with her, that much was clear to me. I couldn't wait to tell her the news I was going to accompany her to her mum's soon, but I had to wait till the meeting with Zack.

"I wish I had been able to find a way to contact you, but you know Zack; too thorough for his own good sometimes."

I rolled my eyes but to my dismay, I still noticed a spike in her vital signs on hearing his name. To be honest though, that could be explained by all sorts, rather than her still having a thing for him. I was getting a little paranoid. In a few days I would confront her about it. She wouldn't be able to hide anything from me and there was no point worrying myself about it for now.

"Hey, Zaph, tell me all the gossip I missed. What has everyone been up to in the last month?"

"Ah, not an awful lot," I started, but she managed to prise quite a lot of detail out of me and by the time we had to go to meet Zack for our meeting, I had spilled the beans on Z's multiple escapades with girls from town. If I were completely honest, I was probably a bit too willing to part with that information, but I couldn't help myself. I wanted to make sure he was no competition for me and shedding some negative light on him was an opportunity I couldn't miss.

I gently touched her arm and caught her eyes with a flirtatious look, though I had to remind myself to take it slowly. Not my forte. I was pleased to see her eyes light up, though she looked down coyly when she caught my eye. It was enough for me.

"The hour is up. We need to go and see Zack." I said regretfully whilst my hand moved down her arm to grab her hand and pull her up. She reluctantly followed and I smiled to myself. She hadn't wanted to break the moment either.

Zack was already in the meeting room, sitting down reading some paper work. He got up when we arrived, an inquisitive look in his eyes but he kept schtum. I could feel him cloaking, making sure he wasn't showing too many emotions, motioning us to sit down.

"Right, I know you've only just come out of isolation, but as per usual, we're rather pressed for time, so forgive me for bombarding you with information and questions so soon. I promise you'll get some time later to digest it all."

"No, yeah. I understand. I'm actually feeling great at the moment, so go for it."

Bless her, she was so cool, I genuinely admired her. Zack wasn't buying her statement though.

"To start with I need to know exactly how you feel about your time in isolation. Saying you feel great isn't going to wash with me. You need to tell me how you feel about being a Sensorian and whether you think you can be loyal to us, even though we have extremely strict rules and harsh consequences when they get broken. No hiding away your true feelings, Eliza. I can tell from a mile off when you're trying to cloak."

His eyes determinedly looked into hers and my poor Eliza wasn't particularly happy about it.

"But Zack, I don't really know what to think at the moment, I.."

"Stop fucking bullshitting me," Zack interrupted harshly and a glimmer of defiance sparked in Eliza's eyes. I wouldn't like to be in her place right now, but I could see she was ready to give it as good as she got.

"Fine then," she snapped. "I resented you immensely whilst I was in there, but I knew you only did what had to be done. I wanted to show you I could cope with it and that I'm a worthy Sensorian, but it was hard at times. I did frequently ask myself what on earth I was doing here and vowed that as soon as I got out I would beg to go back to live with mum and forget all about you lot. Back to my, drugged, but mainly easy, happy life. But then, moments after, I would be cross with myself for even thinking it. I can't turn my back on you or any of the Sensorian community. I would never forgive myself, if I didn't try my hardest to stop my father executing his coup. So that's where I'm at. No frills."

She paused and sought my eyes. I understood completely what she was trying to say and tried to purvey that to her without interrupting Zack. She knew I had her back, I could tell from how she straightened herself slightly, getting ready for Zack's reply, but he sat back in his chair, pondering. I couldn't read him at all which was unusual for me, being his sister. He must have been working on his cloaking skills. Maybe I found it hard to read him because his feelings weren't directly to do with me.

"Okay I see," Zack started, still not giving away whether he was satisfied with Eliza's answer or not. "Is there anything that worries you about being out of isolation, something we might need to work on?" he asked, leaning forward.

Eliza shook her head vigorously.

"No. I feel fine. I'm happy to be out. I just want to get on with things now."

Zack observed her again. I could tell something was bothering him, but he abandoned the idea to confront her. His demeanour changed.

"You'll be happy to hear that we would like you to go and see your mum for a few days. Reflect on what you want to do with your life. Whether you want to stay and become a full member of our Sensorian community and commit to it wholeheartedly or to withdraw and go back to your old life of some sorts, though exactly how far that's possible is still up for discussion. I won't ask you to comment on that any further now. You have made your feelings quite clear, but it will be good to test them."

He leant back into his chair and checked Eliza over for a moment, who was exuding resolve but wasn't given the choice to voice that at the moment. I knew she had made up her mind already, but Zack was right, it was a good idea to be exposed to what living her old life would actually entail.

"Secondly, we want your father to think there may be a way of contacting you and that you're not being guarded impenetrably."

Eliza raised her eyebrows a little on hearing this, but didn't give anything else away. She was clearly cloaking too.

"What did you have in mind?" she enquired matter of factly.

"I hope he'll contact you when you're not in our compound. Zaphire will be with you but I'm sure he'll find a way."

Her heart leapt when she heard I was going to accompany her. It filled me with happiness.

"We'll talk about it some more before you go. We'll have a couple of days in the compound for you to get acclimatised and feel more in control over your senses to avoid a sensory overload. You can go when I feel you're ready for it."

CHAPTER 6
Eliza

I still had to get used to the ultimate control Zack held over me. I could go when *he* felt I was ready for it. I had to take back that control by showing I was ready. Problem was, I didn't really know what he was looking for. I tried to find out from Zaphire when Zack had popped out for a moment, but she was no help. She waved my questions away dismissively and advised me not to worry about it. He'll know when you're ready, she said. But she missed the point I was trying to make. I didn't have much choice but to just take it. Should be used to it by now.

"Come to the Room of Tranquillity with me Zaph. I need to get out of here for a bit."

I noticed Zaph's little glance at Zack, who had returned, asking permission to go and he gave her a curt nod. She got up and grabbed my hand.

"Let's go then," she said energetically whilst she practically whisked me out of the room.

I followed but sighed. She immediately picked up on it and asked me to explain my mood.

"I don't know. It just feels like I have no control over anything anymore. Here you are, practically dragging me off to somewhere I asked *you* to come with *me* to. I know you mean well, but what with Zack taking all my decision power away from me, I need some control back."

"Oh...sorry."

She dropped my hand instantly and looked so disappointed I felt immediately guilty.

"Don't be like that." I said gently and reached out for her hand. "Come."

She allowed me to take her hand in mine, this time I pulled her along and I led her to one of the secluded benches in the beautiful garden room. I made her sit down and I straddled across her lap, unwilling to deny and cloak my urges. I'd seen Zaphire's flirtatious looks and knew she wanted me as much as I did her. My confidence rocketed.

"Mmmmm, I like this assertive Eliza," I heard Zaph mumble.

I looked into her gorgeous eyes and studied her perfect face. She hated her three moles scattered randomly over her face, but I loved them. I kissed all three of them and then her luscious lips. My feelings went wild. A fire inside me unleashed and even if I wanted to, I couldn't stop. It was incredible. Lust overwhelmed me and I could barely keep it civil. Just about remembering we were in a public space, I willed myself to jump off her, but pulled her up and ushered her out.

"To my room," I managed to say, out of breath and gruff. So much for a quiet time in the Room of Tranquillity!

*

"Woooooooow" Zaphy sighed with satisfaction. "Are you absolutely sure you've never been with a girl?"

She couldn't keep her admiration out of her voice and made me blush like a red balloon. I hid my face under the quilt.

"No need to be embarrassed," Zaphy giggled in her light-hearted way.

She leant over me and traced my face with fingers light as feathers. It felt amazing. I was so surprised with my own brazenness. As soon as I felt Zaphire's soft skin and lean body against me, I let go of my barriers, totally engrossed in the experience. It had felt so natural, so loving. Nothing I should have worried about.

"I love you," I whispered in her ear.

Now it was Zaphire's turn to go a deep shade of pink. It was from pleasure, not embarrassment.

"Oh My God. You don't know how much it means to

me to hear you say those words. The last month has been torture. Pure torture," she sighed.

"Same here. Zaph. Same here," I grunted.

"I love you too Eliza," she whispered, her lips softly brushing my ear.

The relief and joy I felt was undeniably the most wonderful feeling ever.

As much as we wanted to just stay in bed and enjoy each other's bodies once more, we had stuff to do. I leapt out of bed, with a positivity that I hadn't felt for a while. I knew I was meant to feel tired and overwhelmed with all the impressions of today. After having been in isolation for a month I was still expecting a come down at some point but I felt happy and as light as a bird. On top of the world! Maybe I was soon to be grounded as a knock on the door preceded Zack purposefully entering my room.

He was momentarily taken aback by the situation he found us in; it couldn't be hidden with the scent still heavily in the air. He shook his head once, like he could shake it off and quickly restored his confident air, ignoring our predicament.

"Give me a minute Zack," Zaphy piped up, hastily

gathering her clothes.

Zack ignored her and addressed me instead.

"You should give your mum a ring. She's waiting to talk to you."

He sounded rather grumpy, not completely managing to hide his feelings.

I nodded and went to find my phone. He fished it out of his pocket and handed it to me.

"Tell her I'll let her know when she can expect you and Zaphire," he ordered, instantly reminding me who was in control. There it was; the bump back to earth. I took a deep breath and envisaged the waves of the sea. I needed to let it go for now. I took the phone.

"Of course Sir," I grumbled quietly.

"Problem?" he enquired sternly.

"Sorry, no. Just a bit tired, that's all."

He didn't look convinced.

CHAPTER 7
Zaphire

Poor Eliza. She struggled balancing being out of isolation and accepting she wasn't in complete control of her own destiny. In fact she was far from it. She'd get used to it. That's just how it had to be and she'll remember soon. Zack won't let her go until she does. I noticed he was testing her, as he had identified the problem the moment she walked out to the Room of Tranquillity. He's going to push her on it. I should tell her, but it won't make a difference. Zack would be able to tell if she faked acceptance anyway.

"It was so good to hear mum's voice again!" she exclaimed happily after she called off.

Her moods were up and down like a yo-yo at the moment. I needed to make sure she wasn't going to be too unstable as it could lead to a sensory overload situation.

"I can't wait to see her," she carried on, still as excited as a little puppy.

Zack put a downer on it immediately by reminding her not to get too excited as a lot of work still needed to be done to convince him she was ready. I saw her face twitch for a fraction of a second but a smile appeared as she announced she would be working hard then. That was better. She was stronger than I gave her credit for sometimes.

"Good. Let's start some long overdue self-defence lessons. Zaphire can do them with you, as long as you are professional Zaph," he warned.

He didn't have to worry about that. The sexual tension had been released. Much easier to concentrate now. We both got down to it and had a great session. She was a bit rusty to start with, but soon got back into her stride. Still moving ungainly but effectively.

"Zaphire, Eliza. Call it a day for now. Eliza needs to eat and rest. We can pick this up tomorrow," Zack decided after about an hour.

I felt a little disappointed as I knew Markus had asked me to meet him after our exercise session and I didn't want to leave Eliza's side. I was looking forward to sharing a shower with her though. But Zack had different ideas and at the moment, where Eliza was concerned, what Zack decided, happened. I am going to challenge him at some point though.

Eliza was still trying to convince Zack to let me go and get changed at hers, but he wasn't having any of it.

I tried to catch Eliza's eye and signal her to back off. It wasn't helping her case at all.

"Do I really have to fucking discipline you, Eliza? You haven't been out for a day yet! Don't say another word. Go. Now," Zack insisted, not in the best of moods. She relented, wisely.

After my meeting with Markus I found Zack hovering around my room clearly waiting for me.

"Hey, want to come in? What's up?" I asked whilst opening the door and gently putting my hand on his arm.

I detected the scent of worry. He collapsed onto my sofa with a deep sigh. I went over and massaged his shoulders gently.

"I'm concerned. Eliza's being obstinate and overly confident. She's not aware of her weaknesses and that can be dangerous. Do you feel her loyalty wavering?"

I shook my head. I hadn't picked up that vibe at all.

"She's just adjusting to having relative freedom again. She's testing boundaries. It's only natural. Don't forget she's only been with us for a relatively short time. She's loyal alright. She wants to find her father and stop him as much as we do. Don't worry about that." I tried to reassure.

"She's fighting me. I don't want to have to punish her, but she needs something to remind her what's important."

He sounded serious.

"What do you have in mind?"

He didn't answer but I could see Eliza was going to have a rather tough time ahead of her in the next couple of days. I knew she would cope. Zack would get the best out of her eventually. He always did. Before we know, we'll be on our way to her mum's. He just needed her to crack a little. She was too confident for her own good at the moment, leading her to think she knew better. And that irked Zack.

"Can I go and see her for a bit now?" I tried in vain. I knew the answer. I knew my brother too well. I tried again though.

"You need to let 'us' happen at some point brother. No use trying to sabotage it."

He just shrugged his shoulders and left me to it.

"Arse!" I shouted and threw a pillow after him.

CHAPTER 8
Eliza

I hated to admit it, but I was actually pleased Zack had resisted my pleas to have Zaphire come to my room. Annoyed as I was with him, he had made the right call. I was physically and emotionally exhausted and needed a break. I wasn't going to tell Zack that though. I was angry with him because he'd also taken my phone off me. Didn't want me on social media as I needed to rest my senses, he'd said. All I wanted to do was contact my friends to let them know I was returning home soon, but he didn't budge. Apparently that could wait till tomorrow. I was going to be eighteen years old next month and he still treated me like a child. Infuriating.

I had nothing much to do so after I had my super lusciously long bath, had some food and watched a bit of TV, I went to bed. It was wonderful crawling into my own bed again and soon I fell asleep.

The next day went without much happening at first. Zaphire was busy most of the day and apart from a quick lunch I didn't see her. I managed to talk to Bella who was insanely excited to hear I was coming home soon. I texted my other friends but I asked my mum to let Kas know. I wanted to speak to him in person, not on the phone. It would be too difficult. For both of us.

Zack was never far away, but apart from arranging a couple of hours exercise and self-defence classes, he left me to it. It was great having a sparring session with Brody and he taught me lots. Afterwards we went for a drink. Freedom felt fantastic.

"So, how do you feel?" Brody began after glugging down a coke.

"Free and happy. Why?" I answered without thinking.

"What do you mean 'why'. You've been in isolation for over a month!" he countered.

"I'm out now, aren't I. So I feel great!" wanting to finish this conversation.

"Tell me what you've been up to, Brodes."

He observed me for a moment but was happy to elaborate on his role in verifying Rick's sightings and stories of nights out with the guys, though he was a bit coy on Zack's participation in those. We said our goodbyes as Zack had requested a meet up at 5pm and I wanted to have a shower to freshen up a bit, just in case Zaphire might pop over later.

I'd just finished getting ready when Zack knocked on the door. To be honest I couldn't be arsed to talk to him, not that I had a choice. I reluctantly opened the door and let him in. To my surprise he looked calm and dare I say it, almost friendly.

"We need to talk," he simply said, before ushering me to the table and gesturing me to sit down.

"About what?"

I knew perfectly well what about. He ignored my remark anyway.

"How do you feel?"

Not that again. I was sick of it.

"I feel great. Why's everybody asking constantly. Can't you sense I'm fine. I thought that was the whole benefit of being a Sensorian."

I knew I sounded irritated, but I couldn't help myself.

"Exactly."

He leant back into his chair and folded his arms, staring at me. I stared back. Not giving an inch. I didn't understand what he was getting at.

"You're in denial. You have just spent a month in isolation with hardly any sensory stimulation. You come out and you act like you've just been on holiday. It's not right."

"I am *not* in denial. I *am* absolutely fine. A bit tired, but fine. Why can't you see that!" I said exasperated.

"That's the fucking point. I *can't* see it. And if I don't sense it, it's not true. You're lying to me and to yourself."

"Oh. So now you know me better than I know myself, do you? Bit arrogant isn't it!" I bit back.

Zack threw his hands up in frustration. He just sat there staring at me whilst I stared back in defiance. After a few awkward minutes, he leant forward and I was getting ready for a bollocking. But it didn't come.

"Okay. So you think you're fine. Good. Get yourself ready then. We're going out."

That took me by surprise.

"Just remember I'm still your trainer and therefore your superior. This is the last time you're rude to me. Your grace period is over and as you think you're perfectly fine, you can be held responsible for your behaviour. Understood?"

"Yes Sir," I remembered my manners.

I texted Zaph, to see if she would come out too. I didn't actually know where we were going but it didn't really matter. I missed Zaphire today and I wanted her to come. Maybe there was a little self protection there too. I didn't really want to be on my own with Zack at the moment. I got an enthusiastic text back, but she said she had to double check with Zack first. A few moments later I heard my phone ping. I checked it eagerly.

Coming crazy girl! Get your dancing shoes on! Plus a whole string of excited face emojis and love hearts. I couldn't wait! I had to find something suitable to wear. I hadn't been out in ages!

I couldn't quite ignore a little voice in the back of my head nagging. I was a little suspicious of Zack's motives. I pushed it to the back of my mind. Who cared what his motives were. I was ready to have some fun.

CHAPTER 9
Zaphire

I knew my brother was up to something. He looked smug and determined. Never a good combination. I wasn't going to let it spoil the fun though. I grabbed a whole load of clothes and went to Eli as she'd begged me to come over and help with outfits. That, I could do. I loved fashion and looked forward to dressing up my girlfriend. I savoured those words in my mind. I hoped she'd look to me as her girlfriend too. It didn't take long to choose an outfit, even though she wouldn't actually take any of my recommendations and she only ended up borrowing one of my jackets. She didn't need my clothes to look stunning.

Brody came along as well. He was always up for some fun. We went to the pub first. Eliza tried to sneak a cider, but Zack wouldn't let her. I gave her a few sips of mine to make her sulky face smile again. I noticed Eli tuning out quite a few times, probably struggling with the onslaught on her senses. As we were mixing with normal people, no one was hiding their sensory outputs as they didn't need to and they wouldn't know how to either. As Sensorians we were used to shielding in public places and only tune into what we wanted to, but it still cost Eliza a great deal of effort. I was about to pass some ear plugs to her to at least dampen one of her senses, but Zack stopped me.

It dawned on me what Zack was trying to do. How had I not seen that coming? I was annoyed as he was clearly setting her up to fail. He could be so harsh. I took him aside for a moment.

"What the hell do you think you're doing, brother," I hissed at him.

"Welcome to the party, sis. You haven't been on the ball at all, have you. Wonder why the fuck that is?" he mocked.

He was right. I hadn't thought of the impact on Eliza at all, I'd just been thinking of myself and having fun with her.

"I'm taking her home," I decided, but Zack grabbed my arm and forbade it.

"She has to be shown she's not invincible. She won't talk. This is the only way she's going to realise. Don't interfere. That's an order."

Bollocks. I had to work hard not to defy him. I longed to just walk off with her and flick him the finger. But I couldn't. He was responsible for her and I had to obey, frustrating as it was. Eliza was blissfully unaware as she was shielding so much, she didn't even notice our quarrel. It was going to be a long night.

The bell for the last round rang and to my relief Zack signalled to go. Eliza was visibly relieved to be outside, but put a brave face on.

"You okay?" Zack asked her.

Tell him you're tired and want to go home. Be sensible Eliza. Please. She needed to show him she'd recognised she wasn't coping, but I couldn't warn her.

"Yeah! Feeling great. Awesome to be out. Wish you'd let me have a drink though," she laughed.

Zack glanced up at me. My heart sank.

"Brilliant. Let's go dance then," he decided.

Brody whooped. He was well up for it, but checked Eliza over, looking concerned. Zack signalled him to leave it.

Eliza threw Zack a bewildered smile.

"Dance?"

She sought my eyes and I felt Zack's death stare burning. I forced an enthusiastic smile. In her state she wouldn't be able to interpret any subtle signals that would have told her I was being coerced.

"Yes, let's go dance, my sweet. It'll be fun!"

I stared icily at Zack. This was such a bad idea.

Eliza had managed to survive the pub but she had realised it was tougher than she'd thought. She would admit it to me tomorrow, I was sure of it. Then he would have achieved his aim to make her realise her weaknesses. No need to push it this far. But he was determined. And I had to play along.

Once inside, Eliza went wild. She leapt onto the dance floor and dragged me along, flinging her arms around my neck and flicking her hair from side to side to the mesmerising beat of the music. I forgot my worries for a moment and lost myself in her crazy fired up eyes, dancing wildly myself. Maybe it would be okay. I just needed to keep checking on her. Don't know why I was kidding myself. Wishful thinking I suspect.

"Eli, if you wanna go outside for a bit, just let me know," I whispered in her ear.

She nodded but kept dancing. I'd never seen her so unleashed. Only moments later the inevitable happened.

She froze on the dance floor. I followed her stare leading to Zack intimately dancing with, and kissing a beautiful brunette. I sighed. *Of course. It would be that to send her over the edge.* I was just about to gently take her outside when she stormed towards Zack, forced the two apart and screamed, wildly flinging her arms around.

The poor brunette looked mortified, slapped Zack in the face *(good shot)* and stormed off. Eliza was in full on meltdown and someone had alerted security, who were fast approaching through the crowd. Zack just stood there watching her, his hands on Brody's chest who had tried to go to her. I lurched forward to try and get to Eliza before the bouncers did, but Zack stopped me forcefully, grabbing my arm.

"Leave her. She needs to sink this low and bear the consequences," he warned.

Eliza lashed out at some people who did try and help her. She looked like a wild animal but then sank to the floor, crying and pulling at her own hair. I felt my tears stinging behind my eyes. I hated Zack for putting her through this. The guys from security roughly lifted her up from the floor and escorted her to the exit. Zack, Brody and I followed.

"Are you responsible for this mess?" one of them asked Zack when they were outside.

"In more than one way," I grumbled under my breath.

Zack just nodded. Face hard as stone, whilst taking over from the men.

"Take her home. She needs her bed," one of them ordered.

They walked off, shaking their heads.

I took over from Zack, pushing him away roughly.

"I'm here, my love. I've got you," I gently whispered in her ear. She relaxed almost instantly.

"I'm so sorry," she groggily mumbled when I gently put her seatbelt on in the taxi home.

I could murder Zack.

CHAPTER 10
Eliza

This was bizarre. Zaphy, in my bedroom at Mum's.

Last week, it felt like this day would never come. After my intensely humiliating exit from the club some choice words were said by Zack and Markus the following day and it really hit home. Reality had sunk in.

I'd been angry with Zack for pushing me over the edge and so had Zaph. In fact she still wasn't on good terms with him, but at least they were just about civil now. To start with Zaph wouldn't even be in the same room with Zack for fear of overstepping the mark. She said she couldn't be held responsible for her actions, if near him.

I understood why he'd done it and harsh as it was it had worked. But I agreed with Zaphire, I would have gotten there anyway. I realised how difficult it was to be fully functioning outside the safe boundaries of the compound the moment we stepped into that pub. But Zack liked to push and secure results quickly. That's how he operated and he wasn't going to change.

In the past few days I had worked hard on shielding, and on recognising my trigger points and weaknesses. I needed to withdraw as soon as I felt myself starting to become overwhelmed. It could be awkward or even dangerous if I ignored those signs again and lost my objectivity or, even worse, had a full blown meltdown. That's what Zack had tried to make me realise.

The day before yesterday he had finally given me the green light to go home and I couldn't wait to tell Zaph. But when I did she reacted less enthusiastically than I'd expected. Last night the cat came out of the bag when she came to my room. I sensed she was on edge. Something was bothering her.

"Hey," I started, taking her face in my hand and trying to kiss her. She moved her head sideways, avoiding my lips. That didn't bode well. "What's wrong?" My heart jumped a beat. I wasn't sure if I even wanted to know. I picked up some very negative vibes.

"I need to know something. I've tried to ignore it, telling myself I was over reacting and paranoid, but I have to ask. It's eating me up," Zaphire tentatively stated.

It was very unlike Zaphire to behave this anxiously so I took her hands gently in mine. She was trembling and her nerves were hurting me. I tried to shield, but she stopped me.

"Let it in, please. I need you vulnerable so I can read you properly. I don't want you shielding or cloaking. It's important."

I reluctantly agreed, still scared of suffering another sensory overload.

She took a deep breath, her heart rate spiked and tiny beads of sweat covered her face.

"Have you still got feelings for my brother?"

I felt slightly sick. I felt myself turning red and hot, unable to control any of the signs I was emitting. I tried to sound calm.

"What makes you ask?"

"Isn't it obvious? The other night...when you froze.."

I realised what she was alluding to. It was complicated and I wasn't sure she would understand.

"Oh that." I smiled a little.

"Yes. *That,*" she nodded, fearing the worst. She looked defeated.

"No. Zaph... It's not like that. Trust me," I pleaded. I took her face in my hands again and looked straight into her eyes. "It's not like that at all," I repeated softly.

"Explain to me what it is like then. *Something* is going on. You clearly feel something for him," she replied desperately.

"I love *you*, Zaphire. You alone."

I tried to reassure her, but her body language showed she didn't believe me. I had to try and explain what this thing was with Zack, but I was scared she wouldn't understand, destroying what we had. It was my turn to take a deep sigh.

"Okay. But promise me you'll hear me out. Please try and understand."

I forced myself to look her in the eyes, but I was struggling. I wasn't sure where to start and how to explain my feelings for Zack to her, I didn't even really know what they were myself.

"I seemed to have this....physical attraction...."

Zaphire jumped up and paced towards the door.

"I knew it!" she hissed.

I went after her and grabbed one of her arms.

"You promised to hear me out!...Please Zaphy. Listen to me," I begged, grabbing the other arm, shaking her, trying to stop her from leaving my room.

She stopped momentarily and I quickly continued.

"It's nothing else. I swear! I can't deny there's something and I can't hide it. But I love *you*, all of you. And I've chosen you. Not him. Please believe me. You must sense I'm telling the truth!"

She sat back down, looking a little dazed. I curled

up next to her, hoping she would give me a chance to explain.

"I don't know exactly why, but when I saw Zack kissing that girl, something just snapped inside. I wasn't myself, remember. It all became too much. I somehow felt cheated by him, even though I knew he'd been seeing girls all along. It was hard to ignore when he came in my cell reeking of sex. I was just angry with him but tried to repress it, and then it just became too much and the frustration spilled out. I am so sorry Zaphire."

I hoped that was enough. To be completely truthful, I didn't quite understand why it had upset me so much. I didn't really want to delve into that too much myself, maybe a little afraid of what I might find out about my true feelings for Zack. I put my hand gently on her arm and she didn't push it away. She felt more at peace. Hurt, but I could feel she was trying to understand. That's all I could ask for.

"So, if our relationship is going to work I have to accept you have a sexual attraction to my brother. Great," she remarked with a sarcastic edge.

"It's only physical, Zaph. Purely chemical, I promise."

I hoped it was enough to convince her .

"I suppose we are twins...," she managed to joke a little.

Resilient as ever.

The next morning I sensed she had made some sort of peace with it. Resolved to make it work and excited to spend time with me at my mum's.

I could hear mum calling us down for dinner. We were going to have a quiet night in and meet up with my friends the day after. I needed to tell my mum everything that had happened over the last month. She had been kept up to date, but she was full of questions understandably. I told her as much as I was allowed and what I thought she could cope with. She didn't need to know everything. I did tell her about Zaphire and me though. It was awkward but I didn't want it to be a secret.

"You and Zaphire are in love?"

She sounded surprised but she smiled.

"Well, that's fantastic. Love is good."

She gave us both a big hug. My mum was awesome.

CHAPTER 11
Zaphire

It was difficult to accept Eliza fancied my brother, though she assured me it was purely physical and she didn't want to act on it. I reasoned it away as best I could and I had put on a good show of acceptance, but there was just a tiny little niggle in the back of my mind that kept me slightly on edge. Eliza had been so preoccupied with her mum and meeting up with her friends that she hadn't completely tuned into me and seemed happy to think I had come to terms with it. I needed a bit longer to think but I also wanted to make the most of my time with her, here in her home town. I locked my doubts away for the moment and tried to concentrate on the conversation that was going on between Eliza and Bella.

".....and then I'm going to move there once the offer is confirmed."

Bella was talking about her University offer and her plans for the future.

"What about you?"

I checked Eliza's vital signs and, though she started to emit some stress signals, all was still under control.

"Not sure. I might take a gap year and work. I could possibly get an apprenticeship somewhere."

"Oh. That's new?"

Bella looked confused. Eliza was seeking reassurance from me, but I thought she was handling it so I just nodded and left her to deal with it.

"Don't you want to take up your offer to study Biology? You were so pleased when you heard you got a place?"

"It was a conditional offer, so I still need to get the grades. Not sure if I managed with all the disruption, so I have just been thinking of other options. Just in case."

I could sense Bella's worry but also her guilt for pushing it. She wasn't going to dig deeper for now, which was just as well because Eliza was starting to struggle with the barrage of signals she had to deal with. She cleverly changed the subject.

"How's Jimmy?"

She prodded Bella playfully in the arm, who burst out into an infectious laugh. It made Eliza smile instantly, though even joyous feelings can be hard to cope with. Eliza had been out for a week or so but she was still a little vulnerable.

"Jimmy's great," Bella swooned.

"But tell me about Kas. What happened to you

two?"

She looked concerned but Eliza stalled.

"What did he tell you?"

Bella shrugged her shoulders.

"Not much. He went off somewhere to meet you, leaving just a text message to his parents and came back distraught! All we got out of him was that he'd managed to see you, but that both of you had decided it wasn't going to work between the two of you anymore. He doesn't want to talk about it, but he's not been himself since."

Eliza nodded her head slowly. She was struggling. I decided to step in.

"It was tricky for Eliza. We had just met at the time and were getting to know each other when she realised she was falling for me. She didn't know how to tell Kas but didn't want to lead him on either. It was a difficult time for her."

Not sure if that helped. Eliza had turned bright red and shuffled uncomfortably in her chair, fiddling with her hair trying to hide her face. She had told Bella about us, but clearly wasn't at ease talking about it. Bella felt awkward too.

"Does Kas know?" she asked carefully.

"No, not yet. Not sure how to, really."

"You should tell him before we all meet up at the party later."

Eliza shrugged her shoulders non-committally and fell silent.

I felt Bella was a little protective over the guy. She must be good friends with him and he clearly had a difficult time with the whole thing. She didn't know anything about it of course. All Bella knew was that Eliza supposedly had suffered a setback in her mental state and that she'd been treated for that. Kas knew different, having been 'arrested' by Zack and everything, but wasn't allowed to talk about it. Finding out Eliza and I were now together was not going to help his state of mind. She was right, Eliza had to tell him, but she was still sitting quietly, not wanting to talk about it. It was Bella's turn to change the subject.

"How did you two meet then?"

I could tell she'd been dying to ask that question from the moment we met. I took it upon myself to answer.

"Eliza had just been allowed to start activities outside of the institute and we met in an art class. I'm not very arty but tried the class out anyway and we found common ground instantly, Eliza also being far from talented in that department." I laughed whilst Eliza slapped me playfully. Bella laughed too.

"You can say that again!" she teased.

We spent the rest of the time talking about Eliza and Bella's school days, some made up stories I produced about what Eliza and me got up to and any gossip Eliza could get her hands on from Bella. When we were about to leave Bella once more urged Eliza to talk to Kas and I reassured her I would make sure she did, though I could feel Eliza was going to resist.

"I truly think it's better if we just don't mention it. He'll work it out and then he won't have time to brood over it," she argued.

Unfortunately I was no Zack, nor her trainer so I couldn't just order her to get on with it. I had to actually try and persuade her but ultimately it would be her choice. I sighed and tried to talk sense into her once more. I'd sort of given up hope, but then I suddenly sensed her change of heart. She got her phone out and started texting. Minutes later she got a reply.

"Right then. He's coming over now. But I want to talk to him on my own."

I wasn't sure if that was wise, but I couldn't budge

her on that, so when he arrived I went down to the kitchen and had a chat with Alice. All I could do was be there for her when she was done, however it would go.

CHAPTER 12
Eliza

I gave in to Zaphy's pressure and told Kas. It was awkward. We didn't hug. We barely looked each other in the eye but I felt his pain and love and his overwhelming need to touch me, kiss me, shout at me, his rage and disappointment. It was hard to shield. He didn't act on any of it. He just stood there one minute defiant, the next despondent. When I told him about Zaphire and me he just sighed and nodded, then left. I think he was there for less than ten minutes. I crashed after he went and Zaphy came to my rescue with a hot cup of tea and a tender hug. I wasn't looking forward to the party Bella had organised in honour of my return. I hoped he wouldn't come.

That hope was dashed the moment we walked into Bella's house. I could hear Kas' booming laugh in the next room, a little too raucous, a little too wild. He was drunk. This didn't bode well. I was hit by a nasty acrid smell and very tense emotional vibes and I saw Zaphy steel herself too, shielding to the max. I wanted to turn around and leave immediately but then I felt Zaphy's hand in mine, giving me a little squeeze and I managed to steady myself. Next minute, I was surrounded by my former classmates hugging and kissing me.

"I've missed you so much!" Freya, my biology mate, squealed in my ear.

It was so loud I nearly shrank away from her. I was quite good at protecting myself from loud background noises like music and the general hubbub of people at parties, but this was a different level altogether. It was physically painful. Whenever us Sensorians had been out in public we never had to shout in each others ears to make ourselves heard, I forgot it wasn't the same for my friends. I couldn't do much about it as everybody wanted to talk to me so I had to just endure it this evening. It was going to be a long night.

I felt Zaph push something into my hands. A set of earplugs. Of course! Why hadn't I thought of that.

"Sorry Eli, I thought you had some in already. I should have reminded you! I keep forgetting you are still new to this. I always bring an extra pair so you can have these."

Thank goodness. It made a world of difference and I thanked Zaphy with an exuberant kiss, which she returned fervently. We got rudely interrupted by loud whooping noises. I quickly realised it was Kas.

"Look achou, kissssin and evrrrthing...whooo," he

shouted drunkenly. One of his mates put a hand on his shoulders and tried to lead him away, but he threw it off and pushed passed several people, finger pointing at Zaphy. This wasn't looking good.

"Sjo, sshhhe's the one? Th'one thaz turned you?"

He was hardly coherent and Jimmy stepped up.

"Come on mate. You're embarrassing yourself. Let's go home."

Kas wasn't budging though, ignoring Jimmy and moving in on us, swaying on his feet. I could feel Zaphire working herself up to take action, but I decided to deal with this one myself. I owed him that.

I grabbed him by the arm and forcefully pulled him aside, and pushed him out into the garden. It wasn't difficult as it had taken him by surprise and his intoxicated brain wasn't working at full speed. I was glad as I didn't want to embarrass him even more by having to use excessive force.

"What the hell do you think you're playing at Kas!" I hissed at him once outside.

"Actually, do you know what? Just leave. You're too wasted to discuss this now." I glowered. Kas hadn't quite given up yet though.

"I miss y'babes. Sjoo much."

He tried hugging, heavily leaning on me, but I

pushed him off. I grabbed his face and looked him straight in the eyes. I got hit by a jolt and, for the second time in my life, I was looking at my own face. It looked rather fierce but a tad blurry. My body involuntarily shivered and I let go of his face instantly. The image went, leaving me a little stunned. I didn't like this Vision Hacking business one little bit. It was out of my control and I thoroughly detested that.

"We'll talk tomorrow. Go home. Now. I'll get Jimmy," I spoke gruffly, trying to cover up my own confusion.

He sat down on the grass defeated and I beckoned Jimmy over.

"Take him. He's ready now. Thanks mate."

I hated seeing him like this. It was so unlike him and he clearly hadn't moved on. It felt shitty. I felt Zaphy approach and I hastily wiped away a tear.

"What an arse. Are you okay my sweet?" she asked with an angry but concerned look on her face.

"Yeah," I lied, knowing she would see straight through it. "Unfinished business I suppose. Don't be too harsh on him. He's had a rough time," I soothed over his behaviour.

"You're too forgiving. He was being a dick in there," she said spitefully.

She couldn't hide the scent of jealousy. I decided to let it go. She would learn he's just a friend to me now. Awkward as it was at the moment, I didn't want to lose him completely.

It turned out that was going to be harder to achieve than I'd thought. Kas didn't return my phone calls nor texts the following day. Then I got a message from Bella saying he didn't want to talk to me and that he wanted me to leave him alone. Difficult as it was, I had to respect that. I sent him one last message saying that if and when he felt ready, I would be there for him.

CHAPTER 13

Zaphire

I knew Eliza had experienced another VH episode, this time with Kas. I wasn't going to say anything to her, as I felt her unease about it. I would report it to Zack. He would know how to coax it out of her and he'd already lined up someone to talk to her anyway. I knew she wasn't keen at all at the moment so I pretended I hadn't noticed.

We'd been staying with Alice for a week now and I noticed Eli was getting restless. There had been no sign of Rick trying to establish contact or anything and it was irritating her.

"He's not going to do it. It's too obvious. You being here and all," she moaned.

"We need to go back to the compound and make another plan," she decided resolutely.

"Zack wants us to stay here. He's positive Rick will try and contact you. You need to be patient," I countered.

"Patience sucks if you haven't got time," she grumbled. "He won't bite. I just know it."

I didn't want to return to the compound yet as I was having far too much fun with Eliza but she was too focussed on her task to be persuaded to let it go and wait. She had already texted Zack with the request to come home, which he'd refused to start with but Eliza wasn't going to take that lying down. She tried about a million times to FaceTime Zack and at the end of the afternoon he finally answered.

"What the fuck are you calling me hundreds of times for? I already told you what I want you to do." His less than impressed face didn't deter Eliza.

"You wouldn't answer," she replied shrugging her shoulders. "I need to talk to you. Face to face. I'm serious; Rick isn't going to make contact this way. It's too easy. He'll suspect it's a trap. If he gets desperate he might try but that won't be for weeks, if not months. I know it, I can feel it."

I could see Zack was thinking it over, but I hoped he would stick to his guns and order Eliza to stay here. It wasn't to be.

"Okay, I'm going to trust your opinion Eliza, but we do need to come up with another plan ASAP. Pack your bags and come home tomorrow."

Eliza picked up on my sulking straight away and teased me about it. I just didn't want our time together to end as I knew as soon as we were back at the compound Markus would have a whole lot of work lined up for me and soon Eliza would be full into the mission and we wouldn't get much time together. On top of that, Laura had joined the team up North, which meant Markus would be more grumpy than usual without his wife by his side.

"I don't like it either, Zaphy, but you should know the mission comes first. I can't believe I have to remind *you* of that!"

She started playing with my hair, pulling little strands softly and surprising me with a few fierce little tugs, making her giggle uncontrollably.

I retaliated without mercy and soon she was on the floor begging me to let her go. I scooped her up, and slung her on the bed. This girl was going nowhere. At least for the next hour or so.

"Do you have to go back already?" Alice asked disappointedly the next morning. "I was just getting used to both of you being here and I kinda liked it. It's lonely without you here."

"Don't you start, mum. I just had Bella giving me grief over the phone. We'll be back soon. I promise."

Eliza was determined to show how strong she was, but I detected guilt and sadness, even though it had been her that had pushed for our earlier than planned departure. Credit to her, she didn't blame Zack or Markus, but hadn't mentioned it was her idea either. Just as well I think, as Alice wouldn't have stopped trying to convince her to stay otherwise. She knew Zack, and if she thought it was his orders, she gathered Eliza wouldn't have a chance of disobeying them. So she let it be, with just a little grumbling.

"You'd better not leave it so long again. Please don't get yourself into trouble and please be safe. Goodness knows what your father is capable of. He always was a very determined man."

"Alice, are you absolutely sure he hasn't tried to contact you? You haven't noticed anything out of the ordinary lately?" I tried once more to make sure she hadn't missed anything.

We didn't want Alice harmed and she was to notify us the moment she noticed anything unusual. But Alice reassured us she hadn't observed anything out of the ordinary and that he certainly hadn't contacted her. Though I did catch just the tiniest of hesitations before she answered and I pressed her on it.

"No, don't worry Zaphire. I just had a strange feeling he was nearby a couple of days ago, but it was based on nothing. I haven't seen Rick or heard from him at all," she reiterated. I believed her.

Eliza pulled me aside just before we were about to leave and asked me to follow her to her bedroom for a minute.

"I need to talk to you before we get back into the compound. Something has been bothering me," she started.

I let her take her time as I saw she was struggling to express what she wanted to let me know. It took her a few minutes to gather her thoughts.

"When I was in isolation I had very confusing feelings about my dad. I can't really tell any of the leadership but I also didn't want to put you in an awkward position. I still don't want to do that, but I need to talk to someone. You know I'm loyal, right?"

I nodded. I felt she was genuinely convinced about her own loyalty to us Sensorians. I didn't doubt her at all.

"The thing is, that even though I want my father stopped, I don't want him to get sentenced to death. How am I going to reconcile these feelings Zaph? I'm scared I'm going to compromise the mission somehow and that is the last thing I want. I know how important it is."

I thought for a moment before answering. I had suspected she was having an internal struggle about something, and she was right about one thing. If the leadership heard about it they wouldn't fully trust her.

"You have to do what feels right for you, Eliza. You can do your best to somehow rescue your father out of this, but in the end it is our law. You have to decide if you can live with that if it did come to it. Ultimately it's out of your hands and you have to decide whether you want to help us or not. It's not an easy decision to make and don't blame yourself for feeling the way you do."

I wasn't sure how much that had helped her, but I think that at least being able to speak about it had lightened her worries a little, as she appeared visibly less tense.

She nodded her head deliberately, as if she was going over everything I'd just said, letting her brain digest it.

"Please don't tell anyone."

She looked worried.

"Don't offend me by even asking that." I scoffed. But though I knew I could keep this from Markus, Michael and Laura, I feared if Zack ever had to question me about this I wouldn't be able to lie to him. I hoped it was never going to come to that.

CHAPTER 14
Eliza

"Before we discuss plans concerning Rick, I want you to explore your VH abilities. I have arranged a meeting with Rob Saunders. Remember him? The guy in the wheelchair you saw before you went into isolation?" Zack asked, just minutes after we arrived back at the compound. I suspected he wanted to catch me off guard.

I nodded, though the last time I saw Rob he was in such a state I doubted I would recognise him.

"He's a Vision Hacker too and damned good at it. He might be able to convince you to develop your skill as he'll be able to tell you how useful it's been for him."

Zack's plan had worked. Before I even had time to think about it and reject the idea, I was sat across from Rob in one of our small meeting rooms. Saunders was much better looking and younger than I envisaged when I remember his beaten up face. Probably in his late twenties at the most. His face, not pretty like a catalogue model, but rugged with strong features. A couple of red raw scars were still clearly visible around his left eye, but it didn't distract from his looks. In fact it quite suited the rather tall and broad man.

I looked out for signs he emitted that could be warning me about his intentions, but he had a clean scent and his body language was open and trustworthy. I didn't even know why I was being so suspicious. I decided to give him a chance.

"Tell me about your VH experiences. How did they make you feel?" Rob asked in his deep, warm voice, making me feel instantly at ease.

"They were very short and made me feel...," I struggled to find the right words for a moment, but Rob waited patiently. "...I dunno, unsettled and out of control, I suppose. I can't see how they could ever be of use to me. It sort of just happened, I didn't do anything to make it happen."

"It did feel disconcerting to me too when they first happened," Rob confessed. "But now I'm in full control of them and it has been an amazing tool in investigations and keeping me safe."

"Apart from your last mission," I interjected.

He looked a bit put out. I felt mean bringing it up.

"Yeah, didn't see that coming, and by the time I did, it was too late."

"So, how did you gain control over it and how do you use it. Do you have to be in physical contact or does it work differently for you?" I asked eagerly.

"Hey, hey, Zack was right. You do bombard people with questions, don't you? Remember your training Eliza."

I slowed down my breathing and started again.

"Fair point. Tell me what you think I need to know then, please?"

"To start with it happened randomly, but usually when I was in some sort of state of distress. Like you, it only happened when I physically touched someone and it wasn't much use to me at all. I decided to practise on my friends to see if it was possible to gain some sort of control over it. I found a way to trigger it, and the more I used it, the better my control got. Now I can just switch to someone's vision at will, without any physical contact. It's taken a long time to get as skilled as I am now, but the practise initially was relatively quick. You just need to find your trigger and be able to tune into it."

"That sounds far easier than it probably is," I sighed. "And anyway, I still can't quite see the benefit of it. How's it actually going to help me?"

Rob looked at me quite indignantly.

"Don't be so reluctant. You're better than that," he gently scolded.

I shrugged my shoulders but felt a little

embarrassed for my negative attitude. He picked up on that immediately of course. It was his turn to let out a little sigh.

"It has helped me countless times in investigations. I can see emails people write, pick up phone numbers, see people's reaction behind me, signals that were not meant for me to see. It's like having an extra pair of eyes, but better. I can literally flip between people's visions to keep track of people or situations unfolding. It's amazing."

I clearly hadn't really thought it through properly, but Rob was right. It would offer incredible options if I were able to control it. I really hadn't seen it that way, I'd just thought of it as a nuisance. I apologised for my less than enthusiastic response from earlier.

"Would you be able to help me control it? Any tips on how to access it?"

"You need to think back to what feelings you had when the episodes happened and concentrate on those emotions. Start with physical contact first. Once you have that under control and can make it happen when you want, move on to remote visual hacking. It's more difficult and it takes a lot of practice, but you'll get there if you really want it."

He got up to leave, but not before he demonstrated

a little remote VH.

"You could have told me I have a bit of green stuck to my front teeth," he laughed.

"Useful as a mirror too. Start practising, girl. Text me if you need some advice."

Rob had been right in that it really didn't take me long to gain some control over it. It was difficult at first, not really getting anywhere. But once I worked out how to tap into those very extreme emotions I had when the hacking had happened previously, it became fairly easy. The jolts became less severe each time I did it, and I was able to VH anyone I touched without much effort after only a couple of days. Zack was over the moon.

"This is just brilliant. You are something else Eliza. You're a natural when you decide to put your mind to it."

"I'm not quite there yet, Zack. I can only sustain it for a short time and I'm nowhere near any remote hacking. Don't get too enthusiastic. It's of limited use at the moment."

I tried dampening his enthusiasm just slightly as I didn't want his expectations too high. Not sure it worked though as he completely ignored my comment.

"We have a meeting scheduled with Markus at 5pm

today. Most of the leadership is going to be there as they want to assess your state of mind."

"My state of mind is just fine," I grumbled. "But I really need to speak to you before that meeting, Zack. You've got to tell Zaph that you need to see me on my own. I don't want her there, but I don't want to raise suspicion. I'll explain later."

I expected Zaph to arrive at my room any minute now, and didn't want to get caught talking about her. I was right, she practically burst into the room, not bothering to knock anymore.

"Oh. You're here," she grumbled, spotting Zack. I could swear I detected jealousy still. Silly girl.

"Yes. And on my way out. Eliza, I'm expecting you in the small meeting room in half an hour. Alone," he ordered as per my request.

Zack threw Zaphire a warning glare as she was about to protest. She shut up straight away.

I nodded my acknowledgement, raising my eyebrows slightly at Zaph. True to his word, he got up and left us in peace, so we could catch up. Zaph was in no mood to talk and within five minutes we ended up in the shower together. I loved every minute of it. Zaphy was amazing.

CHAPTER 15
Zaphire

Eliza left in a rush, hair still wet and dripping but she didn't care. I guess she didn't want to upset Zack by being late and get reprimanded. She's had enough of those and knew it was better to just try and follow Zack's orders to the letter. It made for a much easier life.

I decided to find Brody, even though I was meant to finish off some work. I had spotted him in his room and wanted to catch him before he might leave. I didn't need to worry. He'd ensconced himself on the sofa, feet up and listening to some music. He must be off for the rest of the day as he wore nothing but a pair of joggers and an old T-shirt full of holes, ready to just slob about.

"Hey, Zaphster. What's up?"

He invited me in with a wave of his hand. He wasn't going anywhere, lying back on the sofa after he half heartedly sat up to see who'd entered his room. I wasn't sure how to broach the subject subtly so I just crashed into it.

"What's going on with Zack? Does he talk to you at all?"

Brody considered this for a moment and I could sense his reluctance to spill the beans on his friend.

"Not really," was his short answer.

I realised I needed to work a bit harder to get anything out of him.

"It's just that I'm worried. He's behaving recklessly, very unlike him."

"What do you mean?" still not giving anything away.

"The girls...," I prompted.

"Oh that."

Brody sighed. Clearly still feeling uncomfortable talking about his friend.

"He's just letting off steam, Zaph. He'll get over it."

"Get over what?" I pounced. "Does he still have a thing for Eliza? I knew it!" I started pacing through Brody's room, letting my emotions run wild.

"Calm yourself down girl. What the hell! He's dealing with it, isn't he. Leave him to it," Brody warned.

"But he's not dealing, is he? He's just screwing! Taking advantage of all these girls! Disgusting!"

I couldn't help myself. I full on shouted at Brody, who started to look agitated. Highly unusual for him as he was the most laid back and calm guy ever. He actually got up and strode over, grabbing me by the shoulders and pushing me down to sit on the sofa.

"For fuck's sake Zaphire. You're being ridiculous. Yes, he's acting out of character, but he's not taking advantage of anyone. He specifically targets the girls who just want to have some fun, just like him. He can smell from a mile off the girls who'd be vulnerable. He clearly needs to take his mind off...,"

He stopped and looked sheepish.

"Exactly," I said bitterly.

So, my girlfriend fancied my brother, even though she claimed it was purely physical, and my brother was in love with her. Much more than he dared to admit. *Great.* This was going to test my ability to trust them beyond anything I had endured before. I loved her and I adored my brother, but could I live with this impossible situation? I really missed Sam. She would have been able to help me think through all of this.

Brody stood a little helplessly by my side, sighed deeply, regained his calm and sank into the sofa next to me. He wrapped his arm around me, making me feel instantly much better.

"Look. Zack can't help how he feels, but you can trust him. He would never do anything to hurt you. You know that. Eliza is off limits. He'll get over it. He's strong like that."

"I know, I know. I just wished it wasn't this complicated," I sighed.

I left Brody to his slobbing and retreated back to the office, to finish off the work I had left earlier today. I immersed myself fully in the case and soon was thinking of nothing else. In no time I was done and dropped my report off at Markus' office. Just as I left from there I bumped into Eliza. She looked exhausted. I would kill to know what Zack and her had discussed, but I knew I wouldn't stand a chance of finding out unless he wanted me to.

"Let's go and grab a cuppa," I offered and Eliza accepted gratefully. We only had just under an hour before our meeting with the team and both of us could do with a little break.

Markus, Michael, Lois and Zack were already in the conference room when Eliza and I arrived, feeling somewhat refreshed due to our down time. There was a slightly tense atmosphere, but nothing much out of the ordinary, and I didn't pick up any weird vibes between Zack and Eliza. They could be masking though as I didn't feel, smell or see anything much being emitted by either of them, which was a little suspect. I saw Zack had noticed me checking them over and he stared me out, challenging me. I didn't quite know what to make of it all, but decided to concentrate on Markus for the moment, even if it was just to avoid Zack's intense stare.

"Rick is getting increasingly hard to track, so we need Eliza to get in there as soon as possible. We're losing control of the situation, because we just don't have enough information. We have arrested a couple of his associates but they are not giving anything away that's useful. Rick's been extremely clever as to what information he lets people be part of. He knows if we captured any of them they wouldn't be able to lie to us. We haven't identified any Sensorians working with him, but that's not to say there aren't any. He could have recruited from other countries or we just haven't found out yet. I take it Rick hasn't contacted Eliza yet?"

Zack, Eliza and I all shook our heads in denial. Michael shifted uncomfortably on his feet, he was working up to say something he knew was controversial. Markus looked up, eyebrows lifted.

"Or that you know of...," Michael challenged, avoiding Eliza's eyes. Lois' eyes widened somewhat.

Eliza's heart rate spiked and she was about to

challenge him back. But Zack put a hand on arm to calm her down. I was about to speak up for myself, feeling personally attacked, but Zack was too quick and responded in his usual authoritative way.

"Michael. Eliza's not hiding anything from us. I shouldn't even have to say this but Zaphire has been with her and would have realised if contact was made. You're not pulling into question Zaphire's aptitude and commitment, are you?"

"No, no, not at all," he replied hastily, not quite successful in hiding his guilt when I caught his eye. Michael recovered quickly though.

"But the question had to be asked. We need to see firsthand reaction to these challenges, uncomfortable as it may feel. Don't be offended."

I was though. I knew their methods and I shouldn't be feeling personally affronted, but it was kinda hard not to. I tried to disguise my unprofessional feelings as much as I could, but I knew both Eliza and Zack had picked up on it.

"And? Are you satisfied now that there has been no contact? So can we move on and actually do something constructive now?" Zack questioned.

The slightly prickly undertone wasn't missed by Markus who threw him a miniscule but warning glare.

So many things were communicated by body language and scents, you had to keep your wits about you to avoid missing anything important.

I was with Zack. We just needed to move past this and focus.

"Any ideas as to how we're going to get Eliza in contact with Rick safely?" I started off the conversation to get the ball rolling.

I thought I picked up a slight moment between Eliza and Zack, but I must have imagined it as they were both occupied separately, looking through some documentation relating to Rick's whereabouts.

"We could move up North and join Laura and Frank's team? Be closer to the action?" offered Zack tentatively. Laura had moved up there to help Frank organise the team a few days ago.

"That's definitely an option. It would make it easier for him to try and contact Eliza. He'll know if you moved there. I'm sure he's got close tabs on Eliza's movements one way or the other."

Michael nodded in agreement with Markus' comment.

"They could do with some extra hands up there, so it's probably the most sensible thing to do. All three of you plus Brody can go up there and be of use. Then we can take it from there and see if Rick will make a move."

All of us agreed. I was a little surprised not to hear more from Eliza, considering she had such strong views on what moves Rick was likely to make or not when we were still at her mum's. I assumed Zack must have had a word with her about it in their meeting earlier, and possibly forbidden her to comment too much.

CHAPTER 16
Eliza

Zaphy and I spent an amazing evening, night and morning together. I tried to make it extra special for her and told her a thousand times how much I loved her. Little did she know that if my plan worked, it was quite possibly the last time we would spend time together like this for a long while. She knew something was up, but I let her fill in the details herself. Whatever she was thinking, I doubted she could imagine what the reality was going to be.

It had taken me all my effort to convince Zack to agree with my plan. The idea had formed in my head at my mother's house, and I'd made up my mind. I pleaded with him to trust me and trust me implicitly but only when he realised I would do it with or without his consent, he begrudgingly conceded. He clearly wasn't happy about it, but once he had committed he embraced it wholeheartedly. We perfected the strategy together, although we only had control over the first part. After that it was a waiting game and if Rick wouldn't bite, it could backfire quite dramatically. Zack was putting his career on the line. If this was going to go pear shaped one way or the other he, in his own words, would be 'fucking chained to a desk job for the rest of his fucking life' or even end up in prison. Plus he was convinced if Zaphire found out the truth she would blame him for everything and hate him forever. And I could end up branded a traitor and imprisoned for the rest of my life, or worse, dead. Only time would tell.

The meeting yesterday had just been a show on my part. I knew my own plan was going to be the most likely to succeed, but as I'd thought, Zack was convinced Markus would never allow it. They just didn't trust me enough, or maybe thought I wasn't strong enough to get involved with Rick alone, without proper back up and support. In their eyes I would either be swayed to work with my father, or be somehow manipulated to do so. They were clearly underestimating my loyalty and commitment to stop my father executing his dangerous ideas, even though I had fears about the dire consequences my father would face. Anyway, I knew that for the plan to work it was of utmost importance that as few people as possible knew about it, ideally just Zack and me. Rick would sense a trap if too many reactions weren't genuine to what was about to happen.

The hardest decision had been not to involve Zaphire. My heart bled when I thought about her reaction and what she would think of me. I practically had signed a death warrant to our budding relationship. She would never be able to fully trust me again, but it had to be this way. Zack had tried to convince me to include her, but her reaction would be the one that Rick was most likely to focus on and it had to be real. There was too much riding on it.

I also couldn't deny that part of me didn't want her involved purely to protect her. If it all went wrong, at least she wouldn't have to suffer the consequences. I didn't tell Zack this though, but I knew he sensed it. He didn't challenge me over it, he accepted his role in this.

The first part of the plan had to be executed in a public space with as many witnesses as possible for word to get out. It had to be in the lunch room. We were lucky as it was particularly busy today. Zack and I had engineered to be at some distance from our friends, pretending to be in some discussion or the other and this is where it all kicked off. The show was about to start.

"What the hell! I've had it up to here with your

pathetic orders! I'm not doing it Zack!" I threw my arms up in the air, raising my voice, but not quite shouting yet. It had attracted some attention already. Zack stayed calm.

"What's this Eliza? Are you refusing my order? I thought we'd moved past this stage."

"I can't do it anymore! You can stick your orders where the sun don't shine. I'm done with it. I'm done with it all!"

We had full attention. You could hear a pin drop. People's curiosity spiked and a nervous energy arose.

"Piss off, all of you! Stop listening! You morons!" I roared.

"Eliza. Calm down. This is your last chance. Apologise to me and everyone in the room. Now."

Zack stood tall and imposing with the hardest, sternest look on his face I'd ever seen and never in a million years would I have dared to defy him, if it wasn't part of our plan. He was amazing. I swallowed hard, because even though I knew it wasn't real, I found it hard to stand up against him.

"Go to hell," I hissed. "I want out! I want to go home! I can't do this any more! You can all do one!" I shouted, throwing my arms wildly about, my fingers jabbing at Zack's face.

Next thing I knew Zack had twisted one of my arms behind my back but I just managed to kick back and got his knee. I wished I hadn't done that. Within seconds I was on the floor, both arms behind my back and a knee firmly lodged in the small of my back. *Shit.* Pain raced through my body. The physical pain compounded by the angry vibes in the room nearly crushed me. Gasps echoed around the room.

"Mankuzay. You're back in isolation. You're fucking way out of line. How dare you defy me like this and insult everyone around you. For fuck's sake! I thought better of you," he sneered angrily in my ear, but loud enough for everyone to hear.

He had lost his calm exterior and showed me the full force of his anger. Mostly acted but my well aimed kick had riled him. I could feel it so others must have too. Perfect.

He roughly hauled me on my feet and moved me through the room, arms still behind my back. That's when I spotted Zaphire's distraught face. She made her way towards us. I avoided her eyes. I didn't think I could keep this up if I looked at her.

"Zack? Eliza? This doesn't make sense. What the hell happened?"

She exuded complete desperation and bewilderment.

"Get the fuck out of the way, sis."

Zack pushed his way roughly past her.

"Eliza?"

"Don't speak to her. That's an order Zaph."

I just caught a glimpse of her face, her beautiful eyes distraught and confused. It made my insides churn and bile rose to my throat.

"I hate you all!" I managed to choke out before Zack shoved me out the door.

"Did you have to fucking kick me! My knee kills!" he whispered angrily when we were safely out of earshot.

"It was instinct. But it did make it look real though!" I said a bit too triumphantly.

Zack tightened his grip on my arms and hoisted them up a little higher. I squealed in pain.

"That real enough for you?" he growled as he pushed me in the cell. "Don't make me regret my decision to go behind Markus' back!" he warned gravely, before leaving me to my own devices.

Back in the tiny room that had been my home for a month not long ago, feelings of uncertainty started to infiltrate my previously focussed thoughts. I had done it now. There was no turning back and that realisation hit me hard. I was on my own from now on until I'd achieve my goal. I would have to successfully convince my father I was going to side with him, claiming I just couldn't live in this strict Sensorian community and longed for more freedom. Yesterday, when Zack and I discussed my plan it had seemed so clear cut. All I needed to do was behave in a way that word would get out about my misgivings and doubts about living here. But, my outburst had come out of nowhere and I just hoped it was convincing enough for Rick to react.

I couldn't talk to Zack any more as all communications would be monitored from now on, so I hoped to God he would keep his trust in me and wait for me to contact him again when I was settled in with Rick. It was going to be the most difficult thing I'd ever done. I had no idea how Rick was going to get me out of here, but I knew he would try some way or another, as long as our act had been good enough. I just didn't know when.

Zack came back in. This was going to be hard. The cameras were switched on, nowhere to hide. By now he would have informed Markus and he would be expected to do everything in his power to talk me down or at least find out what was behind this sudden relapse. They will question it and listen in very closely, as yesterday everything seemed fine. I would have to be super convincing for them to believe that it wasn't just a small crisis of confidence that could be fixed.

He sat down and ordered me to sit too. I ignored it and turned around facing the wall.

"What are you doing Eliza? What's happened?" he said in about the friendliest tone I'd ever heard him speak. If this was real, I would have cracked already.

"I'm not playing by your rules any more. So you can't order me. It has no effect."

He thought for a moment.

"Do you think we at least deserve some sort of explanation? Could you not have talked about it? Everything seemed fine yesterday?"

"I'm clearly a master in cloaking then. Or you are just a pretty useless Sensorian."

Below the belt. Zack absorbed it, but I knew inside he was cursing me because his superiors will have him for his lack of astuteness. And Zaphire at that. I cringed inside with the thought of that because at least Zack knew what it was really about whereas Zaphire would be utterly confused. Zack picked up on it. He had to, as the observing leadership would have noticed too.

"Why did you feel hurt just now. Something is clearly bothering you, besides this show you're putting on."

Clever.

"You think it's a show do you? What for? What would I achieve with that? I can't live within the rules of this community. Staying with my mum made that clear to me. Hence my request for our sudden return. I wanted to come back to the compound to check that what I felt was real. And it is. I can't do it. I was hoping to talk about it but it just all came flying out in the canteen. I hate it here. I hate that everyone knows everything you feel and watch every step you do. You've felt it from the start Zack. You must have."

He cast down his eyes. He knew he would have to deal with Markus' wrath over this. He was going to face a lot of criticism. I felt sorry for him, but he had told me he could take it. He just hoped it was going to be worth it in the end.

"You've put me in an impossible situation, Eliza. You may not want to abide by our rules, but I do and you, frankly, don't have a choice. You are a Sensorian, whether you like it or not, which makes you subject to our laws."

"Can you not just let me go back to mum? I will sign secrecy papers, I will do anything. I don't want to cause trouble for the community," I pleaded, changing tactics, trying to sound as desperate as I could.

"No. You can't. Not anymore. You've overstepped the mark, we can't trust you. Not only would it set a precedent we're not willing to make, it would also leave you wide open to be targeted by Rick. I won't let that happen." He paused a second and took a deep breath. "I have to confine you to solitary imprisonment for two weeks. Same rules apply as before. The start of that punishment will be when you decide to comply by the rules you've been set. If you decide to ignore those rules you could be in here for a very long time. We will reconvene after you have done your time, fully complying and talk about your future then," he decided.

"For crying out loud, Zack. I'm a lost cause. What are you going to do with me?"

"I fully trust you'll see sense eventually. I know that deep down inside you are a committed Sensorian and we will prise it out of you. I'm disappointed at the moment, especially in myself. We should have seen this coming and dealt with it better."

He sighed and stood up to leave.

"Undress. Leave your clothes by the door. Your prison clothes are on the bed."

He had played his part well. The door shut behind him.

Silence.

CHAPTER 17
Zaphire

"That was unexpected," Brody said in his calm as usual voice.

I was blubbing. I couldn't help myself. Crying was not my usual response but I just didn't understand how things had suddenly taken this U-turn. *How had we not seen any of this coming?* Brody put a comforting arm around me, trying to shield me from all the prying eyes. I didn't have the emotional strength to move, so we had just sat down on the first available table, which happened to have Jessica, Zack's bitter ex, sitting at it. She was gloating but I didn't have the energy to confront the stupid bitch.

"I just don't understand it. Has everything been a lie? She told me she loved me this morning. What did Zack do to her, or say? I don't get it!" I managed to utter in between sobs.

"Something must have been brewing for her to blow up like that. Think back. Did you spot any little signs, maybe when you were over at Alice's?" Brody mused.

"Nothing mate. Absolutely zilch. Maybe I was too blinded by love and my senses obscured. I don't know. Markus is going to kill me."

It dawned on me that it would be me and Zack who would get the blame for this. And rightly so, we should have picked it up earlier. We were in deep shit. By missing this we'd inadvertently blown our whole strategy to deal with Rick.

"It's not your fault Zaphy. Don't start blaming yourself," Brody tried comforting me, unsuccessfully.

"Yeah right. You don't even believe that yourself. She's a newbie. We should have been able to read her better. I know it's more difficult with our kind, but we should have with her. I always noticed when she was cloaking. I just don't understand. Maybe we were getting too cocky for our own good."

I had to speak to Zack. Find out what he said that had triggered the outburst. See what his take on the situation was, before we were called up by the leaders. I managed to pick myself up somewhat and we made our way to find Zack. Brody texted him and he replied almost instantly. He was in his room.

When we entered we found Zack sat behind the table with his head in his hands, surrounded by a cloud of frustration and worry. Not anger or confusion, I noted. I moved behind him and started giving him a neck massage, something he usually appreciated. He pushed my hands away though, stood up and started pacing. He finally looked up at me.

"We're fucking screwed," he simply stated.

"Yeah. I came to that conclusion too," I sighed.

I usually looked to my brother for solutions, but it looked like today he'd run out of ideas as well.

"We'll just have to go and face the music in a minute, Zaph. There's nothing that I can think of that explains this sudden shift in attitude and I'm sure if you'd noticed anything you would have said something by now."

I nodded. I briefly thought about when Eliza confided in me about trying to somehow prevent her father from getting the death sentence, but she had been truthful about her loyalty to us. She wasn't hiding anything, not that I could tell anyway.

"How could we have missed this? I just don't get it. Maybe she's just a master in cloaking, just like her father," I suggested half-heartedly.

Brody nodded encouragingly but Zack slammed it.

"Then we were fools not to have picked up on that. Whichever way we look at this, the buck stops with me. Don't blame yourself Zaph. She wasn't your responsibility and I will make sure I reiterate that to Markus. I won't have you take any blame for this."

"That's very sweet of you Zack, but we both know if Markus wants to impart blame or punishment, he will."

Zack thumped the table in frustration.

"This is a fucking mess!"

"Was there anything you said maybe, just before her outburst? Something that triggered it?" I tentatively asked.

"I went over it a thousand times in my head. It was a simple order, one that she would normally just have done. She was a bit grumpy, but nothing out of the ordinary, I thought it was because she hadn't really wanted to leave you this morning or something. Nothing that warranted her reaction. It must have been simmering for ages and we just missed it."

I believed him. He had said or done nothing wrong to change Eliza's attitude so dramatically. We just had to accept our oversight and bear the consequences.

*

"I feel like I'm like seven years old and about to be told off for eating all the biscuits," I whispered to Zack just before we entered Markus' office.

"You're going to feel worse than that in a minute, Zaph."

Not very encouraging. I was actually trembling. Zack gently squeezed my hand and I knew he would try his hardest to protect me.

Michael and Markus both stood up and were clearly in an agitated state, but no Dullard would ever have guessed as their exteriors showed nothing but calm. Underneath were raging emotions and frustrations and we both shielded the best we could to abate the physical pain of them.

Markus lifted both hands halfway in the air and his face asked a thousand questions, eyes boring into ours.

"Explain please?" was the only thing Markus could say, I suspected, without bursting out in a rage that was clearly bubbling just below the surface.

"I'm sorry Sir. I don't have an explanation. I did not see this one coming at all," Zack started.

Michael and Markus exchanged angry glances.

"Zaphire? Anything to add?" Markus directed his glare to me.

"No Sir. Nothing at all. No indication."

Zack looked at me peculiarly. He must have picked up on my slight unease about what Eliza had told me about her wanting to somehow protect her father. No one else did though.

Markus uncharacteristically lost his temper momentarily, slamming the desk, breaking a cup with the force of it. He took a deep breath before he continued speaking.

"Is there any chance she'll snap out of this at all?"

He knew the answer to that.

"Not in any hurry. I'm sure eventually she'll comply and see sense but I have no idea when that will happen," Zack answered dutifully.

"We have no time for 'eventually'. Basically what you're saying is that we have lost our main strategy for neutralising and capturing Rick."

"Yes Sir. For now."

Zack stood tall but lowered his head, eyes cast down.

Markus spun round sharply, frustration oozing everywhere. Taking another deep sigh he slowly turned back to face us, eyes glowering.

"I'm deeply disappointed in the two of you. You must have lost focus and I don't have to guess what caused that. I thought you could handle it, but clearly both of your attraction to this girl has cost us our strategy."

Zack was about to protest but was silenced immediately.

"Don't say a word. We'll figure something else out concerning Rick, but that is of no concern to you both now. Zack, I'm dismissing you from your duty to train Eliza. You're no longer responsible for her. Desk jobs for the foreseeable future for the both of you. It will be a very long time before I can trust you on a mission again, if ever."

A desk job! Forever! That was my personal form of hell. It would kill me!

"Permission to speak, Sir?" Zack tried.

"Granted. Make it good."

"I take full responsibility, Sir. This is entirely on me. Please reconsider Zaphire's punishment. Her brief wasn't to look after Eliza's mental state, that was mine and mine alone. Please take into account the excellent record she has on all of her previous missions. This was just one mistake."

"A mistake that may cost us our way of life and threaten all of society." Markus paused for what felt like an eternity and none of us dared to say anything. Even Michael kept schtum. "I'll reconsider Zaphire's fate after we've sorted this mess out and work out a different strategy. But I'm not promising anything."

"Thank you Sir," Zack managed to say convincingly but I knew he was struggling with his own destiny. He hated desk jobs just as much as me and I could just about imagine how much he was cursing Eliza underneath all of it. I hoped Zack had convinced Markus enough to let me go up North at least and join them there, maybe even return to work in the field sooner rather than later.

I wondered if I dared ask to see Eliza, but I decided against it. I would try when Markus had calmed down somewhat.

We turned to leave the room but Markus hadn't quite finished yet.

"And you're grounded. Indefinitely. And no alcohol allowed."

I caught Zack's eye and to his horror, almost burst out laughing.

"Markus? We're nearly twenty years old! You can't ground us!" I said indignantly with half a smile.

"Can't I now?" His voice low and threatening. I didn't quite know where to look and wished I hadn't said anything. "The both of you are my responsibility as I am still your carer. So long as you live under my roof you will bloody well abide by my rules. Understood?"

There was no point arguing with him. We'd just have to endure it for the time being.

CHAPTER 18
Eliza

Footsteps approached and I heard the jangle of keys. It wasn't Zack though. I would recognise his walk and particular jangle even if I hadn't heard it for years. I wondered who was behind the door. I didn't have to wait long as the door swung open and a tall woman in her forties strode in. I had seen her around but hadn't been introduced to her yet.

"Stand up."

Her first words were authoritative but not harsh.

I decided to obey, as I wanted to find out what she was doing here.

"Good girl," she said a little patronizingly. "I was warned you may be uncooperative, but this is a good start. Thank you," she continued.

I waited, unsure as to what to make of her.

"I'm Vivian Johnson, but you'll call me Ma'am. I'm your new trainer as Zack has been relieved from his duties concerning you."

She monitored my reaction closely and I tried to cloak my disappointment as best I could. I didn't want to be an open book to her. She smiled a little.

"My speciality is to see through the most difficult of disguises. Very few people can cloak from me and I can tell you now, you're good, but not that good so you might as well give up."

This wasn't good. Not good at all. Under no circumstance did I want her to find out what my plan was or suspect there was something suspicious about my actions.

"In fact, it makes me wonder how Zack and Zaphire did not pick up any vibes of discontent from you in the days leading up to the little stunt you pulled in the canteen. Care to explain?"

I stayed silent. I decided I wasn't going to cooperate with this woman. It was too dangerous. She needed to be out of here, the sooner the better. I sat down on my chair, and folded my arms, trying to think of nothing so I could give nothing away.

"Right. I see you're not ready to talk. I wonder what you respond to better; punishment or reward?"

Again I didn't even consider her question; instead I tried to think about what animal she reminded me of.

"As I want to start off on the right foot, I will start with reward. I'll come back tomorrow and we will talk. After that you may start your period of isolation if you comply with the rules. If you cooperate tomorrow, I will reduce your time to 10 days."

She reminded me of a fox; clever and sly.

"Miss Mankuzay," she nodded and left me to my own thoughts.

I felt sad that Zack wasn't my coach any more, but I knew it had been inevitable. I had openly goaded both Zack and Zaphire for not having predicted my outburst, and Markus clearly blamed them. I probably won't see Zack now until I'm able to contact him again, hopefully with enough information to stop my father's plans. I had learned Zack's phone number off by heart, an old pay as you go mobile that had been out of use for years.

I forbade myself to even think about Zaphy. I would explain everything to her after the mission, but I couldn't cope thinking of the despair she must be feeling now. I simply couldn't go there, I had to be strong and block it out.

Food came and was taken away again. I couldn't eat. I practised my Vision Hacking on the girl who took my food away by quickly touching her hand. It was easy to hack in and I was pleased to find as she jerked her hand away, the vision didn't disappear straight away. I still needed a lot more practice though to even attempt a remote hack but I was making progress. This extra gift could come in very useful indeed, especially as Rick wasn't aware I had it, and even in our compound only a few people knew.

I watched my hour of television and as I didn't have any books to read I just went to bed. Morning took forever to come, but it did. And so breakfast arrived, and left again hardly eaten. I practised some more VH on the unsuspecting boy who was responsible for my food today. Then I nervously awaited Vivian's inevitable arrival.

She came. I didn't co-operate. She left, this time with a threat of punishment. No reward.

I sighed. I didn't know how long I could keep this up for and hoped Rick would make his move sooner rather than later. I hadn't lost confidence, but a little seed of doubt had crept into my consciousness. I didn't dare ask myself the 'what if' question yet. It simply had to work.

CHAPTER 19
Zaphire

"I hate to admit it but Markus is damned clever. Replacing you with Vivian was a master stroke. No way Eliza is going to cloak from her, she sees through practically anything."

I observed Zack for a moment. He looked worried and mighty pissed off.

"Humph," he grumbled, not giving much away. "Markus is a master at everything, Zaph. That's why I admire him so much. But he can be such an arse with it!" he conceded after a while.

We were both struggling with our confinement and it had only been two days. Markus had lectured us again yesterday, well mostly Zack to be honest, about his clubbing and drinking. He was convinced it had contributed to his failure and was now adamant our grounding and no alcohol rule was to last for quite some time.

Zack had tried to reason with him, saying he had only been doing that when Eliza was in isolation and *he* was adamant it hadn't impaired his judgement at all. But it was a weak argument, because the fact of the matter was that we had ballsed up. Plus his arguing had done nothing but make Markus more annoyed. I had kept quiet. I didn't want Markus to forbid my relationship with Eliza, because he could if he thought it was necessary. And I trusted Eliza would get through this and see sense. We could be together again, and I wasn't going to endanger that by winding Markus up even more.

"I'm so bored already Zaph. I mean archiving! Really! I didn't even fucking know we still did that!" His whole body exuded frustration and exasperation. "And it's not just the fucking job; it's the fucking people too. I swear they're all dead on the inside."

"A bit harsh Zack," I couldn't help giggle a little. "I'm sure they're all quite nice really. You just need to coax it out of them. See it as a challenge. It will keep your mind occupied at least."

"How's your job looking Zaph?" ignoring my suggestion.

"Just fantastic. What I've always dreamt of doing," I answered sarcastically. Working in the office, doing administrative tasks was my kind of hell. The most exciting task I had was typing up reports as at least I kept a finger on the pulse as to what was going on in the real world. I had already come across a titbit of information that would at least keep my mind occupied.

124

"Did you know last week Rick was actually near Eliza and me? He was followed right into the village next to Alice's. He stayed one night but didn't go out of his room or meet anyone at all, then returned up north the following morning." I thought about the feeling Alice had experienced. She had been right after all. Pretty intuitive for a Dullard.

"No! How come we weren't informed! That's a vital piece of information!" Zack jumped up and started pacing the room frantically.

"I thought it was a bit odd, because it was almost like it had been filed away without having been read. It was a one page report stuck inside a folder that had nothing to do with Rick's case," I remembered.

"Do you know who tailed him?" Zack asked urgently.

"No, but I can find out. I will look into it tomorrow first thing and let you know." A disconcerting feeling crept into my mind. "Do you think it has anything to do with Eliza's behaviour?"

Zack nodded, deep in thought.

"I don't know. It didn't seem like he contacted her and if he'd done so by phone, why travel all the way down there. Maybe he wanted to check her out, but was warned off and turned back? It's all a bit strange and I wonder who knows about it."

"Should we ask Markus?" I wondered.

"Let's find out as much as we can and then contact Markus," Zack decided.

I agreed. He had been clear about not wanting us involved in the mission, but if we had stumbled across something important he wouldn't deny us a meeting. We just needed to be sure first.

The following day I was keen to start work and my colleagues picked up on my change of mood instantly, making irritating comments to highlight that fact. I ignored them and immediately delved into the pile of stuff I did yesterday to try and locate the report I had spotted. My heart jumped a beat when I found it almost instantly. The person who'd written it was someone I recognised the name of, but I never really had come across. I decided to give Harish a call immediately, though I had to move out of the office so people couldn't overhear. I went into the toilet and checked each cubicle before making the call.

"Harish speaking?" a softly spoken man answered, his voice betraying a little curiosity as he wouldn't have recognised the number.

"Hi, it's Zaphire Mackenzie."

"One of Markus' twins?"

Excitement spilled over into his voice.

"Yes. Can you tell me anything more about what happened when you trailed Rick down south?" I tried to be as to the point as possible.

"Err, nothing much happened. I didn't think it was important as my message was never followed up. I guessed you all knew everything about it."

He was straight into self defence.

"No need to worry, Harish. I'm just tying up some loose ends. Do you remember who you gave the message to?"

"Err, let me see. It was a girl. Yes, it was a girl called Jessica. Can't remember her surname. I passed the notes to her to give to Markus and Zack directly."

"Okay Harish. That's all for now. Thank you very much."

My heart had started pounding so loudly I thought the people in the office next to the toilet might wonder what was going on. The door opened and I quickly ran the water and washed my hands vigorously. It was Selma from my office.

"Are you okay Zaphire?" she enquired curiously.

The room must have reeked of sudden excitement and urgency and I still hadn't managed to calm my heartbeat down. I walked off quickly, mumbling something inaudible and nodding my head, unable to think of a believable excuse. I had to get to Zack. He'll explode when he hears his disgruntled ex-girlfriend is somehow involved in this. If Rick was made aware of us following him, it might explain why he didn't make contact with Eliza. Frustratingly, I had to wait till morning break, as the working hours were rigorously adhered to in this department.

CHAPTER 20
Eliza

No books had arrived. Part of the punishment. I'd given myself a couple of exercises to do to keep myself occupied. I'd got up to fifty four press ups when I heard someone approach in a hurry. It wasn't a scheduled visit. Vivian wasn't due back till tomorrow and it was nowhere near time for more food. I fleetingly hoped it was Zack or Zaphire but, the footsteps didn't sound familiar.

The door opened and no other than Jessica rushed in. My heart jolted. She took off her hoody and trousers and all I could do was stand and stare at her for a second or two.

"Wh... what...," I started to stutter but was interrupted immediately.

"Don't ask questions. Listen. We have to be quick, Eliza. Take off your trousers and put these on. Take the hoody too and cover your hair. Here's my pass and the keys," she ordered hurriedly.
I did what she said. My heart nearly exploded in my throat. This was it. This was Rick's move.

"Listen carefully as I will only say this once. Get out of the building as quickly as you can. Under no circumstances look up. Just keep walking. If someone tries to talk to you, cough and mumble your excuses. When out of the compound, turn right, take the first right and a dark blue BMW will be waiting for you. Lock the cell door before you go otherwise an alarm will go off when you open the exit door. Move. Now."

She pushed me out of the room and there was nothing for it. I locked the cell door and walked. My body ached to run but I managed to contain it to a purposeful walk. I didn't want to alert anyone who happened to be monitoring the security cameras. The first obstacle was ahead. I held my card out in preparation for the scanner by the door. There was no reason to be nervous as it should work; it didn't rely on eye recognition or anything, but my adrenaline was pumping and the nerves raged through my body. I sincerely hoped I wouldn't bump into anyone as the scent I emitted was intoxicatingly strong. In a crowd it wouldn't be so bad as it would at least take a little time to locate who was causing the stench, but alone in this corridor there would be no denying it was me, and would raise suspicion instantly.

The door reliably bleeped and clicked and I pushed

it open, glancing quickly into the next corridor. No one to be seen, so I carried on walking quickly towards the lobby, which wasn't far away. I could see people through the next set of glass doors. It was relatively busy, which was good.

Just before I got to the door, a young man approached it and opened it for me, politely stepping aside to let me through. I mumbled a 'thank you' without looking up at him, but managed a quick touch of the hand to access his vision. All he saw was a hooded figure walking off, then the vision disappeared. I hurried into the crowd.

As if in slow motion I noticed him realise the suspicious scent hanging in the corridor, and I could feel his searching eyes looking for me in the crowd. I didn't look back, heading straight for the exit. I quickened my step slightly, getting my card ready again on approach of the door to the outside world. I picked up a slight commotion behind me, but kept stoically walking. The scanner was slow, but after what seemed to take an eternity it bleeped and I opened the door. I immediately took a deep breath of crisp outside air, blowing it out slowly in a vain attempt to calm my heart down and focus on cloaking my output of signals. I didn't want to leave an obvious trail, in case they were following already.

I turned right out of the door, kept walking and headed into the first road. True to Jessica's word, about a hundred meters on I spotted the blue BMW waiting for me. I didn't dare believe I'd made it until I was in that car. I could swear I heard footsteps running after me, but resisted wasting time by turning around and checking. I practically ran the last bit, grabbed the door handle, opened it and threw myself inside. The driver didn't hesitate and, wheels screeching, drove off. I glanced out of the back window but couldn't see anyone. If they had been following me, they'd lost me. Relief flooded over me.

I couldn't believe I pulled it off. It had only been about ten minutes since Jessica had entered my cell. I couldn't believe she'd helped me get out, but I was under no illusion she'd done it out of the kindness of her heart. She must have been contacted by Rick. Maybe even recruited. Had she sacrificed herself for him? She was stuck in that cell and she wouldn't be able to escape the consequences. Security will go up a hundredfold once they realise what happened, so another miraculous escape was not on the cards for her.

Shit. She could face the death penalty.

I wondered if she realised what Rick had asked of her. I felt sick to the stomach. My father was utterly ruthless.

CHAPTER 21
Zaphire

Finally the clock struck eleven. Coffee break. Everyone started to clear their desk and close their computer files readying themselves to go. I shoved my papers in a pile and rushed off to find Zack in archiving. He should be on his break too.

I peeked through their door window to see Zack looking horrendously bored, listening to one of the guys explaining the inner workings of an internal combustion engine, as far as I could gather through the thick glass. I banged on the door and Zack's expression was utter relief to have an excuse to go.

"Zaphy! Have you found something out?" he asked eagerly.

I pulled him across the corridor and into a small room. No CCTV to be seen. Excellent.

"You won't believe this. You'll never guess who took that message. Bloody Jessica!"

I waited for his reaction, shielding instantly. A wise move on my part.

"Little bitch! She never fucking passed it on, did she! Jesus, that's just one step too far. Undermining our mission just to fucking spite me. Let's get her," he bellowed.

"Wait a minute Zack. I think you need to go to Markus with this. This is too big for us. She may have other reasons, besides being spiteful. What if it's more than that?" I urged.

"What. You mean she might be involved with Rick? No way. Fuck it. You're right. We need to see Markus immediately. Fuck archiving. You with me?"

He waited for my response. He had given me the choice to withdraw and he wouldn't mind. He would do it by himself, not blaming me for pulling out. I had done my bit as far as he was concerned and wouldn't want to force me into something I wasn't prepared to do.

"What the hell. Of course I'm with you. Let's go."

"Zack. Your shift has started."

A little knock on our door preceded the warning.

"Yeah. Err... Stefan. Could you cover for me for an hour or so?"

The young man's face darkened. He wasn't willing to comply with Zack's request. I felt Zack's irritation rise. He stood up tall and looked bloody imposing. Face hard as stone and eyes throwing daggers. He might have been temporarily demoted to archives, but there was no arguing with his natural authority. Stefan's attitude changed rapidly.

"Of course, Sir. No problem," he mumbled as he scuttled back to his office.

"Well done brother," I whispered, though slightly annoyed that I couldn't hide my admiration. He really didn't need the encouragement.

We rushed to Markus' office, but on the way I noticed something was off. Weird vibes emanated from the lobby. Confusion and stress mixed with adrenaline was in the air and a man was asking several people questions, looking extremely hassled. My instinct took over and I grabbed Zack who had noticed something was up too, but was so keen to get to Markus, he wasn't fully tuned in. I made him stop and listen.

"....hooded girl....something's wrong. I can feel it... did you see.."

I couldn't quite make out what the young man was asking or telling everyone, but I knew it was important. I got an overwhelming sense of determination to investigate. *Did I catch a little whiff of Eliza?* No, I couldn't have. She was in her cell. I turned to Zack.

"We need to find out what's going on here. I feel this is something crucial."

He was reluctant. I pressed on.

"Trust me Zack. My instinct is rarely wrong. It won't

take long."

I walked resolutely towards the guy who'd caused my interest to pique, hoping Zack would follow. I felt him hesitate but then was behind me grumpily sighing.

"What the fuck. You better be right," he grumbled.

"Hey, what's up mate?" I directed myself straight towards the fellow. He looked round, with a slightly panicked look on his face. I recognised him now. He was slightly older than us but I remembered him from school. "You're Archie, aren't you?"

I tried to make him feel a little more at ease. He was clearly struggling, looking at the both of us in bewilderment.

"You're Zaphire and Zack."

"Yeah. We know who we are," Zack responded rather sarcastically. "But why are you causing bad vibes, dude. Tell us what's happened."

Patience and tact weren't his strong point.

"That's what I was trying to find out. A girl with a hoody came out of that corridor just when I went in. I didn't recognise her scent but the stench she left in there was unmistakeably adrenaline mixed with fear and guilt. She was up to, or had been up to something bad, man. She moved so quickly that before I had put two and two together she was out of the door. I ran to go after her, but by the time I was out I couldn't see her anymore. I tried to follow her scent, but it disappeared, mixed in with everyone else's odours out there. I was just trying to find out if anyone had seen her and sensed it too."

"Thanks. We need to look at CCTV and check the log. Did she use a card to get out?" I enquired urgently.

"Yeah. I think so?" he nodded, slightly unsure of himself.

"Come with us, please."

We made our way to the front desk and got Olivia, the receptionist, to alert security. They soon checked who had left the building in the last half hour, and the name just before Archie came up as Miss J. Summers. Zack banged the desk with his fist.

"What the fuck did Jessica do?" he growled.

"This is weird. We need to let Markus know now. We'll access the CCTV footage there," I decided.

CHAPTER 22
Eliza

We'd been driving for about four hours. The driver hadn't said a word, ignoring all my questions, so I'd given up and just looked out the window watching the world go by. I tried to sleep a little, but the adrenaline in my body stopped me from being able to relax enough. Anyway, it was good to be alert as I could keep an eye on the road signs and work out exactly where I was.

The car finally came to a stop after we'd been driving around in a town called Bradstone. I'd never heard of it, but I knew from other towns mentioned on the signs that it was located somewhere in the North East. The house we parked outside of was situated in a slightly dilapidated residential area on the outskirts of Bradstone.

The driver got out of the car and had a good look around before opening my door and gesturing for me to get out. Once I was out he held my arm and gently but forcefully encouraged me to walk up the garden path towards a dark looking house, its foreboding appearance not helped by the dark brown curtains being drawn. He let us in; the dank smell from the corridor greeting us hit me like a suffocating blanket and made me feel most unwelcome.

He seemed to be unaware of the awful impression the house made. He took his coat off and swung it over a chair, turned the light on in the sparse kitchen and filled up the kettle.

"Brew?"

I nodded. I was parched.

"Y' must be hungry, lass."

I nodded again as he got some bread and butter out. He showed me a cupboard full of cans of soup, baked beans and whatnot.

"Help yersel' to whatever ye like," he offered not unkindly.

I rifled through the slightly sticky contents of the cupboard and found some cream of mushroom soup. I poured it in a bowl and looked for a microwave.

"Nah, ye have to cook it on the hob, lass. Here's a saucepan."

I offered to make him some too, but he declined politely in his broad northern accent. He carried on making our tea, assuming I had milk and sugar as that's how it came.

After about an hour of eating, drinking tea and awkward silences, someone else arrived at the house.

It was a not unattractive, brightly dressed woman in her forties who immediately came over and introduced herself.

"Hi, I'm Tina. You must be Eliza." She offered her hand and gave me a firm handshake. "You must be wondering what on earth is going on?" she opened the conversation.

"I have an inkling," I said measuredly.

"Well, tell me. What do you think is happening here, then."

I ignored her slightly irritated tone.

"My father has taken it upon himself to free me from my isolation cell, in the hope I would join him in his quest? It's just a guess." I added the latter part slightly sarcastically.

"So where is he?" I asked looking around as if I expected him to walk in at any moment.

"He's not here. You won't see him for a couple of days yet. That's if you want to see him of course. He doesn't want you to do anything against your will. We can return you to the compound if you wish us to do so," she answered, not denying my presumption.

"Okay. I'll stay here, thank you. I wish to meet my father," I said rather formally.

"You'll have to stay here for a few days, until we're

sure you're not tracked. Just in case you've swallowed a device like you did before. As you know it can take some time to pass through your system, so we're taking this precaution. All they'll find is you and me, and I know nothing."

"I'm not being tracked. I had no idea this was going to happen," I stated indignantly.

"Well, I'm not a Sensorian so I can't tell whether you're telling the truth. We have to take this precaution. Your father seemed to think you would understand," she replied matter of factly and slightly accusingly.

"I do understand. Doesn't mean I have to like it." I sighed and sat myself down at the kitchen table again. "How are we going to kill the time then, Tina?" I tried to sound a little more friendly. Might as well make the best of it, since I wasn't going to change anyone's mind about this arrangement.

"Mattie is going to get us some provisions and entertainment before he'll be off. He'll come and pick us up when Rick decides it's safe to do so."

She said my father's name with such reverence and admiration, it made me wonder if she was in love with him.

"You like my father?" I tried.

"He's amazing. I've only met him a couple of times

but I know he can change the world, Eliza. He's a true leader. The world would become a better place with him in charge."

I nodded non-committally.

"Where did you meet him?" I asked, hoping to find out some information about his whereabouts.

"Different places. At meetings in halls and hotels. He never stays in one place for long, except for at his base. But I don't know where that is. Not many people do."

"How many people are with Rick? How many followers does he have? Have you any idea?" I dug a little more.

"I know he's gathered a core of other Sensorians and he's hoping you'll join them. There are about a hundred of us, common people, spreading the word."

"Spreading the word?"

"Yeah, about all the good things he's done for us already. Helping to get the truth out of people and punishing those that lie. Can you imagine a world where no one can lie, because they always get outed. No more conmen out to get your money, no more cheaters, or people getting away with crimes. You don't need a body of evidence. All they need is to put be on trial and a penal of Sensorians assessing them."

143

"If only it was that simple," I half mumbled. "Do you know how many Sensorians he already has recruited?"

"I'm sure he'll introduce you to them in due time, if he trusts you. I don't know who they are or how many. He keeps most of the organisation close to his heart. Your dad's a very clever but cautious man."

Mattie, the driver, came back with supplies and a TV box. He set it all up for us, though Tina insisted she knew how to do it. The next few days were going to be less than exciting so I gave into it. I briefly tried to blag access to a phone, but was told that under no circumstances I was to have access to any phone, computer or tablet. So, I had myself a shower in the rather drab and uninviting bathroom. At least the water was hot. I put on some pyjamas that were laid out for me on a bed and ensconced myself in front of the small but functional flat screen. There was not much else to do than wait for Rick's next move.

CHAPTER 23
Zaphire

"Let's track her movements backwards, starting from the moment she left the compound," Markus decided.

He had listened to our account of what happened so far, immediately telling us off for not informing him straight away. The news that Jessica had failed to deliver an important message about Rick's whereabouts was received with concern and raised eyebrows. Her odd behaviour leaving the compound in such a rush and leaving such a stench did nothing to alleviate that worry.

"Wait a minute. Look where she's coming from." Zack's interest piqued. I heard his heart quickening. "It's the bloody isolation cells. What the fuck is she doing there? She's coming out of Eliza's cell!"

Zack rushed out of the room heading for the cells before Markus could stop him. I hot-footed after him and I heard Markus and Michael follow not far behind. Markus contacted Vivian and ordered her to come straight away too. I noticed Zack fishing the keys out of his pocket. He'd clearly 'forgotten' to hand those in after being relieved of his duties. He opened the door.

"What the...where the fuck is Eliza!" Zack thundered.

Jessica sat on the bed; looking up at us triumphantly.

"Wouldn't you like to know?" she taunted.

Realisation of what had happened hit us instantly.

Markus entered the room and pushed us aside. Jessica's face dropped. Her demeanour changed immediately from cocky to repentant and submissive. It didn't fool anyone.

"I'm sorry Sir. I never...," she started but was roughly interrupted by Markus.

He walked over and hauled her to her feet, then pushed her down to kneel in front of him.

"What have you done Jess." his voice low and threatening, but mixed with an undertone of surprise. He'd never imagined anyone would actually undermine him and our society like this. And this was big. A huge betrayal. "You need to tell us everything you know. Now!" he demanded, eyes cold as steel.

Zack looked like he was going to kill her there and then, but I felt stricken. Eliza had run. She'd betrayed us. I felt sick as a dog and puked my guts up, just when Vivian arrived. I sat myself on the bed and watched

146

everything as if it was a film. I couldn't believe Eliza had left like this. Something or someone must have made her. She wouldn't do this to us. Not to me.

"All I know is that I came here, swapped clothes, gave her my card and she left. There was a car waiting for her a couple of streets away. I didn't make her go. She chose to."

She glanced maliciously at me and Zack.

"What street," Markus barked.

"Duress Road," Jessica whispered.

"Michael, get CCTV from the surrounding roads. We need to find out what car she travelled in and what direction it went."

Michael turned around and rushed out of the room. Time was of the essence.

"Where's she heading."

Markus stared Jessica deeply in the eyes. She wouldn't be able to hide anything from him.

"I don't know. I don't know anything. I was coerced," Jessica squeaked, in a desperate attempt to save her skin.

Markus turned around, disregarding Jessica's pleads.

"I'll deal with you later Miss Summers. And I can guarantee you'll wish you'd made a different choice.

You know the consequences of betrayal. You're done."

His words dripped with anger and contempt.

Markus marched out and signalled us all to follow. I hesitated looking at the pool of sick I'd left behind.

"Leave it," Markus growled. He was in no mood to be slowed down. We walked back to Markus' office. "Zack, you're going to assist Vivian in trying to locate Eliza. She's a fugitive and needs to be captured. We have to assume she's colluding with Rick and it needs to be treated that way. You will follow Vivian's orders to the letter. Understood?" A threat sat hidden amongst the words.

"Yes Sir," he answered dutifully, but I knew my brother. He wasn't happy about having to obey Vivian at all, but relieved he was on active duty again so soon.

"Zaphire, first of all, well done for being so alert at your job to have picked up the missing message. However, you're too close to Eliza to be of any use at the moment. So, go back to your job, for now."

What the hell. He couldn't do this to me! There was no way I was going to go back to that boring admin job now. No way.

"Markus. Please. I can be of use. I know Eliza better than anyone. You need me," I tried, to no avail.

"Zack knows her well enough. He can ask for your input if Vivian requires it. I don't need you on this job. You're too emotionally involved and I can't have that. The job is too important. Not another word about it."

Arsehole. Why was Zack allowed and not me! It took all my strength not to have an emotional outburst and prove him right. Instead I turned towards Vivian.

"If there's anything you need me to do, please let me know, Ma'am."

Vivian accepted gracefully. Not wanting to ruffle my feathers or defy Markus.

"I will certainly do that," she answered dutifully.

At least Zack was in the loop so he could keep me updated. I wanted to prove Markus wrong. I convinced myself that Eliza hadn't betrayed us. There must be a different reason for her escape. There simply had to be. I couldn't wait to talk to Zack later. See how he felt about it. I knew he would think the same and together we could find out, under the radar, what was going on.

"Thank you Vivian. I'll go back to my office now and leave you to it."

I made a good show of being obedient and mature about it and I think I managed to cloak my true feelings well enough to not raise any suspicion from Markus, but I noticed Zack's expression. He wasn't having any of it. He could read me too well.

"You're both still grounded by the way. Don't think you're exonerated, and this job is just because it's an emergency, Zack. And you need to apologise to Stefan. You used your authority to bully him into covering for you. You weren't on a mission so you shouldn't have abused your power. Don't roll your eyes at me, Zacharya."

Zack was so pissed off. Markus knew exactly how to punish him.

"I'll give you some advice though. Next time find someone to cover for you who can actually cloak. Stefan is an open book to everyone."

Markus smiled to himself, annoying Zack even more. I made myself scarce, back to my office. I didn't want to bear the brunt of his wrath.

CHAPTER 24
Eliza

If anything, my father was indeed a careful man. Three days in, and no sign of him. Nothing from the Sensorians either, unless they found me and were waiting for Rick's move. If Rick had spotted them, we would be stuck here forever. He wouldn't make contact, and it would all be for nothing. I would never be able to prove what my intentions were and would probably be tried for betrayal. I only have Zack as my witness, and they might not believe him as it may look like he was covering his own arse.

I hadn't gotten much more information out of Tina, and though she wasn't unpleasant, we didn't have much in common either. I got bored of practising VH on Tina, but I was getting good at it. I could keep the vision alive for a few minutes now. My constant touching of her hand or arm really weirded Tina out though, so I had to stop doing it after a while. Something needed to happen soon. And as if someone heard my musings, Mattie arrived just after lunch.

"It's time, lass. Get yer stuff. We're off."

Clearly no time for small talk. I ran upstairs to get

my toothbrush, towel and the few items of clothing Mattie had purchased for me. I was downstairs and ready to go within five minutes. Mattie nodded appreciatively. Tina said her goodbyes as, to her dismay, she wasn't coming. She'd really hoped to accompany me, mainly to meet Rick again, but her desires were denied. I started to feel nervous. I was going to have to dig deep to pull this off. I had to start believing this was for real, otherwise he'd know straight away. I had to immerse myself in the Eliza that had chosen to run away from the Sensorians, looking for something else, hoping Rick would interpret that as a chance for him to convince me to join him.

Mattie blindfolded and handcuffed me, mumbling an apology, saying he was just following orders. I cursed within as it would mean I couldn't check the road signs. Once again Rick proved himself an extremely careful and clever man. However, he didn't know I could hack someone's vision and I hoped I would get an opportunity to use it. If only I could do it remotely.

I tried to concentrate on the direction the car took but I lost track within a few minutes. I think we took the motorway at some point, but then were back on little windy roads. At this moment, there was no way I could give Zack any useful information on where I was headed, even if I was able to contact him.

I'd lost my sense of time completely. I could have been in the car for forty minutes or two hours. No music was played, so I couldn't even count the number of songs and estimate the time. It was time to somehow get physical contact with Mattie.

"Can we stop somewhere, please. I need to adjust the seatbelt. It's hurting me."

I knew he would never let me go for a wee, but I thought I may have a chance with this request. He didn't answer straight away. I felt he had a little internal conflict whether to permit it.

"Cannit you hold on fair longer?" he answered gruffly.

"No, it's so uncomfortable. You know we feel things a lot more intensely than ordinary people, don't you. It's driving me insane. Please?" I pleaded.

I could feel a shift in his attitude. He was going to stop. And a couple of minutes later I felt the car slowing down and veering off to the left. I had to concentrate to make use of the slight opportunity that was coming.

"Could you...," I lifted my handcuffed hands, implying I couldn't unbuckle myself. He took the hint. I moved my arms slightly and felt his arm brush past. His vision hit me straight away.

Damn it. He was looking at me, keeping his eyes firmly on my hands. I adjusted my position slightly.

"Buckle me up again, please."

He brushed past again which would help keep the connection just a little longer. He finally looked up and I saw we were in a lay by. Some bins, yellow. A burger van parked up about ten meters away. He checked his mirrors for traffic and moved off. Glanced over at me for a second.

"Are yee feeling rites?"

I lost his eyes. *Shit.* Not sure how useful the information I managed to see would be but it was better than nothing. At least when we'd arrive there I would be able to see what time it was and estimate how long I'd been driven around. It wouldn't have given me a guarantee of how far we'd driven as he could have just gone in circles for all I knew, but any indication would be helpful.

When we arrived, Mattie took off my blindfold but left my hands tied up. I squinted to shield from the bright light suddenly penetrating my eyes. We had parked on the drive of a large but modern looking place.

154

It looked a bit like a mixture between an office and a residential house, with its stark metal beams and enormous windows. It easily contained ten or more bedrooms.

A man and woman were waiting for us. They were dressed smartly, but ever so unremarkable. They could blend in anywhere easily without drawing attention to themselves. The woman took off my restraints and led me to a room straight away. There was not much in it, apart from a bed, a chair and a table with some books on it. A little chemical toilet shoved in the corner. The scent of it too pungent for my sensitive nose. I just had to get used to it. No window. It felt awfully like my isolation cell and I hoped I hadn't just been transferred from one cell to another. No one had spoken to me at all, not even Mattie. I had not been able to sneak a view of the time, no clocks, no phones or computers or anything in sight. I decided to grab a book and read for a while. There was enough light coming from the rather dull orange bedside table lamp, though in my previous life I would have struggled due to the medication dampening all my acute senses, including my vision.

I hoped someone would give me something to eat soon, as I started to feel a little peckish. At least I didn't have to wait too long. A gorgeously smelling plate of roast beef with all the trimmings was passed to me, and I happily tucked in. Still not a word was said to me, but my month of isolation had prepared me for that, so I tried not to let it bother me too much. I trusted I would find out soon enough what would happen next.

A knock on my door woke me up after a fitful sleep, and a girl not much older than me beckoned me out of my room. My eyes could hardly cope with the brightness out there, having been accustomed to the relative darkness I'd been living in. I finally caught sight of a clock, telling me it was 8.30 in the morning. That made sense at least. The girl led me to an open plan kitchen with one side that completely opened up onto the patio. It was a magnificent sight. A table fully laid out with breakfast waited for me giving off the most delicious smells, which I eagerly approached.

A familiar scent hit me, and I noticed Rick standing right in the corner, observing me. I broke out into a sweat, I couldn't help it. A wave of panic engulfed me and it took all my strength to calm myself down and get control over my senses. I took a deep breath and envisaged a calm sea, with little waves licking the beach. I no longer used Kas riding the waves as my calming strategy because that had quite the opposite effect on me now.

I waited for Rick to make the first move.

"Hi Lizzie. How are you feeling?" he asked, slowly walking towards me.

I shrugged my shoulders, trying to look indifferent to his approach, but I knew my goosebumps gave away how I really felt.

"I feel I owe you an apology," he said after a little pause.

I didn't answer, just looked at him curiously.

"The last time we saw each other, I put you in a precarious situation. I'm sorry that had to happen."

Well, that was the type of apology I'd tried to make to Zack many times before and got punished for. It wasn't really an apology at all, but I wasn't going to challenge my father. Not yet. I didn't have to anyway, as Rick was perfectly tuned into my feelings.

"Okay. I understand. Let's move on. It seems you are in a slightly different situation now? Let's talk about it." He pulled a chair back for me and after I sat down, he took a seat opposite. "Have some breakfast, Lizzie. I'll have some too."

He put a croissant on his plate and started

smothering it with jam, just like I like it too. I hadn't said a word yet, but I knew it wouldn't be long before he got me to talk.

CHAPTER 25

Zaphire

"Hey, Zack!" I shouted at the fast disappearing figure in the corridor. "Come back!"

He slowed down reluctantly.

"Not now, Zaph," he said slightly irritatedly, doing his utmost best not to look me in the eyes.

I caught up with him nevertheless.

"I get the distinct feeling you're avoiding me. I haven't seen you in days and you're not answering my messages," I accused.

"No, no. It's not like that. I'm just incredibly busy."

He blatantly lied. He couldn't cloak that sentiment to save his life.

"Oh, come on Zack. You can do better than that! We need to talk. Please?"

I meant business and Zack responded, realising he wouldn't be able to fob me off today. I ushered him back to my room and pushed him inside. He stood in the middle of my room, feeling awkward and still busily avoiding eye contact.

"What the hell is up with you? Do you know something? Is it bad?" I pressed.

No answer. He turned his back on me again, making his way towards the door. I blocked the exit. He wouldn't push past me. I could feel it.

"Look Zaphy, I need to go and see Vivian. You'll fucking get me in trouble," totally ignoring my questions.

"No. You don't get to do this. We need to talk, think of a strategy to find out why Eliza left and try to get to her before Markus does," I pleaded, talking fast.

Zack turned to face me. He stepped towards me and put his hands on my shoulders.

"Listen Zaph. You need to let this go. Eliza betrayed us. I know it's difficult to accept but it's the truth and you need to face up to it sooner rather than later. This desperate belief of yours that there's a different reason she left is just self-preservation. I get it, but it's not going to help you in the long run. You have to accept she's gone and move on, heartbreaking as it is."

His eyes were filled with compassion and urgency. I detected cloaking too though.

"What are you not telling me, brother. There's something. I can feel it."

"Stop Zaphire. Trust me. There's nothing else. I'm just worried about you. Please don't do anything stupid." His turn to plead.

"Why are you saying that? What would I do?"

"I don't know, Zaphy, but I know how stubborn you are. You're hurt and you'll do anything to avoid dealing with that pain. I know you." His voice soft and caring now.

I started to lose control over my emotions but I I fought hard not to give in to them.

"You've given up on Eliza," I stated despondently.

"She's given me no choice, Zaph. She fucking absconded. What else can we believe. She had a choice to stay. No one forced her to run."

"Maybe she got it into her stubborn little head that she would challenge her father herself or something..."

Zack interrupted me abruptly.

"Stop fucking torturing yourself, Zaphy. Get over it."

His voice had turned all gruff. He spun around and left the room. He was hiding something from me and I vowed to try my hardest to find out what it was. And what I did know for sure, is that I was going to get to Eliza, with or without my brother's help.

I had not given up on Eliza.

CHAPTER 26
Eliza

"Look, I understand you're uncomfortable with me for now, but I also know of your difficulties settling into the Sensorian community. I wanted you to have a chance to find a different lifestyle; with me. Then you can decide, for yourself, where your loyalties lie," my father proposed.

I had so many questions and things to say that I reluctantly lifted my silence. Though I tried to reign in my curiosity and just tackle one thing at a time. It was going to be of no use if I looked too keen to find out all the secrets about Rick's organisation. I kept it personal, at least to start with.

"I took the opportunity to run away because I want to find out more about who you are Rick. You're my father and I know so little about you. What I do know is that you care so much about changing our society, you were willing to sacrifice me."

I couldn't let it go. I needed to hear his regret, at least.

"I know what you want to hear, Lizzie. But you'll be disappointed. It was a risk, but I knew the likelihood I actually had to follow through and hurt you were minimal. The gamble paid off, as I had predicted," he insisted.

There was no remorse.

"However, I'd much rather spared you the ordeal, had you chosen to stay with me. Maybe I can have a second chance this time?"

He observed every little sensory output I produced for minutes on end. I felt like I was under a microscope.

"You feel uncomfortable, but not completely adverse to the possibility of staying with me. That's a good sign." He nodded to himself with a satisfied smile on his face. "You'll understand I have to take it easy, introducing you to my world. You're still a risk."

Again he checked my reaction, thoroughly. He seemed to be happy with whatever he could read in me. It wasn't so difficult to cloak at the moment, because I focussed on the other feelings that were real to me too. I wanted to get to know my father better and I wanted to find out more about the world he had created for himself. I understood why he didn't fully trust me, so it didn't make a spike in my outputs. As long as I didn't think of my long term goals of being here and the inevitability of my subsequent betrayal of my father, I was convinced I could pull this off and make him trust me.

"I'm happy you helped me escape my cell in the compound. I have to find out what my path is in life," I offered. Still more or less truthful, so shouldn't raise any suspicion.

"What will happen to Jessica?"

He didn't like that question. Possibly because it would shed a bad light on him.

"She was desperate to help out. I gave her that chance. She'll face her punishment feeling content she helped the cause."

"But she could be..."

My thoughts went black. They could sentence her to death.

"Don't worry about her. She's under twenty one. They won't give the maximum sentence. We can help her when we've executed the first stage of my plan."

I sensed his instant regret in mentioning that. He didn't want to talk about his strategies yet. I couldn't help prodding him a bit. I felt he was referring to the Sensorian community specifically.

"What is the first stage then, Rick?"

"In due time, Eliza."

Ah. He used my full name. Bad sign. I wasn't going to find out anything about that yet.

He made his excuses and disappeared off with no clue as to when I would see him again. He'd left me in the kitchen and just when I was about to explore my surroundings I was joined by a young man, early twenties with a head of long strawberry blond curls. I couldn't help but notice he was bloody handsome and smelled divine.

"Hi, I'm Daniel. I'm here to look after you."

He strode up to me and firmly shook my hand. I rolled my eyes.

"Pleased to meet you Daniel, but I don't really need looking after," I sighed.

"Boss' orders. He seems to think you do, so here I am. I'm going to take you to meet some people later so whenever you're ready, let me know."

He had a pleasant tone of voice and it calmed my initial misgivings down a little. He wasn't ordering me around at least.

"Okay. Can we take a walk first?" I wanted to see what the house and area was like and suss Daniel out at the same time.

"Of course, we can go to the garden if you want?" he suggested.

"Is that your way of saying we're not allowed to go

outside the house boundaries?" I challenged. He looked up, slightly perturbed.

"Just for now. But if you want to go, just say so. You're not a prisoner. You'll understand we have to be careful about our location. If you want to leave, we'll take you back, but blind folded."

We walked in silence towards the patio, stepping over the runners, the only reminder there normally would be a glass set of sliding doors there. The garden was huge. It wasn't well kept, but beautiful nonetheless. I sniffed the fresh air. It made me instantly feel good. There was something about the smell of grass and trees that reminded me of my childhood, playing in the garden. All that was missing was the sea air. We were definitely in the countryside, not a hugely built up area and nowhere near the coast. The slight breeze felt like little feathers tickling my skin, giving me goosebumps. I zipped up my fleece a little.

"So, what's your story Daniel? How do you know my father?"

He didn't answer straight away, but I could see he was thinking about what to say. He knew there was no point in lying, but he also wasn't bound to tell me anything. I didn't pressurise him, instead sat down under a tree in a patch of slightly shorter grass and waited. He squatted down next to me, picking absent-mindedly at the daisies in the grass.

"He helped my family find justice. There wasn't enough evidence to convict my sister's rapist and he walked out of court a free man. She was only thirteen when it happened and she has never fully recovered from the ordeal. She's seventeen now. On the outside she looks fine, but inside she feels broken." He spoke with such anguish it hurt. His anger and disappointment with the system still raw. "That would never happen in the society your father wants to create."

"It must be hard, knowing he's out there living his life as if nothing happened," I probed a little further.

"He's not though. Rick made sure of that. As I said, we got our justice in the end."

"What did he do?" I asked reluctantly, fearing the answer.

Daniel looked at me in silence. He didn't have to say anything, I knew.

I sighed, shaking my head. Rick had been recruiting people by meting out his own punishments to people who he thought deserved it, but had escaped the system somehow. Clever but dangerous. People like Daniel would be loyal to him forever, but he would also make enemies, not to mention the risk of being caught himself.

"Don't judge your father too harshly. He won't have to go to these extremes when he puts his own system in place. In the end there wouldn't be a death penalty for a start. He believes once people know they can't get away with lying and covering things up, they won't try anymore and crime will be so rare it will be easy to deal with."

"But we have to go through this phase first?"

It was a rhetorical question and Daniel picked up on that. He just nodded.

"Are you ready to meet some more of us? You may be surprised. We're quite a nice bunch."

He smiled a little and it made me feel at ease. I was ready to face anybody or anything at that moment.

CHAPTER 27

Zaphire

I needed to get in touch with Laura. I thought I might be able to persuade her to let me join them up North. It had been the plan to go there anyway, before Eliza decided to run away, but now I was made redundant of that job there was no chance Markus would include me to go. Laura would not go against Markus, unless she thought it was absolutely necessary, so I had to be clever about it. When I had a moment, I sneaked off to my room, avoiding the endless nattering of my colleagues at break time and decided to be brave and give her a ring.

"Hey sweetheart, what's up?"

She'd picked up straight after the first ring. Her voice slightly worried as I hardly ever rang.

"I...I'm not good. I'm not coping. Laura, I need you," I managed to squeeze out a sob.

"Oh honey. I'm so sorry sweetie but I can't come down South. You know that right?"

I sniffled loudly and sighed deeply.

"I need to see you, Laura. Please?" I tried to sound as desperate as I could, which wasn't difficult because I needed this break. I had to get away from Markus' watchful eye and to a certain extent, away from Zack.

"Can't you talk to Zack, sweetheart? You know he's always there for you if you need him."

"I know, but this is different. It's difficult. He's a man, you know. It's not the same."

It went quiet for a while on the other end of the phone

"I'll sort it," she sighed, but sounding determined.

She blew me a kiss through the phone and rang off.

Markus came to my room not long after the phone call and told me curtly that his wife had told him I was to come up and see her, no questions asked. He felt my relief and instantly realised this request had not materialised out of thin air. Laura had played the 'mum' card and Markus knew better than to challenge it. Even though we never called them mum or dad, and they referred to themselves as our carers, it was exactly what they were. I knew they loved Zack and me deeply and would always want the best for us, though what I thought was best for me and what they thought was, didn't always match.

The next day, I was booked on the train to go up North.

"I told Laura you're grounded and she supports that. She won't be able to pick you up from the station so she'll send Sam," were Markus' parting words before he dropped me off at the train station. I was happy it was going to be Sam. I missed her so much.

I'd wanted Zack to take me so I could have a last ditch attempt to convince him not to give up on Eliza, but he was nowhere to be seen and Markus wouldn't have let him anyway. It was probably for the best as he would only have tried to persuade me to stay, or worse, ordered me to do so. I would try and ring him later and explain my actions as he'd be wondering what I was up to. But for now I switched off my phone, to avoid confrontation. He'll be less likely to kick up a fuss when I'm already with Laura.

"Sam!" I couldn't help but shout excitedly, when I spotted her freckly face and bopping curly hair in the crowd of people waiting on the platform. She moved effortlessly through the crowd, anticipating everyone's moves and embracing me within seconds of first laying eyes on each other. Her familiar scent nearly made me cry. I'd missed her so much. She whisked me to the car park and in no time we were on our way to our new compound.

"Things have gone a bit crazy over at your side. Wow. Who'd have thought Eliza would turn like that?"

Sam looked at me inquisitively, noting my ambivalent feelings towards the events. I wasn't going to tell anyone my intentions yet, not even Sam. I had to figure this out by myself, so I just shook my shoulders and said nothing. She didn't press any further and instead we just caught up with general chit chat and enjoyed each other's company for the rest of the journey, singing along to Queen classics.

When I saw Laura, she gave me a proper hug and strong as I was, I really needed that. It made me feel safe and able to cope with whatever life threw at me. I knew that just being up North and therefore probably nearer Eliza wasn't going to solve everything, but I felt I had a better chance. If only I could get an opportunity to talk to her, I was certain I would be able to find out what was behind this stunt of hers. But I had to be patient, find out as much information about Rick's whereabouts as possible and then work on Laura to abandon Markus' stupid grounding punishment. I had more chance of that here than being around Markus, but it would still be difficult to achieve. For now, I just enjoyed being looked after by Laura who looked genuinely concerned and went out of her way to make me feel better.

"Come talk to me, sweetheart. When you're ready. You must feel heartbroken."

She gave me a kiss on the head and left me in my room to freshen up somewhat.

As I'd expected, when I turned my phone back on it was full of missed calls and text messages from Zack asking what the fuck I was thinking leaving, and to get my arse back to the compound straight away. The messages getting more irate the longer I hadn't answered. Bless him. I decided to give him a call.

"Hey."

"Hmm."

Okay, he was still pissed at me.

"It was killing me staying down South, not being able to do anything to help Eliza."

"She doesn't need to be helped. She betrayed us."

"I need to speak to her and ...."

"You'll do nothing of the sort. Stay the fuck out of it Zaph. I mean it."

His voice was low and threatening. Something else was definitely up. I just knew it.

"What do you know Zack? Tell me. Please."

"You need to leave it. I told you before, I just don't want you to get into trouble...or hurt."

"I can't," I simply stated.

"You fucking can, sis. Listen to me. Don't. Get. Involved."

"I'm sorry Zack. I have to."

Zack growled frustratedly.

"Vivian plans to be going up there in a few days. You won't be able to fucking avoid...."

I quickly ended the call and switched off my phone. I needed to think and prepare a plan. I could do without Zack's verbal abuse for now. As I suspected before, I was absolutely sure now that he wasn't telling me everything and I simply had to find out what it was. If he wouldn't tell me, there was only one way to figure it out: Find Eliza.

CHAPTER 28
Eliza

Daniel was right. His sister, despite her terrible ordeal, was a lovely girl. Easy to talk to, warm and friendly, but in her eyes lay a deep sadness. His friends, who I assumed were all fans of Rick, were a jolly lot and accepted me into their group with ease. I felt no negativity at all, apart from Helen, a pretty girl who clearly fancied Daniel, and initially observed me warily; looking for signs that gave away I was after Daniel. It was mild though and didn't bother me. She soon relaxed and focussed on flirting with Daniel again. The guy was so oblivious, it made me smile. Mark, one of the 'Rickofants' came and sat next to me. The name I'd come up with for them made me snigger.

"Inside joke?"

He nudged me gently with his shoulder. I was acutely aware of the pheromones he emitted, betraying his more than casual interest in me. I tried to ignore them.

"It's just funny to watch the group's interactions and the undercurrent of emotions that everyone is oblivious to."

"Isn't it tiring to always know what people feel?"

His curiosity for my gift was refreshing. I've never really had to explain anything to anyone, because all the people who were allowed to know were Sensorians themselves, or my mum, who was in some sort of denial about it and never really asked anything. A world where we wouldn't have to hide our gift suddenly felt quite tempting. I was cautious though, knowing if I said too much I could eventually be in trouble myself.

"Sometimes," I nodded non-committally.

He didn't pry any further, instead making small talk and trying to make me laugh, rather successfully. Mark was charming and witty and made me feel at ease.

It wasn't long before I was hit by a rather acrid scent and the source was near. Daniel came over, looking all protective and clearly unhappy with Mark's attentions to me. Maybe he was suspicious of his intentions. Funnily enough it had taken another boy's affections to awaken Daniel's feelings. He covered it well, claiming his overall responsibility for me as tasked by Rick.

"Are you okay, Eliza? I think we should head back and I'll show you to your room. You look tired." he said with a slight edge to his voice. He offered his hand to pull me up and I gladly took it. I wanted to spend some more time with Daniel on his own and see if there was possibly an opportunity to exploit his newly awakened interest in me. Maybe Helen did have something to worry about after all.

As it happened we stayed in the kitchen for a bit. Daniel decided he was going to cook us something and I offered to be his kitchen aid. He was pleased I did and forgot his previous concerns about my perceived tiredness. He teased me about my ungainly cutting skills and I retaliated by throwing the cut carrots at him. I playfully flirted with him and he responded predictably, oozing the sweet scent of desire. But, to his credit, he kept himself in check and never overstepped the mark.

He finally escorted me to my new room. It was a far cry from the dingy cubbyhole I stayed in for the first night. It was light and stylishly decorated in white with different shades of grey. I could still smell a hint of paint in the air. It had a walk-in cupboard filled with clothes, all simple and exactly what I would wear. Someone had done their research.

A couple of days went by, and though my days were filled with pleasant company and I was steadily gaining Daniel's trust and affection, I grew restless. I needed to move on from here and get more access to

Rick. This wasn't going anywhere nearly fast enough for my liking. Luckily Rick had decided to show his face again and was in an unusually talkative mood with minimal cloaking, but it was all useless chit chat, which I needed to change.

"I want to talk to mum. She'll be worried if she doesn't hear from me soon. I have no idea what Markus has said to her or whether she even knows that I've left the compound. Anyway, I need to get my exam results soon too, so she would want to be there."

I thought I'd get it all out in one go and see how he'd react. It wasn't as relaxed as I'd hoped. His barriers went up straight away and I could not read him at all.

"How would you see this occur?" he asked measuredly without giving his feelings away.

"Well. Duh. I'll phone her," I mocked.

"Don't try that smart ass tone with me, young lady. It's not going to get you anywhere," he growled, scowling as he walked off, leaving me to regret my sarcasm.

I got another opportunity fairly soon as within the hour he returned to my room asking me to come for dinner with him.

"I would like you to meet Jean-Pierre and his wife Angelique, fellow Sensorians and instrumental in realising my world view. You may remember seeing them when you first got to the house. They'll join us for dinner this evening."

No mention of our previous conversation but still, I rejoiced inside. Finally, I'd meet some people of importance. I covered my feelings instantly as Rick picked up on it immediately, scrutinizing my body language.

"I'm just happy to meet people you work with. It'll help me, being able to talk to someone who can give me an honest opinion on what you're like to work for. You have nothing to worry about unless there's something you're not telling me," I reasoned, hopefully convincing him I had no ulterior motives.

"Have you had a thought about me contacting mum and collecting my results?" I asked, changing the subject.

"Yes. And the answer is no," he said resolutely. I wasn't going to give up that easily though. I pushed a bit further.

"I don't think that's a wise decision, even though I understand your reservations."

I didn't elaborate, letting him think it through

himself. Maybe risking a telling off for my slight cockiness, but I could sense a slight change in attitude.

"It's too risky," he concluded.

I still hadn't given up.

"For whom though? What is the worst that could happen?"

"I could tell you a long list of things that could go wrong, Lizzy. For starters; you could betray me," he accused.

"And why would I do that? Plus, if I did, it would be better you knew now anyway, wouldn't it? I practically know nothing," I challenged back.

He took a moment to think about that one.

"You could be captured by Markus' henchmen and I would lose you," he countered.

"I'm not talking about going on my own. We'll have security all around me. They wouldn't try. Trust me."

"They will definitely try and contact you."

"Let them," I said shrugging my shoulders.

"You seem to think you have an answer for everything, don't you? Let me think it through and I'll come back to you on that one. Let's concentrate on this evening for now. Agreed?"

I nodded. I counted that as a win and was sure he would let me go one way or another.

Jean- Pierre and Angelique were indeed the unremarkable looking couple who I laid eyes on when I first got to the house. Tonight though, they were sparkling and distinct, the complete opposite from before. They oozed power and their scent was strong. It was interesting talking to them. They were from France and were part of a similar set up as the one Markus led in England, albeit much smaller. However, they had the same strict rules on secrecy and the couple were also fugitives from their leadership as they had broken that vow. It surprised me how certain they were that they could use their skills to their and everyone else's advantage with little fear of reprisals. They just didn't see the necessity for secrecy. I thought it was either ignorance or arrogance to think that society wouldn't either condemn you or use you to their advantage, whether you'd agree or not. With Rick I knew it was arrogance. He simply didn't think any ordinary person could actually touch him, being completely convinced his gift would protect him from any ill intentions people might have. I remembered how he had let on to me that he believed Sensorians were superior to ordinary people. I bet he hadn't told his non-Sensorian followers that.

Anyway, informative as the conversation was, it didn't give me much more insight into Rick's plans as to how he thought he was going to achieve his coup, and the minute I broached the subject, however casually or subtly, the walls went up immediately.

"She wants to know what I'm like to work with," Rick restarted the conversation after a rather awkward moment when my seemingly innocent questions were met with cloaking and evasion again.

"That's an easy one to answer," Angelique replied instantly. "He's inspiring and completely trustworthy. A man of his word."

Her face lit up with admiration. I expected some sort of reaction from Jean-Pierre, a little jealousy or hint of annoyance with his wife's adulation. But nothing. Not an inkling. Instead he nodded.

"Totally agree. This man can make anything happen and he'll reward everyone's loyalty. It's an absolute pleasure to work with him."

"What. No flaws whatsoever? There's got to be something? Surely?" I half joked. I must have looked incredulous as both of them started laughing.

"You must think we work as his personal promoters but I can assure you, you have nothing to worry about if you decide to join us. He's always up front with us and his methods are completely transparent and well thought out," Angelique continued.

"Once he trusts you completely, you'll find out. I would never go back to the way it was now I've seen the alternative," Jean-Pierre added, reading my doubts about my father's seeming perfectness.

Rick smiled and looked rather smug, but waved their praises away.

"I think my daughter needs time to trust me. She's new to all of it and the only source of her knowledge about me stems from Markus and his followers. She thinks I'm some sort of crook and a danger to Sensorians."

To that Jean-Pierre and Angelique laughed heartily.

I didn't know what to make of it all. Could my father be the person Angelique and Jean-Pierre saw, rather than the dangerous renegade Markus professed him to be? Could the world they envisaged really be possible? An image of him strapping the explosives to my leg surfaced and my body chilled. He would have a lot to prove to convince me.

CHAPTER 29
Zaphire

It turned out my luck was about to change when I got a phone call from Eliza's mum. I froze momentarily when I saw her name flash up on my mobile, but answered eagerly. Alice's voice betrayed slight confusion and worry when she uttered my name and it put me on edge.

"What's up Alice? How are you?"

A second or so passed before she answered.

"Hi, yes, I'm fine thanks. I called you because I got this rather short text message from a withheld number, claiming to be Eliza?"

"Okay. What did the message say?" I enquired matter of factly, but feeling excited.

"It said to meet me at exam results day in the reception area at 2pm. With three kisses and a smiley face. She does always sign off like that. I just thought it a bit weird she didn't just ring me."

"I haven't seen Eliza for a bit as she...," I didn't quite know how to put it, so I kept it simple.

"...she's very busy."

"Oh?"

She didn't sound convinced.

"When's results day again?" I slipped in quickly.

"It's this Friday at the school. Are you going to be there? Is everything okay between you two?"
I hesitated. I decided not to answer. She needed to know the truth but I wasn't allowed to speak about it.

"Have you spoken to Markus at all?" I was curious to know what they had told her. After all, he's meant to be responsible for Eliza and at the moment, he didn't even have a clue as to where she was. I wondered how he was going to explain himself to Alice. I'd quite like to be a fly on the wall when that conversation took place.

"Well, briefly but he said he was busy and would phone me back, but that was a couple of days ago."

"You need to talk to him, Alice. It's important, but wait till after the ceremony."

"Now you're making me worried. Should I be worried?" Her voice went an octave higher with concern.

"You'll see her at results day, don't worry. Phone me once you've spoken to Markus."

I needed to see Eliza. I needed to find a way to get up there without Laura knowing. She would never let me go and if I mention anything, there would be no way of sneaking out. If I got caught there would be hell to pay, but if I did make contact with Eliza it would be worth the risk. I had two days to organise something and I desperately needed an ally. I had to convince Sam to cover for me. I needed a moment alone with her and soon.

*

"Zaphy, really?" Sam sighed disbelievingly.

I looked at her in desperation.

"Can't you tell me at least a little bit about your plan for me to risk months in the isolation cell?" she asked, hoping it would help her justify the risk she was taking. I looked away, knowing I couldn't give anything away.

"You just have to trust me. Please. I need you to do this for me," I pleaded, holding out, believing she would yield.

"I guess it's something to do with Eliza?" she tried again, her eyes dark with trepidation.

I kept silent, quietly shaking my head. I tried once more.

"I can't tell you, Sam. But believe me, if I could, I would. I know I'm putting you in an awkward position and if there was any other way, I would have chosen that."

Sam sighed. I picked up instantly that she'd made

up her mind. I knew she would help me.

"Thank you so much, Sam. I won't forget this."

"When?" she asked matter of factly, all focussed on the task in hand.

"Tomorrow."

A spike in her emotions betrayed her calm face. She hadn't expected it to be so soon.

At 4.30am the following morning, we sneaked out of our temporary home, switching the alarms off and back on again as we left. The click of the door sounded as loud as a canon ball dropping on a stone floor. We held our breath for what seemed like minutes, but it remained quiet in the house. I prayed it would stay that way until I was long gone and Sam had safely returned. She dropped me off at the nearest train station where the first train would leave at 5.30am. She'd be back before the earliest riser in the house would be up. I anxiously awaited her text message to say she was back home and undetected. It came just when the train arrived at the platform. I breathed out heavily with relief having successfully carried out the first part of the mission. Now, Sam's task would be to stall for as long as possible the moment Laura would notice I was missing, without implicating herself, as far as that was possible.

I watched through the window as the train moved swiftly through the countryside, leaving my brain free to contemplate my impending meet with Eliza. My heart started to beat just that little bit faster.

CHAPTER 30

Eliza

Funny. I was more nervous about seeing my mum than getting my results. The significance of those results was minimal at that moment. The task I had set myself for today was huge and I didn't think I had much chance of succeeding.

I just hoped someone would show up other than my mum. Zack must have at least considered the possibility that I might be at the school to collect my results. Whether he would be allowed to leave the compound was by no means certain. Maybe mum had spoken to Zaphire. That was the most likely scenario as mum would have preferred to talk to her than either Zack or Markus. Though I wasn't sure how Zaphy had taken it all, so it might not be a good thing if she was the only one that got the message. I didn't even know what I'd do if it was her that turned up. Would I be able to keep up the facade? I couldn't be certain. However, if she had told Markus and he was the one to come, I feared that he wouldn't be in a listening sort of mood.

It looked like I had to rely on my improvisation skills to create a chance to give Zack a sign of some sort that I was still working on winning my father's trust, via whoever it was that might turn up. I started to realise more and more that this plan had so many ifs and buts and was not very likely to succeed. However, I was determined to try. I had to do something. Then an opportunity presented itself a little sooner than I'd anticipated.

Just before I was about to leave I heard a gentle knock on my door.

"Can I come in?"

The door opened slowly and Daniel's face peeked around the corner. I nodded and sat back down on my bed. Daniel sat beside me. I could tell he wanted to say something, but he wasn't sure how to.

"Out with it," I demanded.

More silence.

"I need the toilet."

He rushed up and made it to my bathroom. Bit weird, but I left him to it. Then my eye spotted the phone he'd dropped on the bed and my heart leapt. *Shit.* A chance I couldn't miss! I grabbed it and typed in the unlocking code, hoping he hadn't changed it from when I last worked it out.

I was in.

The numbers of Zack's phone, imprinted in my

brain, rolled of my finger tips and I typed as fast as I could.

Exam results today. Bradstone on way to house countryside no sea lay by yellow bins burger van. Not trusted yet

I hit send, waited a couple of seconds to make sure it went, then as soon as I deleted it I threw the phone back on the bed just before a sheepish looking Daniel returned. If he'd been a Sensorian I would never have gotten away with it, as my blood was pumping and sweat was forming on my face and the palms of my hands. All the tell tale signs of having been up to no good. I hoped the garbled message made some sense, but at the very least Zack would be happy to have heard from me. A sign I was still on board. He may even be able to wangle a visit to the school.

"What's up Daniel? You're acting strangely," diverting the attention to his erratic behaviour, to prevent him from noticing my own flustered state.

"Just be careful today. I kinda like you, so please don't do anything stupid." he pleaded, his face a little red from embarrassment and a flicker of worry.

"Why would I be doing that?" I countered and laughed it off. "I have to go. See you when I get back, Daniel," blowing him a little kiss as I left.

Once Rick reluctantly agreed to let me go, it had been his mission to fit me up with an entire protection detail. He had me strip searched before we went in the car, made me swallow a tracker, stuck a mic under my bra and I was flanked by three security guards, one of them being a Sensorian. Not seen her before. She was called Irena and was an imposing woman with a slight Eastern European accent. Her voice was reassuring and she emitted a natural sense of calm.

Despite the blindfold I was able to pick up where we were driving as I had manoeuvred myself close to Irena, and was able to tap into her eyes regularly. I knew exactly where we were and couldn't wait to let Zack know the next time I had access to a phone. I hoped it wouldn't be too long.

I spotted my mum immediately on arrival. She was nervously waiting by the entrance door and I couldn't help myself from sprinting towards her, the three guards trotting alongside me. It must have been quite a sight. My mum's eyes spoke volumes. She knew something was up but I didn't give her any time to react or say something. I threw my arms around her and smothered her with my body.

"I've missed you so much," I sobbed.

After a few minutes she pushed me gently away from her and looked me over with concerned eyes.

"What's all this?" she exclaimed as she waved her arms around wildly at the guards around me.

"What?" I joked, looking quasi confused. But mum gave me a withering look. She wasn't in the mood for jokes.

"Long story; I'm staying with dad for a bit. It's all fine though. Don't worry. I'll let you know more when I can." I felt her whole body go cold. She wasn't taking it well. "Mum. I'm safe. Really. It's complicated, but I'm fine. Let's go and get my results," I tried moving on. Mum wasn't buying it. I felt her worry and fear coursing through my body. I had to shield or it would cripple me.

"But...," she tried again.

"No Mum. Leave it. Please," I implored and finally she sighed, shrugged her shoulders and started walking to the hall where the envelope with my results was waiting for me.

CHAPTER 31
Zaphire

I could smell her before I saw her. Flowery, with a hint of patchouli, so fabulously sexy. I nearly stopped breathing. My Eliza, diminutive but looking determined and strong, exactly how I remembered her. *I love her so much.* She hadn't picked up my scent yet as she was shielding heavily from her mother's emotions, making her less alert. Maybe that was just as well. It gave me a chance to work out a plan. Part of me was scared she didn't want to see me at all and may try to avoid me if she was aware of my presence. I kept my distance, just in case.

I noticed the three guards who kept close contact to her. It was going to be damned difficult to get anywhere near her. Then I picked up another complication. The unmistakably scent of my brother. I spotted him, brazenly moving within the crowds of students and parents with the distinct ease of a Sensorian. How had he managed to convince Markus to be working the field on his own? Maybe Vivian was here too, but I couldn't trace her at the moment. Unless he was doing it secretly. I better keep out of his way, even though I was under no illusion he wouldn't have picked up my scent. We were super aware of each other. He knew. Nevertheless, I stayed hidden behind the huge pillars in the lobby trying not to interfere with whatever he was trying to achieve. I'd made him angry enough as it was.

About ten minutes later I heard Eliza and Alice approaching. Eliza sounded pleased and excited. She must have done well in her exams. Alice was proud and exuberant. For a moment I forgot why I was here and could barely stop the impulse to run towards Eliza and congratulate her. I was brought to my senses when I heard other excited voices calling Eliza's name. It was Bella and a group of her school mates enthusiastically running towards them. The next few minutes were filled with high pitched squeals, hugs and kisses and some berating by Bella as to why Eliza hadn't let them know she was going to be there. I felt Eliza's stress levels rising, but Alice came to the rescue with some half arsed excuses of 'being busy' and 'last minute arrangements'.

I gathered myself and waited for their next move. I overheard them planning to grab a drink at the school's canteen so I hurried over there and hid in the nearby toilets. I didn't really need to see them to keep track. I could hear and smell them anyway, even over the typical school loo's odours. I hoped she would take herself to the toilet at some point so that I'd get a chance to speak to her. I didn't have to wait too long. I heard everyone going their separate ways after meeting up in the canteen and soon after I sensed her presence getting closer and her scent becoming strong. I quickly stood on one of the toilets in one of the cubicles, just in case she wasn't alone. I heard the door open and her footsteps approaching. My heart beat wildly. She knew I was there. She stopped. I heard her breath falter.

"Where are you?" she mouthed, barely any sound leaving her lips and rustling a piece of paper or something at the same time to cover the sound, but I picked it up.

"Cubicle three," I mouthed back, safe in the knowledge she'd hear it.

In less than a second she stood in front of me. I jumped down from the loo, grabbed her face and kissed her passionately. She returned my kiss feverishly but after a second or two she pulled back. I heard someone approach and a look of panic raced over Eliza's face. Before I knew anything I was on the floor, Eliza sitting on top of me with my arms yanked back.

"Irena!"

A woman appeared immediately. She must have been the person entering seconds ago. Eliza hauled me up to my feet but she held onto my arms, pushing them up so I could hardly stand straight.

"I thought I smelt another Sensorian!" the woman growled. Her face inches away from mine, I could feel her spit spraying on me. *Gross.*

"What are you doing Eliza. Get the hell off me!" I yelled and kicked back violently. Her iron grip didn't loosen at all. We trained her well. "Who's this bitch!" I nodded aggressively towards the woman she'd called Irena. She was a Sensorian but not one I knew or recognised the scent of at all. I caught sight of Eliza's eyes in the mirror. They were like ice. Her face determined and distant, nothing left of the seconds of passion only moments earlier. My blood ran cold. Her voice came sharp as a knife.

"Shut up."

She pushed me forwards for Irena to take over. The woman held my arms tightly. It hurt. I felt a gun push into my back. *Christ!* This was serious.

"Take her to the car but wait until I've rejoined mum. I don't want her to see Zaphire," she ordered and Irena nodded.

"You go see Alice. I'll update the men."

What the hell was going on? It looked like Eliza was in charge. Maybe I'd been wrong about her all along and she had actually turned and betrayed us. Everything was pointing that way but I still detected something off in her manner which gave me a little bit of hope. The dark look she threw me on her way out did nothing to confirm that though.

CHAPTER 32
Eliza

Bloody hell. I'd acted completely on instinct and as soon as the adrenaline had ebbed away, I had no clue as to how to handle the consequences of what I'd done. I hoped the mic hadn't picked up our kiss. It could blow my cover or, at the very least, it would need a lot of explaining. Why did Irena have to come into that toilet just at that moment. It had ruined everything. I could have tried giving Zaphy some sort of message, even though it would have confused her. She would have listened, she clearly still loved me. But it had all gone horribly wrong; she probably hated me now.

Zaphire's look of shock and hurt at my perceived betrayal had been excruciating to endure. I don't know what she'd expected but it clearly wasn't this. Our kiss, brief as it was, had been so passionate and full of longing. I would have given everything to have had it last longer.

I needed to put it behind me now and concentrate on my mother, pretending nothing had happened only minutes before. My acting skills were being called upon again.

"Hey, sweetheart. I've ordered you another hot chocolate. Come, sit with me. Are you okay? You look all flustered." she asked, her eyes full of worry.

I felt close to a sensory overload, but I could not afford a meltdown. I started visualising the sea and willing my heartbeat to slow down, to some effect.

"I'm okay, mum. Just a bit overwhelmed with the whole occasion. I can't believe I have officially passed my A levels!" I managed to say fairly confidently. "And seeing all my friends again just made me realise how the decisions I have made will affect me, and what I have had to leave behind." I added, quite truthfully.

I felt elated to see my friends again, especially Bella, but drained at the same time. I still found it hard to deal with all their unbridled and uncloaked emotions. It was hard work keeping it all together and I realised the choice to live as a Sensorian was probably the only one that I could have made and stayed sane. But that didn't mean I didn't miss my friends and the relatively uncomplicated life I'd lived before.

"Hmmm. You've done amazingly well considering what you've been through. You should be so proud of yourself," mum mused for a while, but then started grilling me again. "I was expecting Zaphire and Zack to be here?" She stared at me a little too intensely. I tried to avert my eyes but she pulled me up on it.

"Look at me Eliza. What is going on?" she dug a bit further.

I put my hot chocolate back on the table, too hard. The content spilled over.

"We...er...split up, mum. I don't want to talk about it."

The room went cold. Or at least for me it did. It was as if every soul literally left the building. I glanced up and caught Zaphire's eye as she was ushered past the entrance of the cafe by Irena, just at that very moment. All I could feel was her pain. Her despair. Her glum eyes, bereft of all hope, told me she'd overheard me. I felt sick.

"Oh sweetheart. Please talk to me. You look like you're really hurting, baby. You know I'm here for you, I won't judge."

Mum's voice was so full of compassion, I wanted to tell her everything. Right there and then. But I couldn't. I had to get out of there, away from mum before I cracked. I had to get back to the house. Work out what to do next, and deal with the consequences of capturing Zaphire in my mad moment of desperation. I slowly shook my head and, without looking at mum, got

201

up and left, the two men in close pursuit. I couldn't even stay to work out how to get a message to Zack. I knew he was here. I caught his scent earlier. The whole thing had been a disaster. Mum's confusion and pain hurt like hell. I needed to put distance between us as quickly as I could, and was grateful to get outside.

Irena was nowhere to be seen and neither was the car we had come in, but then the BMW raced around the corner and screeched to a halt in front of us. I was pushed into the front seat, one of the men piled in the back, leaving the other on the pavement to sort his own transport home out. I caught a glimpse of Zaphire, passed out in the back seat. My heart grew dark. This had not gone to plan at all. I desperately hoped she could forgive me. Once in the car, I was blind folded again. I didn't care. I knew where we were going.

I wasn't expecting the welcoming committee on my arrival back at the house. Rick came up to me and gave me a hug, whilst the car with Zaphire in it sped off.

"You've given me exactly what I need for the next phase of our mission. I'm proud of you. Welcome on board," he beamed, with Jean-Pierre and Angelique making appreciative noises.

It left me reeling. *What the hell had I done?*

CHAPTER 33
Zack

Fuck. Something had gone down. The atmosphere was rank. The stench of utter distress, worry, guilt, disbelief and fear all hung heavily in the air. I'd only just come down from my own struggle with my emotions on first glimpsing Eliza earlier. I hadn't counted on them being so raw and fierce. I'd been fooling myself to think I could just switch off my feelings for her. I'd fallen for her and it wasn't just going to go away. It took all my energy to refocus and push the feelings back where they belonged, buried deeply. And now this.

I quickly glanced through the room and just caught a glimpse of Zaphire being pushed past the canteen entrance by a woman who I was sure was a Sensorian, though unknown to me. What the fuck happened to her. A few minutes earlier when I sensed her here, I gave her a mental bollocking. But I never gave her enough credit for her resolve. If Zaphire wanted something she clearly always found a way of doing it. I admired her but was equally furious.

Eliza had clocked Zaphy, but I noticed she tried to distract her mum from spotting her. The dynamics between Eliza and Zaphy was puzzling. Eliza knew what was happening to Zaphire and, though I found it hard to believe, I felt she was responsible for it. What the fuck was she up to? Had I been wrong to trust her? I had a moment of doubt as to why I even agreed to her plans, which were against everything I had previously believed in. I would never have gone against the leadership's wishes, or behind Markus' back before I'd met Eliza. She had affected me in more ways than one. I shook the feeling off. She must have had her reasons. I wasn't prepared to think about any other explanation.

I could do with a partner and regretted not being fully honest about my whereabouts today. I hadn't expected anything much to happen. I just thought me being here may have given Eliza a slim chance to make contact. I sensed Eliza knew I was here, but she suddenly got up and left, followed by the two men who had flanked her side all day. Trust my fucking sister to put a spanner in the works. I had told her to leave it. The stubborn woman clearly hadn't listened and now it looked like she was in deep trouble. On top of that she had screwed up my chance to get some more detailed information from Eli, rather than just that garbled text message. *Fucking frustrating.*

I quickly moved through the cafe, blending in as much as I could with the crowd, trying to get a glimpse of where they had taken Zaphire, but by the time I got to the door, there was no sign of them. I followed Zaphy's scent which was not hard to pick out, heavy with stress and fear, but it came to a dead end. I could just about see Eliza get bundled into a blue BMW and speed off. Just when I focussed in on the number plate, a little girl ran into me and I lost sight of the car.

"Watch your fucking step!" I hissed furiously, making the poor thing scuttle off to hide behind her mum, who threw me an angry glance.

The man who just seconds ago had pushed Eliza into the front seat had also disappeared from sight. *Bollocks.*

I knew there would have been no point in trying to follow Eliza, even if I had seen where they went. Rick would have prepared for us to be here and he would have taken precautions to prevent anyone from pursuing them. Not only would it be a complete waste of time, it would also alert them and might push them into doing something stupid. I didn't want to be responsible for that. There was nothing for it than to fess up about my little outing to Vivian. I couldn't sit on this. They got my bloody sister and we needed to find her. Eliza better find a fucking way to send me some useful info. And fast.

Back at the compound I headed straight to Vivian who was in her office agitatedly talking on the phone. As soon as I entered she excused herself from the conversation and stared me down.

"What have you done?" she asked in a low threatening voice, moving slowly in my direction. She knew something was up within milliseconds of me entering the room. She was amazing at reading people.

But I was pretty good too, and had sussed out that although she knew I'd done something she wouldn't agree with, she had absolutely no inkling of what it might be.

"Ma'am. I may have showed a little too much initiative today..."

The start of my confession was met with flared nostrils. Not great, but I persevered.

"I decided to check out if Eliza would attend her exam results day at her school. I thought there was only a slim chance that she would, so I didn't want to bother anyone else with it. I went on my own. Sorry Ma'am."

She looked me over, silently. I felt her annoyance rising.

"That's not all though, is it? There's more to this confession as I would bet my arse on it that if you went there, found she wasn't there and returned, I would never have heard of it. Would I?"

Her dark voice rumbled menacingly through my body. I had to shield somewhat. She was absolutely right. I would never have fessed up had it not been completely fucking unavoidable. I didn't quite know how to explain the next bit, without triggering a major outburst.

"Two things happened. I did see Eliza there. She was flanked by three guards, one of which was a Sensorian, but I didn't recognise her scent or appearance at all. Eliza must have picked up my scent but she didn't show it or try to make contact with me. She received her results, met some friends and had a drink with her mother. Then left."

I paused there. Vivian's eyes trained on mine. I kept my composure; just. *Fuck*. It was hard.

"And the second thing?" she asked through gritted teeth.

"Okay. So, try and remember that if I hadn't been there we would not have known what I'm going to tell you and we would have been blindsided by it..."

Vivian raised her eyebrows and, I swear, she growled like a bear. Her whole demeanour uncompromising.

"Out with it," she demanded fiercely.

I took a deep breath to steady myself.

"The room went thick with heightened emotions and I spotted my sister being ushered past the canteen by the Sensorian. Zaphire was in distress and I think I picked up guilt from Eliza. They must have ran into each other or something and somehow Zaph got captured."

Silence. Pain. I had to shield again. But no shouting. It was Vivian's turn to steady herself.

"Right. Tell me everything you know," she asked matter of factly.

"I don't know anything else. That's all. It all went very quickly, Ma'am. Wait. Eliza sped off in a blue BMW."

"Number plate?"

"Didn't get it."

That annoying little bratty girl bumping into me! Vivian wasn't impressed but carried on. Cool as a cucumber.

"What did the Sensorian look like?"

"Tall, five foot eleven-ish. Dark blond hair and broad. Stern face. Name might be Eilena, or Rena or something. I heard Eliza mention a name like that."

"We need to inform Markus and get a team on it. We want to know as much as we can before they contact us. Because, that, they will. I'm absolutely certain they will use her as a pawn or some sort of bargaining chip. I'll deal with you later. Time is of the essence now."

She stormed out the door, clicking her fingers at me, fully expecting me to follow her like a dog. I didn't think it wise to challenge her, so I gritted my teeth and sped after her.

CHAPTER 34
Eliza

A soft knock on my door woke me up. I must have fallen asleep the moment I'd thrown myself on my bed after we came back. Being so on edge and having to prevent a sensory meltdown all day had exhausted me mentally and physically. The welcoming party threw me off even more and I just had to withdraw from everything and flee to my room.

It was Daniel. He came in and sat on the edge of my bed, his hand nonchalantly placed on my legs. All my worries flooded back and I sat up in a slight panic.

"Where's Zaphire?" I tried to say as calmly as I could muster. Daniel looked puzzled.

"Who?"

"Zaphire," I emphasised as if that would jog his memory. It did seem to bring something to the surface.

"Oh her. What do you mean. How am I supposed to know where your ex is right now?"

He still looked utterly confused. He clearly didn't know anything about what had happened earlier today. I shook my head and felt irritated. Everything was a battle. All the time. I was growing tired of it.

"Just forget it," I snapped to add to Daniel's

bemusement.

"Fine. I just came to see if you were alright, but I'll go."

He moved abruptly and made his way out.

"No, no. I'm sorry. I didn't mean to upset you. Stay. Please?"

He slowed down, turned around and smiled. He forgave easily. He was a kind soul. He sat back on my bed and sighed.

"Do you want some food? That always helps me out of a grumpy mood?" he winked.

"Grumpy? Me?" I playfully threw my pillow at him and we both laughed. "Let's get some," I agreed. "And then I want to see my father."

*

"Where is Zaphire?" I demanded to know as soon as Rick walked into my room. He stopped dead and observed me for what seemed like an eternity. It turned my legs to liquid and made my stomach somersault, but I held his gaze. With difficulty.

"She's in a safe house. She'll be brought to our main compound when we're sure she's not followed," he answered finally.

I could feel he was still assessing my allegiance. Though he had welcomed me 'on board', it was by no means a done deal. I had to keep up the facade, and convincingly at that.

"We have a main compound?" I redirected the conversation slightly.

"Yes and, in fact, I'm inviting you to visit it tomorrow. Interested?"

"Absolutely. It'll be nice to see where my father hangs out most of the time."

He picked up on my slightly sarcastic tone, giving me another stare.

"Given we're family, and we're supposed to be able to read each other quite easily, you are a bit of a hard nut to crack, Lizzy. I hope my trust in you won't bite me in the arse in the future."

I laughed loudly, trying to cover up my anxiety. I took a deep breath and steadied myself.

"I believe you have good intentions and I'm fully behind those. But, I have issues with trusting you which, I'm sure you'll understand, stem from you abandoning me and mum. It will take time, so you'll always pick up some ambiguous vibes from me. You'll have to cast them aside or decide to cast me aside," I answered.

This time I stared him down. He lowered his eyes,

nodded and walked briskly out of my room. I think I won that round. Though I was still none the wiser where Zaphy was and what Rick wanted to use her for. Round two was coming up.

I bumped into Daniel on the way to the gym. I call it a gym, but it was basically a bedroom with a few bits of gym equipment and it was heavily overused. In the short time I'd been at the house I got so frustrated that nine times out of ten it was full, I had devised a spreadsheet for people to sign in and it worked a treat. I did suspect Daniel manufactured it so that he would end up in the gym at the same times as me, but I enjoyed spending time with him so I didn't challenge him about it, too much. I couldn't help myself but poke some fun though.

"Hey, what a coincidence Daniel. You're here again."

He went slightly red in the face and his heart jolted a little. *Bless him.*

It was nice pounding away on the running machines in unison. We didn't feel the need to talk but enjoyed listening to the same music so we shared headphones. He always got a bit frustrated as I kept turning the sound down and he would sneak it back up again, not realising it would physically hurt me. When it got too much, I stepped off, opened up another window to let some fresh air in, and then did some weights. It felt good challenging myself and keeping my mind off Zaphire.

"Have you worked out where your ex is?" Daniel asked hesitantly.

I sighed. My temporary sanctuary was disturbed and my brain went into full worry overdrive. I grunted in frustration.

"In a safe house somewhere. Do you know how many of these houses exist?"

I noticed Daniel got slightly excited.

"I know of four, not sure if that's all. I can try and do a little bit of digging for you?"

"Would you? I don't think Rick would approve."

Apart from a few tiny muscle movements, he didn't flinch. He looked me in the eyes and spoke with reverence.

"I don't think he would mind. He would see my good intentions; to help you. Even if he wouldn't agree with it, he wouldn't be angry with me. He's a fair man, Eliza. It's time you start seeing that."

There was not a part of him that wasn't convinced of this. I wasn't so sure about it. In fact I would like to see Rick's reaction when he finds out. It would tell me an awful lot about him.

"Okay then. Yes please. See what you can dig up. That'll be great. Thanks," I smiled and I felt his body warm up instantly. Poor boy. I didn't want to take advantage of him, but I needed all the help I could get.

CHAPTER 35
Zack

"What else do you know Zacharaya? Answer me, damn it." Markus slammed the table in frustration. I told him all I could but I had to keep Eliza's text message to myself. There was no way I was going to betray our plan yet, even if it meant enduring Markus' relentless grilling.

"You are hiding something from me. Why? It doesn't make sense. Your sister's life could be at risk. It is of utmost importance you tell me everything you know!"

His stare was steely cold and it made my insides physically chill. Never had I kept anything this important from him and it was hurting me, but I firmly believed it was possible to find Zaph and keep Eliza's mission alive.

"Sir, please. Stop. There's nothing more to tell. I'm sorry I can't be more useful but I swear I will do everything I can to help find her." I pleaded, pouring all my sincerity into the last statement in a bid to convince him to let it go. He grunted and paced up and down the room.

"What I want to do is lock you up until you tell me

the complete truth, but I need your help now. You better have an explanation for withholding from me, because when I find out you will need it to keep your arse out of isolation. Understood?"

"Yes Sir."

I waited for further instructions, trying to be as compliant as possible. I hoped to fuck it would all work out and that Eliza would come up with something soon. I didn't allow myself to think I could fail Zaph. That simply wasn't an option. I needed to find her, without compromising Eliza, but if push came to shove, I would choose Zaphire. To hell with the whole mission.

"You will go over the CCTV footage and locate the car they used to transport Zaphire, then see if you can track it down. It's highly likely the same car that you saw Eliza get in as they probably would have waited for her to come out. Tristan managed to give us access to all CCTV in the area, and we will be given it for any area we need. It's not going to be easy as the CCTV just outside the school is corrupted, so you need to look at the surrounding streets. Don't come out of that room until you find me something useful. That's an order."

Markus had regained his calm but I knew not to mistake that for complacency.

"Yes Sir. Permission to go?"

"Granted. Vivian, a word please."

I didn't hang around. I needed to find something on that CCTV and fast. Tristan was a fucking legend. He worked for the police and had been able to tap into CCTV on more that one occasion for us. We needed something soon as the phone in my pocket stayed awfully quiet. No news from Eliza yet.

"Hey mate!" Brody shouted, slightly out of breath from running to catch me up. "Where are you heading? Haven't seen you for a while?" He gave me a friendly slap on the back and laughed, but picked up on my mood immediately. "What's wrong, man?" he suddenly asked seriously.

"Don't ask," I sighed, paused but decided to ask a favour.

"Are you busy or can you give me a hand with something?"

"Whatever I was doing can wait. What do you need me to do?"

Brody was a legend too.

Whilst trawling through the footage I told Brody what he needed to know. He was worried for Zaph and furious at Eliza.

"That fucking bitch. She has really screwed us

over," he cussed.

"I don't know," I tried to say as neutrally as I could. He picked up on it straight away.

"How can you not be cursing that girl? She got your sister captured!"

"Well, that is what I picked up from her sensory output, but I can't be sure," I tried to explain.

"Since when are you ever wrong Zack? Just accept it. She's the enemy and needs to be put away."

"Easier said than done, Brodes. She's under Rick's full protection. It's all so fucking messed up," I sighed.

"Yeah, and you still have a thing for her," Brody whispered under his breath, knowing full well I could hear him just fine. I snapped. I grabbed him and pushed him against the wall, my face inches away from his. He didn't flinch and stared right at me, not fighting back. I let him go.

"Sorry mate," I mumbled slightly embarrassed.

"No probs. Probably deserved that," he shrugged, straightening his top.

We carried on trawling through the footage in silence for a while. Still we found nothing note worthy. At one point Brody had to go, leaving with the promise to come back later. I lost complete sense of time and when he did come back hours later, I hadn't moved, bar from taking a piss in a bottle, which I'd shoved in the corner of the room.

"Ugh, fuck, it reeks in here!" he exclaimed with disgust on opening the door. "Open the bloody door for some fresh air, mate! You've got to come out and get a bit of exercise and food. Have you actually had anything to eat or drink since you started?"

"Nope," I answered absent minded, focussing totally on the images in front of me. Brody grunted in frustration.

"Come with me Zack. You'll be able to concentrate better after a little break," he tried, but I knew I couldn't leave that room until I found something. They were Markus' explicit orders and I wasn't going to give him any more reasons to punish me.

"I'm concentrating just fine. Just leave me the fuck to it," I replied rather grumpily. Brody sighed and left, leaving the door wide open. I didn't really pay much attention and carried on staring at the footage, though my eyes were stinging from the hours of continuous screen use. I singled out a few images of cars that caught my eye that could possibly be the one they'd used. *If only I got the damned registration number.* I just couldn't be sure, but they were worth following up. I passed on the number plates of the cars from the

CCTV to Tristan and was waiting for some results as to whom owned them, but in the mean time I kept checking more footage, hoping to spot something obvious.

The most delicious scent of Chinese take away entered my nostrils, way before Brody swanned back into the room and slammed the food on the table.

"Eat," he ordered. No point resisting and I was extremely hungry, so ate eagerly, indulging in the sumptuous smells and tastes. Next minute, I felt the phone in my pocket vibrate. A message from Eliza. My stomach lurched and my heart skipped a few beats. The hunger deserted me immediately. Brody looked at me with suspicion. I leapt up from my chair, grabbed my stomach and sped out.

"I need a shit," I grumbled on the way out as if in pain. Didn't think it fooled him but it bought me some time.

CHAPTER 36
Zaphire

I was in deep shit. When I was bundled into the car, the bitch had injected some drug into my arm and I was out for the count within minutes. I don't know how long I had been unconscious for but when I woke up, I was locked up in a dark room with nothing in it, apart from a mattress and a bucket. I had no idea about time or how long I'd been there but it couldn't have been more than a day. I felt lonely and betrayed and my anger for the girl who I'd thought loved me started to fester.

Why the hell is she doing this to me? I had trusted her and given her the benefit of the doubt when everyone else thought she'd turned her back on us. They were all correct. I should have listened to Zack. But even after all this, I still had the tiniest bit of hope that it was all a mistake and she would open that door and embrace me, making it all go away. I knew I was kidding myself. I had to face up to the fact that Eliza had shown her true colours and it was up to me, me alone, to get out of this mess. The trouble was that as long as I was in this room there was fat chance I could get out. I had to wait till their next move, whenever that was going to be.

It turned out I didn't have to wait long for some action, but if I thought I could somehow use the change of scenery to my benefit I was sorely mistaken. These guys knew what they were doing and before I'd even moved I was gagged, blindfolded, my arms and feet bound simultaneously and I was sprayed with something so overwhelmingly powerful, it deadened my sense of smell completely. They placed something which I assumed were noise cancelling earphones over my ears, so I could barely hear. I had never felt so claustrophobic and disorientated before, being deprived from all my senses. I was helpless and I felt absolutely enraged. I wanted to kill Eliza. Right there. Right then.

I was carried out, shoved in a car and we drove a few hours. Why had they not drugged me again? They did this on purpose. They wanted to hurt me and make me weak. Intimidate me. *Never.* I wouldn't give them the satisfaction. All I would show them was my contempt.

I must have passed out eventually, as when I opened my eyes I was sat in a small study. The blindfold and gag were removed and I was able to breathe freely. Books were everywhere, a huge desk with piles of paper scattered about so there was not much space left to work. A laptop was balanced on top of a couple of books. I tried to lean forward to have a little peek at the computer, but I couldn't move. I was strapped into the chair. *Shit.* I tried to control my breathing and simmering anger. I had to stay calm.

I heard someone approach and stop a few metres behind me. The spray still obscured my sense of smell somewhat, but I could just about detect that whoever it was, it wasn't Eliza or Irena, There was something familiar about the scent, though. Then it hit me. It was none other than Rick himself. I suddenly became uber aware of him. My adrenalin kicked in and made my senses even stronger than normal. I heard his heart beating, it was only slightly raised. His breath was steady but just the tiniest of hitches gave away he was tense too. I could feel his heat increase as he approached slowly. He was now only about thirty centimetres away from me, and I felt his breath caress the back of my neck. Goosebumps reared their ugly little heads all over my body. I was fed up with being the victim and took the lead.

"Why am I strapped to this chair? Are you scared I'm going to overpower you?" I sneered.

"I don't trust you. But given that Eliza so easily beat and captured you, I don't think I need to be scared of your fighting skills," he scoffed.

I huffed.

"She took me by surprise," I admitted slightly sheepishly.

"You thought she would fall into your arms and regret everything she'd done, didn't you?"

He laughed sarcastically. I could punch him. The annoying thing was that he was more or less right, even though I didn't want to admit that, even to myself.

"Well, she doesn't regret what she did. But there may be a chance of you two being together again, if that's what you want? I want Eliza to be happy and if that involves a relationship with you, then so be it."

I couldn't believe what I was hearing. The cheek of it.

"Is that why I'm here? Is that what she wants?" I couldn't help asking though.

"No and yes undoubtedly. In that order," he answered measuredly, trying to work out where I stood in this.

He must have felt my scorn, but also my longing

for a chance we could somehow work this out and be with Eliza again. I knew it was impossible but my heart was aching for her, looking past her betrayal. My brain couldn't though. It hurt. A lot. I let out a deep sigh that probably told him everything.

"You have a choice. You could join us, be with Eliza and help 'persuade' Markus to give us access to the compound to address all Sensorians and give them the opportunity to work with me, without repercussions for them or me. Or you could refuse. Then I have no choice but to use you to force Markus into submission. However, I would never allow you to see Eliza again."

He paused to give me a chance to answer. I would give him an answer alright.

"Over my dead body," I hissed and exploded. "Who the hell do you think you are! Trying to use my love for Eliza to break my loyalty for the one person who took me in, looked after me and raised me to be a good person and who loves me! You don't even know how to love, abandoning your only daughter when she was only two!" I turned my head and spat at him, hitting him full on in the face.

He slowly wiped it off with the back of his hand, stood in front of me and slapped me hard. Searing pain. Not only where he'd hit, but all over my body. I was getting pounded by the full force of his anger and didn't have time to shield. Another blow landed. His ring cut my eye. I could feel the blood trickle slowly down my face.

"We shall find out how much Markus loves you. You've left me no choice," he growled and marched out of the room.

CHAPTER 37
Eliza

"What are you doing with that?" Daniel nodded accusingly at his phone in my hand. His tone was cold. His stare hard. I was thrown for a second and felt myself go red. No way to hide that. I had managed to sneak Daniel's phone out of his coat pocket and when he busied himself putting on Netflix and finding something to watch, I used it. I recovered quickly. I never forgot how I was slightly peeved and embarrassed when Zack pointed out my prowess in improvisation and deception, but it had come in useful so many times and now it was called upon again.

"I'm so sorry Daniel," I simply said, waiting for Daniel's reaction to work out how I was going to play this.

"Sorry for what exactly, Eliza? I may not be a Sensorian but you sure have a guilty look on your face." His voice angry, clearly feeling betrayed. I looked up at him, eyes wide open but then I lowered my lids slowly.

"This is so embarrassing," I started, squirming and fiddling with the phone still in my hand. I quickly gave it back to him. He sat down beside me. I felt his anger slowly dissipating, but I was not out of the woods yet.

"What did you try and do? Contact your ex? She won't have access to her phone anyway," he sighed.

"No! That's not it. Not at all!" I exclaimed, trying to sound surprised and slightly offended. "It's far more embarrassing than that. I wouldn't betray Rick or you after you've just helped me so much."

I hoped to God I sounded convincing, because that is exactly what I had done and any other Sensorian would have picked up on that huge lie.

He got up and threw his hands up in the air, looking baffled.

"Well, what was it then? You had my phone; you clearly did something by the look you gave me when I caught you with it. Tell me, no matter how embarrassing it is."

"Oh my God," I buried my face in my hands and sighed deeply seemingly trying to muster up the courage to confess to him. "I tried to hack into your messages," I mumbled.

"You did what! What on earth for?"

He now looked positively puzzled. Bless him. He had no idea about deceit and jealousy. He was so blissfully naïve and trusting.

"I tried to get into your phone and read your

messages, Daniel. I wanted to see whether you had talked to anyone about me or whether you were seeing other girls. I know you like Helen and she's really into you, so I just wanted to find out where I stood with you..."

I looked up to see his body language and face to put together the signals I was getting from his scent and vibes. He was totally unsure how to take this and what to make of my feelings of insecurity that I led him to believe I had. He wasn't stupid though.

"But you're a Sensorian. You don't need to do that kind of shit to know how I feel about you." He wasn't convinced. I had to persevere.

"No I don't have to. I know you like me and maybe even more, but I can only see that when I'm with you. I was just insecure, you know. It was wrong, but it was just that."

I grabbed his hands and looked up, searching for his eyes.

"I shouldn't have taken your phone Daniel. Can you forgive me?" I cast my eyes down. I felt his anger and confusion leave his body and it was replaced by something else.

"Does that mean you like boys too?" he teased. He lifted my head and moved in. His lips gently caressed mine and I let him. He was nice, uncomplicated and genuine and for just a moment I could actually imagine a future with him. But it would all be based on a lie. I returned his kiss softly but then recoiled gently and put a finger on his lips.

"It's too soon, Daniel," I tried to soften the rejection somewhat, a little smile playing on my lips.

"Does this mean you've forgiven me?" I gently teased.

He broke out into a smile.

"Yes. It does. But you worried me. I thought...Never mind what I thought. Let's forget it even happened."

He gave me a soft kiss on my forehead, before he stood up and offered to get me a cuppa, which I gratefully accepted. Once again reminding me what a kind soul he was.

It gave me a bit of time to digest what I'd just found out and what I'd done. Daniel had told me he'd discovered where Zaphire was staying, and also where she was going to be in the next couple of days. She was meant to be going to the main compound where Rick had planned a big meeting the day after tomorrow. Daniel had no idea that I didn't know where that was, so he'd let slip the town name where Rick was based, assuming I knew what he was talking about. I was absolutely sure if I got that information to Zack, he would figure out where the building was, and get Zaph out of this mess, if they didn't manage to get to her before she left the safe house.

I'd been able to text it to Zack and managed to delete the message just in time. Now all I could do was wait and find out as much as I could about the organisation and who else was involved. It was time to use my VH skills to the max.

CHAPTER 38
Zack

Fuck, this was good. I knew Eli would come up with something useful at some point but this exceeded my expectations. I had to find out where exactly Rick's main compound was, and now I knew the town, it would be do-able. All I needed was some time and people power, sadly neither of which I had. I doubted Zaphire would still be at the address Eli had given me but I had to check it out anyway, just in case. I had to convince Markus that the CCTV footage had shown something worth checking out, but I had to get round Brody first. He suspected something was going on and I had to convince him somehow to let it go and leave me to it. Brody was loyal to me but he also had a strong sense of duty to Markus so I knew I had to pull it out of the bag with this one. I returned to the room where Brody was waiting for me, his arms crossed defensively and a stoic look on his face.

"Hey man. You okay?"

His face betrayed a sliver of concern but mostly suspicion. I nodded vaguely not quite knowing how to start.

"Brody. I need to ask you something and you're not going to like it."

I waited to be hit by his sensory output, but apart from a little apprehension, I didn't get much. He was fucking cloaking. He had anticipated this and was prepared. That made my job much more difficult as I wouldn't be able to tell if I could trust him fully. I had to carry on regardless.

"I'm going to tell Markus I found and tracked the car that highly likely carried Zaph. I'm also going to tell him that the CCTV showed the same car driving into a housing estate. I found the nearest addresses and we need to check them out, one house in particular. I know that you know that isn't true, but I need you to keep that to yourself and trust me."

The silence was killing me, but I gave him time and didn't push it. Although Brody was cloaking, I could still see the conflict playing out in his mind. He finally answered after a few minutes, which had felt like an eternity.

"How did you get that address? I assume it has something to do with that text message you received earlier? And you need to tell me the truth Zack, if you want any chance of me putting myself in this position."

He meant it, but I couldn't give the truth. Not yet.

"Brody. You know I would never do anything to put my sister in danger and that I would give my fucking life to save hers. I need you to do this for me. Make yourself unavailable if you don't want to actively lie, but please let me do this my way," I pleaded fervently.

"For fuck's sake Zack! You owe me big time." He dropped his guard and I felt he meant it. I tried to give him a hug but he turned away from me. "Just go. Before I change my fucking mind."

"Thanks mate. I knew I could count on you."

He flicked me the finger. I had some apologising to do after this was all over, if he would ever speak to me again.

Markus was impressed with the lead I 'found' and sent Vivian up to investigate straight away. I asked if I could join her, full well knowing Markus was going to deny me, but he would have found it odd if I hadn't asked. I protested a little to give him a chance to assert his authority over me but it was all for show. I needed to stay here and find a way to discover where Rick's main compound was, and I didn't think Zaphire was still going to be at the address I gave them anyway. I had no idea where to start though and on top of that Markus had given me a stack of paperwork to do in his office.

He hadn't forgiven me yet. Whatever I needed to do, it had to wait. I would have to work through the night if necessary, but without access to the entire workforce I didn't really stand much of a chance. I had to try though. There might be a way.

After about three hours Vivian reported back. As luck had it, I could hear firsthand what she had discovered as he had the phone on speaker and I was still there doing admin.

"Zaphire has been at this address, Sir. Her scent is still lingering, so she hasn't long been gone. There is nothing in the house now though, so it looks like they moved to another location. Get Zack to follow up with the CCTV. There must be more footage. However, question him as to how he got the address as there were no cameras near the location."

Fuck. I had to think fast.

Markus turned to me, face stern with questioning eyes boring into mine. You would have thought I'd gotten used to that by now, but it still made me feel sick to the stomach. I had to fucking man up and answer quickly to divert suspicions.

"It was an educated guess Markus. I googled the area and checked the census and that looked like the most likely house to be used as some sort of safe house," I lied. Markus took a moment to process my answer and nodded.

"Okay. But you're nervous. Why?"

He knew something was up.

"Because I lied about knowing the address. It was a guess and I was worried you'd be angry with me. I haven't been in your good books lately."

I managed to look at him, but cast my eyes down under his stare.

"Fair enough. And you still aren't. In my good books that is. Stop lying to me and go back to check the CCTV again and focus on that area," he ordered.

"Yes Sir," I quickly replied and practically ran out of that room. I had to conjure up some more CCTV from the area as it wouldn't be long before he would check in on me and I better have something.

Brody hadn't left the room and in fact had a massive grin on his face.

"Oh dude. You really owe me now. I may have just saved your arse."

"What the fuck, why? What have you found out?" I exclaimed, surprise written all over my face. I could do with some good news though.

"I had a look in the area of the addresses you came up with and it actually shows a BMW coming in and leaving the area nearby on several occasions. I guess they didn't find her there, did they?" Brody searched through some images and pointed at one he had enlarged.

"This was taken about five hours ago and I'll be damned if that's not Zaphire in that car, a few streets away from the house."

"You're a fucking genius Brodes! That's exactly what I need. How can I thank you, mate!"

He looked at me and paused.

"By never putting me in that position again. I'm serious, Zack. Promise me."

"You have my word Brody. I'm sorry I asked you to neglect your duty to Markus. It won't happen again."

This time he didn't shirk away from my hug.

I had some work to do to see if I could follow the car to its next destination, but CCTV in the surrounding area was sparse and quite a few cameras were not functioning at all, and after about two hours of searching, the car had all but vanished. But I had one more trick up my sleeve and that was the town where Rick's headquarters were. She might not be there yet, but if I could get my hands on CCTV of the town and surrounding areas, I could spot them arriving there. It required another lie though.

"Why don't we look at the towns surrounding the area and decide which ones could be likely candidates for Rick's headquarters. He might want to take her there so if we could find it then we could monitor it," I suggested. Brody gave me a strange look and sighed.

"You know we have been trying to locate his main compound for weeks now, don't you? That is what Laura and Frank have been working on. Nothing yet, but for a few tiny clues, but it could be any of those towns round there. Where do we start? We simply don't have enough people to scour through that much footage!"

"What if I tell you I have a feeling it's this town here, pointing at the map."

"Oh for fuck's sake Zack. You just promised me no more shady deals!"

"No. I promised I wouldn't put you into a position where you'd have to compromise your duty for me. You wouldn't have to. It's just a hunch. Markus understands hunches, trust me."

Brody growled and muttered some choice words under his breath, but once again he came through for me.

I contacted Tristan and he was able to get us access to all the CCTV we needed, and we set to work. We'd only just got into it when the door swung open and Michael burst in. The stench of panicked urgency barrelled into the room.

"Go to Markus' office. NOW!"

Both Brody and I leapt to our feet and raced to our leader's office, hearts pounding and nervous as hell. What had Markus found out? Whatever it was, it didn't sound good. When I opened his door, one look at the screen told me enough. Shit had hit the fan.

CHAPTER 39
Eliza

I found myself roaming the house during a rare moment of solitude. Daniel was working on something and I hadn't seen my father in the last few hours. My feet had taken me to the room they used as a little office where a few of Rick's staff were glued to their computers. It smelled stuffy and sweaty in there. A Sensorian wouldn't be able to work in this room for very long!

How I wished I could VH remotely, but I still needed a slight moment of contact to set it into motion. I desperately wanted to see what they were working on and see if I could discover some more names of people who were involved. I decided to enter and hover. I'd met a couple of them before and when one of them looked up I pounced and asked him if he wanted a cuppa. He eagerly nodded his head and then the other two gladly accepted the offer too.

When I put down the first cup, I made sure I brushed passed the man's arm and tapped into his vision straight away. I quickly read the email and made a mental note of the recipients, none of whom I knew or even heard of before. The email was a reply to a request to intervene in a law suit involving several companies, but I couldn't quite make out what it was all about before the vision faded. It didn't look relevant.

I moved on to the slightly older woman called Sophie, who, by the looks of it, was compiling a list of guests. This could be interesting and I made sure I got some good contact with her, though it made her look up at me in a peculiar way. I got a good connection and I chose to stick with it so I quickly put the next cup down in front of the other bloke and got myself a piece of paper, nonchalantly sat down on a spare chair and started writing what I could see through Sophie. My eyes honed into two names and my heart fell. Why were they on this list? I'd seen Irena on it, Daniel and his mates, lots of foreign sounding names and then Lois Langfield and Ned Peterson. There was no chance they were undercover, so why were they included? I feared the worst and I had to get a message to Zack as soon as I could. They shouldn't trust anyone. I hoped to God it was a mistake of some sort. I couldn't believe Ned would betray Markus. Not after he worked so hard to redeem himself. They must have gotten to him one way or another. He wouldn't do this out of his free will. But his name was there. That was a fact. I hadn't come across Lois a lot but I knew she did carry quite a lot of power. She was on a par with Frank and Michael, so definitely a worry for us and a coup for Rick if she had turned.

"Hey, Eliza!" an enthusiastic voice belted from the back of the room.

It was Daniel's friend, Mark. I could really do without this but I turned around and smiled at him as much as I could muster. He was beckoning frantically for me to come over. I hastily stuffed the piece of paper in my trouser pocket and reluctantly went to see him, not wanting to raise bad blood or suspicion.

"Nice to see you again, lovely. How are you doing?" he said, genuinely pleased to see me. I felt a smidgen of guilt only perceiving him as a nuisance to be dealt with quickly. I might as well have a look and see what he was working on, but I didn't think he had much to do with the organisation and I was surprised to even see him here. I just saw him as Daniel's friend and never given him another thought. Maybe I had been wrong.

"I'm fine Mark. Thanks. Are you busy? I won't keep you long."

I planted my exit strategy early.

"Extremely. I've been run off my feet what with Rick

arranging this big meeting so last minute," he sighed a little exasperated.

My interest immediately piqued. I tapped into his vision but he was only looking at me. Not helpful.

"Can I help you with anything?" I slyly suggested. He hesitated for a second, before breaking out into a broad smile.

"Are you kidding? Yes please. I actually really need this document checked over. Just spelling and grammar and such, but it's taking me ages and I have to get on with arranging the catering. The document needs to go out in an hour. Do you think you can handle that?"

The desperation in his eyes was obvious. This was almost too perfect an opportunity to be true. I jumped on the chance.

"Of course. No problem. Where shall I sit?"

"Brilliant. You take my computer as it's all here. I just started, so carry on from where I left off, please."

He stood up and sat down at the desk opposite, leaving me to it. Completely trusting me.

The document was an absolute goldmine. It contained all the information I needed. The venue, date and time of the event were all there. I was absolutely sure Zaphire would be at the meeting as if I knew Rick at all, he'd want to make the most of her capture one way or another. Plus it was more or less alluded to in the document. Now all I needed to do was get the information over to Zack.

I sensed trouble. Daniel's scent rapidly became stronger, and it stank. He was furious and worried at the same time. I was expecting a Zack-like telling off and braced myself, but Daniel's anger presented very differently. There was silence but his eyes spoke a thousand words, and none of them were particularly nice.

"Hi Mark, I have to talk to Eliza. Do you mind if I take her with me?"

He didn't look at me but solely addressed Mark, who looked a little bemused but was really none the wiser of Daniel's foreboding mood.

"Yeah of course, Daniel. She was just helping me out a bit. Thanks Eliza. Did you get it done?" he asked hopefully. I nodded, saved my work and hastily stood up to follow Daniel, who was already by the door, waiting for me. I held my head high. I needed to give the illusion that I didn't think I'd done anything wrong.

"What is it Daniel?" I asked pretending I wasn't aware of any issue. "Why do I feel these tense vibes coming from you?" again, simulating innocence. He ignored my questions and instead opened a door to a small room and expecting me to go in. He pointed to a comfy chair for me to sit down and sat himself down on the opposite chair. Leaning back as if relaxed but arms crossed.

"What are we doing here Daniel? I don't understand. Has something happened? Is Zaphy okay?" I tried anything to make him believe I really didn't think I did anything wrong.

"You know full well that you're not supposed to access computers. What were you thinking?" His voice betrayed a little of his state of mind, but was still calm as anything.

"Is that what you're worried about?" I countered. "It wasn't for my personal use. I was just helping Mark edit some files. I was bored so it kept me busy for a while."

"Mark should have known better than to ask you. We were all told not to give you any access," Daniel grumbled and carried on.

"I shall have to report this to Rick and see if he wants to ask you any more questions. I won't be able to tell if you are telling the truth, but he will."

That wasn't good. I had to stop him doing that. I could try and spin the truth for my father a little bit but if he were to ask me direct questions, he would know I was hiding something. We could shield and cloak as much as we wanted but the familial bond was much tougher to deceive than just another Sensorian.

"You don't want to bother Rick with this. He has his hands full organising the upcoming meeting and I promise I was just helping out Mark. You can ask Irena or another Sensorian to check me out if you really feel it's necessary?" I suggested, hoping he would drop it. I wanted to concentrate on finding a way to get in touch with Zack, rather than spending energy and time on deceiving other Sensorians. On top of that, I might not succeed in lying to them. What was it with people just walking in at the wrong time! I would have been out of that room not ten minutes later and no one would have been any the wiser.

"You've put me in a horrible position Eliza. I like you and I do believe you. But I still think I should mention it to someone. I think you're right not to get Rick involved, so I'll get Irena to come and meet us," he decided.

Bollocks. I really could do without this but it was going to happen, so I needed to prepare myself quickly for the impending interrogation. I started visualising to relax. Nothing more convincing than a steady heartbeat. I didn't have long though as unfortunately Irena was just in the vicinity and promised to be there in a few minutes and sure enough there was a knock on the door already.

"Hi Irena. Sorry to bother you with this but I hope it will reassure Daniel to have you corroborate my story," I smiled whilst taking the lead. I was determined not to look the victim or guilty. She smiled back. Thank goodness I gained her respect dealing with Zaphire before. It would definitely work to my advantage.

"So, what is the problem Daniel? How can I help you?" she asked, curious to know what the issue was. When Daniel explained she looked a bit dubious and my heart rate just rose a little, gaining her attention.

"What files were you editing Eliza?" she asked, holding my gaze. I knew where this was going and there was nothing I could do about it. Mark would be able to give the answer to that question so I answered truthfully. This wasn't going my way.

"So you know where and when the meeting is," she concluded and I just nodded.

"Thanks for informing us Daniel. And Eliza, I believe you didn't do anything else but edit the files, but you weren't supposed to know that information. Though Rick is beginning to trust you, he's not willing to test that trust yet. You will have to be under constant observation from now on until the meeting," she decided.

"Irena, please, is that really necessary?" I pleaded. "You can trust me. How many times do I have to prove myself? No one needs to waste their time babysitting me," I sighed.

"I'm sorry Eliza. I do trust you but you have to understand it's our duty to make sure nothing gets in the way of Rick's plans. He's just cautious. And I'm sure Daniel will be happy to oblige," she said with a cheeky twinkle in her eye.

Shit. How on earth was I going to contact Zack now?

CHAPTER 40
Zack

"Look who joined us," a voice boomed from the computer screen followed by a sarcastic laugh.

"We were waiting for you, Zacharya. We couldn't start without Markus' prodigy, could we now," the voice continued.

Bollocks. It was Rick of course. Fucking mocking both Markus and me. I saw Laura and Frank had joined the video conference as well and both looked shocked. The screen didn't show Rick. Instead it was the bruised face of my sister staring helplessly at us. Her mouth gagged, and wearing noise cancelling head phones. She looked scared but still her eyes shone with resilience. She was coping. For now. Rick removed her headphones, but left the gag in.

"Hey, my sweet. Don't worry. We will sort this out," Markus said, ignoring Rick's sneers. "We're all here now, Rick. Why don't you tell us what this all means?"

Markus' calm voice belied the inner turmoil I sensed. But he was putting up a good show for the camera.

"I'll admit that I hadn't planned on using Zaphire as a tool to realise what I need, but Eliza gave us this opportunity and it was too good to miss. It will help my cause greatly and much more quickly than I could have hoped for, so I'm not apologising for it," Rick stated bluntly.

I cringed on hearing Eliza's name.

"I'm not asking you to apologise. Just tell me what you want," Markus interrupted brusquely.

"Don't get your knickers in a twist, I was getting to that," Rick smirked. "My request is to have full access to your compound and have a meeting with all Sensorians. You'll let me show them the future society I envisage and give them the choice to join me, without any repercussions for me nor all the people who choose to follow me. I don't think that's too much to ask in return for your daughter."

"What will happen to her if we don't comply?" Markus questioned icily, stalling any decision that had to be made. Zaphy's eyes went wide. She didn't want to hear this.

"You can't seriously...," I butted in but was hushed up by a stern look and a growl. The atmosphere was unbearably tense. It fucking hurt.

"She will live the rest of her life in a dark cellar deprived of all her senses. You will never find her and she will die alone."

Markus averted his eyes from the screen.

"We might have to take that risk. But before that would happen, we'd hunt down your arse and sit it in our court room. And you will not get out of there without a death sentence. Hand her back now and I will give you amnesty. Turn yourself in and reform. You could be an asset to us once more."

Sweat poured out of every single pore I owned. Everyone's heart pounded fast and loud and the stench of stress was stifling. I had to get out of that room but my feet were stuck and my legs were lead. I wasn't going anywhere.

"Interesting offer Markus. But you forget that I hold all the cards. I'm not giving up my vision to end up working with you again. If you won't let me talk to your community now, it won't be long before I have another opportunity. I'm in no rush; I'm stronger than ever, especially with my daughter by my side. I'll give you an hour to decide, but say goodbye to Zaphire now. You won't see her again, unless you honour my request."

I looked at Zaphire's eyes, full of despair but resilient still, as they shoved a bag over her head and hauled her roughly to her feet and out of sight. Rick had signed off and it was just the distraught faces of Laura and Frank staring at us now. Laura looked straight at

253

Markus, she took only a second to speak.

"I can't let you gamble with Zaphire's life. We have to give him access. Our Sensorian community is not stupid. They will see through his mad ideas and realise it's not the right way forward," she insisted.

Markus turned away from her, eyes down and shoulders hunched.

"I can't let him blackmail us, honey. However right you may be about our community, we can't give in to him."

I feared he might say that. Too fucking principled for his own good. I had to get Zaphire out of there at all costs. I had to convince him to let Rick have his meeting.

"Sir, there may be another way."

I paused to make sure I had his attention. He turned to me and I took his silence as a cue to carry on. He hadn't cut me off.

"What if we let him have his meeting...."

Markus started shaking his head.

"No." he immediately decided.

But I persevered and jumped in again.

"Please, Sir. Hear me out. We can try and find Zaph, whilst he's here, liberate her and then you can arrest him whilst he's at our premises. It's a risk but it could mean we can capture him and deal with him for good. It must be worth considering, Sir."

"Zack, the chances of us finding her are close to zero. That's not good odds to gamble with."

I had to let him into my secret. It was the only way. *Fuck. This was going to be hard.*

"It might be a lot more than that, Sir."

"What. Why? What do you know?"

Markus' face was nearly touching mine now. I backed away slightly. Everyone looked at me, slightly confused, but urging me to spill the beans. I was fucking shitting myself.

"Promise you won't freak out or get angry, Sir?" I tried in a feeble attempt to protect myself.

"No promises. Out with it. Now!" Markus looked like he was going to burst. He could hardly contain his emotions, but took a deep breath and remained on right side of the edge. It was my turn to take a deep breath.

"Eliza still works for us. She didn't want anyone to know but me, but she is loyal to us, Markus."

It was as if I'd dropped a bomb. Markus, Brody, Michael, Vivian, Lois, Laura and Frank all stared at me. *Fuck.* My stomach churned, my heart raced uncontrollably, but I had to focus. It was crucial I was able to convince them.

"You're delusional if you believe that," Laura hissed. "She captured Zaphire!" each word dripping with her indignation.

"I don't know why she made that decision, but it must have been an improvisation that when set into motion she couldn't stop. She must have been taken by surprise or something. I tell you, she is determined to convince Rick she's loyal to him, so she can discover all the information we need to close his whole operation down."

"You kept this from us! Who else knows?" Markus barked, fuming.

"No one knows. Not even Zaphire. It was essential that as few people knew as possible to make this work. But let's not focus on that. She has already given me some vital information about where they are. I'm just waiting for her to make contact again."

I knew it was wishful thinking but I hoped sincerely they would just overlook my choice to leave them in the dark about our strategy, but the vibes were dark and angry.

Markus blew. *Fuck*. He flung the remote he was

holding through the room, it crashed against the wall and broke into smithereens. In seconds he stood right in front of me and before I knew it he'd punched me full in the face. My nose exploded, my face burned with pain. Another blow connected with my eye. I saw black and wobbled but felt Brody's arms around me, steadying me. Michael and Vivian rushed in between me and Markus, who was still beside himself. Vivian passed me some tissues to stem the bleeding, which I grabbed and stuffed onto my nose. Markus had never lost it like this before. I'd had a few kicks up my backside and a smack now and then when I was younger, but he never punched me before. It hurt and not just physically. This wasn't the man I respected and admired so much. Zaphire's capture must have rattled him much more than he let on.

Despite the pain and shock, I carried on talking. Too fast, stumbling over my words, only just able to get them out.

"I'm sorry I had to do it this way, but it was the only way to keep it real. Focus Markus. Focus on the positive. When Eliza makes contact again we have a real chance of finding Zaphire and set a trap for Rick at the same time. Please, Michael, Laura, you can see this, right?"

I caught a glimpse of Laura who stood staring at Markus and me, her hands covering her mouth, eyes full of worry.

At last, Vivian stepped in. She seemed to be in control of her emotions the most and told everyone firmly to calm down and get a grip. Markus shook Michael off him and straightened his suit. He walked up to me and offered his hand. I took it, uncertain of what would come next. His senses were all over the place.

"Sorry Zack. I apologise. I was out of control and shouldn't have done that. That was unforgivable. We'll deal with your insubordination at a more suitable time. But you're right; for now we need to focus on getting Zaphire out. Are you okay to carry on?"

"Yeah. I'm fine, thank you Sir," I managed to groan, though I felt far from it. I needed some painkillers soon, now the adrenaline had subsided. He'd fucking broken my nose for sure. My eyes were stinging from the tears that were trying to edge their way out. I fought to hold them in. No fucking way was that going to happen. Not in front of Markus of all people.

"How have you had contact with her?"

"She's been texting me, but she had to get hold of

someone's phone. I can't contact her. But I know she'll make contact soon. We have to be patient and buy some time. Make Rick wait at least a few days to have his access to our compound," I urged, albeit woolly mouthed due to the pain.

"It's a hell of a gamble, Zack. I hope, for Zaphy's sake, it pays off. And yours," Markus added menacingly. "Now, get your arse over to Dr Eccles and get your face seen to."

I prayed to fuck that phone in my pocket was going to buzz soon.

CHAPTER 41
Eliza

This wasn't good. Stuck in a room with Daniel until tomorrow. I needed to fix this problem but I couldn't think of any solution that wouldn't blow my cover. Maybe this is how far it would go, but I was reluctant to admit to that. When my betrayal was out in the open, I would lose my father and even though ultimately I wanted him stopped, I wasn't ready to let go yet. I wanted some more time with him. But I shouldn't put my needs before the Sensorians' or Zaphire's. *Shit.* This was hard. But I knew I had to get a message to Zack, one way or another.

"I ordered us some food to be brought to your room. Hope you like pasta?" Daniel spoke chirpily. He looked a smidgen apologetic, smelled a little guilty but my overriding sensation from him was pleasure. His anger had all but gone. Irena had been right.

"You seem to be enjoying my predicament a little too much, Daniel?" I joked.

I wasn't going to let the opportunity to tease him somewhat pass me by, even though my mind was frantically going round in circles at to what to do. I decided to be patient and have some food first. Let my brain think around the problem for a bit. Something might come to me.

He turned a little red in his cheeks and gave a shy smile.

"No.. er...I just thought you might be hungry," he stammered .

"Yeah. I am a little peckish. But don't think you're fooling me," I winked.

"That bloody Sensorian thing," he sighed, going even more red as he realised he couldn't hide his true feelings. I noticed him regrouping and shaking off his embarrassment. "Fair enough. You know how I feel about you and I thought maybe we can make this bad situation, a little better."

He sat himself next to me and moved in. Surely he wasn't expecting a kiss! I was saved by a knock on our door as our pasta arrived. I heard him groan a little, but ignored it whilst I jumped up to open the door.

We ate our dinner. I was trying to make small talk, avoiding awkward silences but all the while a plan was forming in my head. It was going to be risky and horrible, but I hoped I could pull it off. I had to wait for the right moment.

I scanned my room for things I could use. Daniel offered to find a film on Netflix to watch. I agreed. I spotted his phone on charge by the bedside. I made myself comfortable on the bed and took my socks off. I waited until the unsuspecting Daniel took his place next to me, a little too close, clearly still hoping to have another go at kissing me. His scent was full of pheromones. It tempted me and I felt bad over what was in store for him. I had to concentrate and took a moment to visualise the sea. I took a deep breath. It had to be done. He didn't suspect a thing.

I flung round, shoved a knee in his stomach then flipped him over. I snatched the lead that dangled off his phone and yanked his arms behind his back. He started to fight back after the initial cry of surprise and we landed on the floor. I could only just hold him whilst binding his arms. He kicked me viciously in the crotch but I had him. I shoved a sock in his mouth. The room stank of adrenaline and his consternation. It wouldn't be long before the other Sensorians in the house would pick up the scent of distress or heard the noise. I had to control it. I looked around to see what I could use and grabbed the lamp off the table. I didn't hesitate for a second before smashing it over his head. He stopped resisting instantly and fell into a heap on the floor. *Shit.*

I stood there. In shock. Looking at him lying lifeless on the ground. I quickly kneeled by his side and checked his pulse. I heard and felt a steady beat. Relief poured over me, and I put him in the recovery position. I had to cloak my own output quickly to make sure no one would pick up any suspicious vibes. I had to act rapidly, otherwise it would all have been for nothing. I searched for his phone. It had been flung somewhere during our struggle and I frantically searched the room. I spotted it behind the sofa leg and made a dash for it. My fingers trembled whilst tapping Zack's number on the screen. It buzzed twice before I heard him answer, calmly but urgency seeping through his voice too. Despite the situation we were in, my heart still did a little flutter on hearing Zack. I physically shook it off and tried to concentrate on getting all the information I'd found out across to him. I could hear his breath stop when I told him about Ned and Lois. I emphasised I was going to try and talk Daniel round not to let on to Rick, but that I rated my chances of that minimal. So we should probably assume my cover was blown.

"You need to get out of there as soon as you think they realise what you're doing," Zack warned urgently, his voice full of concern.

"Don't worry about me. I'll sort something. Concentrate on getting Zaphy out of here," I pleaded, still feeling guilty about capturing her.

I could hear Zack taking a deep breath before telling me to remain calm, but that he had some bad news for me. When I heard about Zaphire's predicament, I could hardly breathe. How dare my father treat and threaten her like that. I was absolutely fuming. The bloody maniac! Zack urged me to focus. He told me their plans to let Rick come to the compound and use that time to hopefully free Zaphire so they could arrest him. I wanted to discuss the plans in more detail but I needed to hang up as I spotted movement from Daniel. He was regaining consciousness. I had my work cut out.

Daniel groaned and blinked, quickly realising what had happened. Luckily he was still somewhat groggy, so he wasn't making too much noise or attempting to free himself. I gently sat him up, but I still hadn't removed the sock from his mouth.

"Promise you won't shout and I'll remove the sock," I spoke gently but firmly. He nodded and I kept my word. His eyes full of accusation and confusion. I put a finger on his lips when he tried to talk and held a glass to his mouth with some water, which he gratefully sipped from. In the mean time I texted Zack to send me some footage or photos of Zaphire's ordeal, if there was any. I anxiously waited for the message to arrive.

"Daniel, I can explain," I started. It was difficult to look him in the eyes. I felt guilty for hurting him.

"What the f...," he spluttered, but I interrupted.

"Don't say anything yet. Please. Let me say my bit first," I pleaded.

The phone pinged. I didn't want to look, but I knew it was necessary. I opened it and watched. I wanted to puke. What had I done? Poor Zaphy. I had to succeed in persuading Daniel to back me. If I didn't raise Rick's suspicions, Zack and Markus would have a far better chance of liberating Zaphire. I didn't think Rick was going to bring Zaphire to the convention looking like that, so we had no choice but to go ahead with Zack's plan and free her whilst Rick was at our compound. I needed my cover to be able to find out where she was being held, which meant Rick couldn't know about me. I had to convince Daniel. I simply had to.

CHAPTER 42
Zack

The relief I felt when the phone rang was immeasurable. Eliza had not let me down. She gave us locations, dates and names. We couldn't believe Ned and Lois were on the invite list. We had to find out what was going on there and their motivations.

"Could it be that Rick is specifically targeting some of us, who he has identified as potential sympathisers? Ned hasn't had the easiest time here, and so could be perceived as malleable," I offered as an explanation. I couldn't believe Ned would turn his back on us. Michael nodded.

"Maybe you're right. I think we need to keep an open mind. I'll deal with Lois but you'll have a better chance with Ned. They might only just have received the invitation and haven't had the chance to report it," Michael agreed.

Markus got agitated, but soon recovered. Clearly determined not to lose his composure again. I could tell he wasn't happy with something though.

"No. we need to act strongly and swiftly. I need them to be apprehended immediately, Michael. I don't want them to get wind of anything and disappear. We'll talk to them once we have got them safe in a cell," he ordered.

Michael didn't object and promised to locate Lois straight away. I wasn't so sure it was the best idea. If Rick found out, he might get suspicious. I didn't want to do anything that could endanger Eliza's cover, just in case she managed to preserve it. I nudged Michael.

"Make sure it's done as discretely as possible," I added quickly. Michael understood where I was coming from, but it earned me another searing glare from Markus. I was not helping my case.

"I doubt Zaphire will be at the convention tomorrow and there is every chance Eliza's cover is blown. So how are we going to find out where Zaph is?" Markus questioned,

He still wasn't completely convinced with the whole idea. We had five minutes before Rick would contact us again.

"Sir, we have so many more leads now. We're in a far better position now than we were before. We'll still check out the convention. We just have to take the gamble. Let him come to our compound, Sir. It will feel like a win to him, and he may even take his eyes off the ball," I offered, surprised he even let me talk. I fucking hoped I convinced him though.

"It feels like wishful thinking Zack. But, I think it is the best chance we have," Markus conceded eventually. Just in time. The chime of the video call pierced our ears.

"Get out of shot, Zack. I don't want him to see your face. No need for him to suspect discord between us."

Markus ushered me out of the way. It had come out quite swollen and the bruising was starting to show, despite the doctor's attentions.

This time it was Rick's rather smug face staring at us. Laura and Frank had already joined. Brody managed to muscle his way into the room again too. Markus hadn't objected as he was there when Rick contacted us earlier, and he was probably too preoccupied anyway.

"Where's Zack," Rick barked.

"I'm here," I shouted from the back of the room.

"I need to see everyone's faces when you give me your decision. I need to be able to read you all," he insisted.

I checked with Markus and he gave me the tiniest of nods. I moved into shot and waited for Rick's reaction. He suppressed a little smirk. I wanted to fucking punch him.

"It's not what you think," I sighed. "Brody did it. He blamed me for not looking after my sister. He's got a bit of a thing for her." I threw an accusing look at Brodes in an attempt to misdirect Rick. Something else to apologise about later. Rick seemed to accept it though and whilst he directed his stare at Markus, Brody punched my side, but he understood. There was no real sting in it.

"So Markus, what's your decision?" Rick didn't beat around the bush. He wanted an answer.
Our leader sighed.

"It was a difficult decision as I don't like to be blackmailed into making stupid choices. However, we decided to give you access as we trust our fellow Sensorians to listen to your bullshit and value it as just that. We have nothing to fear from your ramblings, so you are welcome to visit us," Markus answered with a huge portion of contempt.

"Good. You'll have Zaphire back with you after we have left your compound safely and made sure you don't take any actions against us. I will be coming the day after tomorrow. I'll confirm a time by email," Rick tried to take the lead but Markus wasn't having that.

"I'll give you two hours to return Zaphire to us afterwards. If we don't have her I will unleash a full scale hunt for you and your followers, and there will be no leniency. And I will send you a mail with the time we will be expecting you."

The two men stared at each other, neither of them flinching or backing down. The seconds felt like minutes. Our faces were dead pan, not giving anything away apart from determination, as Rick scanned over all of us. Finally he spoke.

"Four hours. That's my final offer. Otherwise I will pass this opportunity over and you can say goodbye to your precious Zaphire."

My heart rate sped up, but I noticed I wasn't the only one. Tiny sweat beads appeared on Michael's face and Brody was a total open book, anxiety spilling out all over the place. Laura was white as a ghost and bursting to yell at Markus to accept it.

Markus took his time though. He must have been cloaking to the max, because there wasn't a hint of sensory output on his part. I literally could not tell what he was inclined to answer. So we waited. I trusted he would make the right decision, whatever that might be, but I hoped it would be to accept.

"Deal," he simply stated, causing the room to be filled with a collective sigh of relief. A choice was made.

CHAPTER 43
Eliza

I watched Daniel closely when I showed him the footage of Zaphire. You could hear the conversation between Rick and Markus in the background whilst looking at Zaphire's terrified and bruised face. It was horrific to see her so powerless and vulnerable; a mere pawn in the men's power play. I could barely contain my anger, but I had to stay cool, attempt not to look like some wild banshee in front of Daniel.

The video had the desired effect on Daniel's state of mind. He was mortified, yet I could still sense huge loyalty towards the man who revenged his sister. I had to play this carefully. Not completely vilify the man he clearly worshipped.

"All I want to do is get Zaphire out of there, Daniel. And to do that, I need your help. I don't want my father caught, but he has overstepped the mark here. You understand that, yes?"

Daniel wasn't convinced.

"He must have had his reasons, just like you had. You knocked me out, Eliza."

The accusation still heavy in his voice. He wasn't

going to forgive me for this easily, if ever.

"I didn't plan that. I just ran out of options. Rick did this deliberately. It's different. And he won't hesitate to carry out his threat either. I fully expect Zaphy to disappear if somehow Markus breaks his promise."

He took his time, deliberating my answer carefully.

"The deal sounds solid. If they agree to Rick's demands, Zaphire gets to go home. No need to do anything else," Daniel decided.

"But therein lies the crux. Will Markus agree? And if he does, will he actually stick to it? I'm afraid they might try something and that will anger Rick. You don't know them. Their motto is 'Mission before Everything', and they mean it. It's a very rigid community they live in and they all abide by it. That's why I had to leave, remember. I don't work like that."

I laid it on as thick as I could. I had to sew a seed of doubt in Daniel's mind about Zaphire's safety. He was a good guy, his conscience would nag him. I could see my strategy starting to work. His demeanour changed slightly. I didn't tell him I just got another text to confirm Markus took Rick's deal. Zack clearly gambling I still had access to the phone.

"How would I be able to help though? I don't know

anything about this," he sighed, still quite reluctant.

I took his hand in mine and caressed his face gently.

"Just keep quiet on what I did, just for a few days. Until she's safe? I'm so sorry I hurt you and you have every right to refuse, but I am begging you; please let me help Zaphire."

His anguish was painful. I had to shield to keep from physically shrinking away from him. I hated myself for putting Daniel in this position and I was in no doubt about Daniel's anger towards me at the moment. He struggled to come to a decision and it was hard to make out what he was thinking as he kept changing his mind.

"Daniel?" I whispered softly so as to not antagonise him after a good ten minutes.

"I need time to think. That's the least you can do," he bit back, glaring at me.

Training under Zack with his impossibly prickly and demanding attitude paid off here. It had definitely taught me that at this point it was best not to push and be submissive, at least on the surface. So I cast my eyes down and moved away a little to give Daniel some space and time to think more. It's all about the signals we emit. We sat quietly next to each other for ages. The clock's ticking sounded like a nodding donkey and the fly buzzing around the room like a helicopter, but I didn't want to tune down my senses. I needed to be alert for any signs and changes in Daniel's mood. Then I detected the tiniest of intake of breath by Daniel. He was about to tell me his decision. But I already knew what he was going to say.

"Okay," he sighed.

I could let my relief out that I'd felt seconds before his answer.

"You won't tell anyone? You promise?"

He nodded in answer to my question. I had to ask to test his response for anything that would give away a lie. There was nothing. He smelled clean, he looked clean and his voice sounded sincere.

"Thank you so much, you have no idea how much this means to me."

"I have one condition," he added gravely.

"Of course. What is it?"

"As soon as Zaphire is safe, you tell Rick what you have done. I cannot let you deceive him any longer. Were you ever even in our camp?"

His indignation and hurt showed through once

more.

"I will tell him. But it's far more complicated than you think. I just wanted to have a chance to get to know my father better. It was never just about what side I'm on."

That, at least, was partly true. I knew I had to make the most of the next few days as our days were numbered now. When Rick finds out, he won't ever speak to me again, even if he does manage to escape after the meeting. Daniel didn't know about Markus' intentions of course. I would have my dad's company at our convention, our last dance so to speak, and that's what I had to focus on, besides the fact I had to urgently find out where Zaphire was held. Zack was relying on me. I quickly texted I had a few days grace from Daniel and that I would do everything I could to try and locate Zaphire.

A groan interrupted my conversations with Zack. It was so wonderful to be able to freely use the phone, I sort of got lost in it.

"Can you untie me, please? And I need some painkillers. My head is killing me."

"Oh my God, yes of course!" I exclaimed, a little embarrassed. I scanned all his sensory output once more, before I released him, but I could not sense anything suspicious. His intentions were pure. Just like he'd promised.

CHAPTER 44
Zack

"Really! You twats arrested me for that! Why did no one just fucking ask me without going so bloody heavy handed! What a load of bollocks. Sir."

Ned nearly spat the last words at me.

To say that he was not best pleased would be an understatement. I knew he would react like this. Earlier, I did have a little 'eyes to the sky' moment with Ned over Markus' order to arrest him, to show some understanding. But even though I had my doubts over the rather brusque approach, I could see where Markus was coming from.

"It was just a precaution. You know what it's like. There is a lot of tension and stress at the moment, so please bear that in mind." I explained. "And mind your language. Calling me Sir does not make it okay to fucking swear at me."

I had to remind him that though I was his friend, I was also his superior.

Ned relaxed a little, so I decided it was time to push him on some answers, as he hadn't offered an explanation as yet.

"So, did you receive an invitation to attend Rick's convention?"

My radar was out to spot any sensory output that would indicate Ned was telling the truth. He looked at me indignantly but answered affirmatively.

"Why did you not report it instantly?" I asked matter of factly, trying not to be too confrontational.

Ned hesitated, making me tense. His sensory output was minimal, but his body highly strung. I suspected he was cloaking, but it was hard to tell. I changed my posture slightly, leaning into him more and looking directly into his eyes.

"Just tell me the fucking truth, Ned. There is no other option."

I kept my voice quiet, but he knew there was no messing with me. After a few intense minutes Ned let out a deep sigh, losing his defensive demeanour.

"I didn't want to draw attention to it. I was embarrassed. Why would Rick send me an invite? Did he think I was likely to turn my back on our community? I thought if I said anything it would somehow put seeds of doubt in people's mind. That, somehow, I would be blamed for having been invited. I don't know," he sighed.

He rubbed his hands warily through his hair and he

suddenly looked defeated and exhausted. He let his guard down completely, making it easy for me to read him.

"I worked so hard to be trusted again, Sir. I didn't want to jeopardise all that. I thought if I just deleted it, no one would ever know. Once again, I made the wrong decision. Maybe I should be punished for that."

"No one is talking about punishment at the moment, Ned. Don't be down on yourself. We just needed to find out for sure where everyone's loyalties lie. You understand that. Don't you? I knew you would have a sensible explanation. Relax."

He looked at me slightly doubtfully and to be honest I didn't blame him. Markus was in a foul mood and would happily vent his frustration about the lack of control he had in the current Zaphire situation on Ned. But I had a much better plan. Rather than one of us trying to infiltrate the meeting, Ned should go, eliminating the risk of us being spotted anywhere near the convention. I would do my best to convince Markus to let him go, but I didn't say anything about it to Ned yet. I didn't want to get his hopes up. He could still end up with a stint in isolation.

"Anyway, what happened to your face, mate? It looks bad," Ned enquired, as if he'd only just noticed.

"Don't ask," I answered grumpily.

When I left Ned's cell, I bumped into Michael. He clearly had a different experience with Lois than I just had with Ned. He stank of stress and anger. The muscles in his face were twitching manically. Of course an ordinary person wouldn't have noticed a thing. He just looked a tad hassled to the unknowing eye.

"Hey. Bad news?" I guessed.

"She's bloody unbelievable. She stone faced lied to me, thinking I couldn't see through her cloaking. Who does she think I am? Some bloody amateur!"

I groaned. Lois was instrumental in running our compound. Markus had always relied on her. He'll be gutted to hear of her betrayal and it won't do anything to calm his state of mind.

"Did you crack her in the end?" I dared to ask, slightly risking a bollocking. Instead he just sneered, my question clearly undeserving of an answer.

"Lois actually approached one of Rick's followers herself. A lady from France, Angelique I think she's called. They knew each other years ago and had been in touch sporadically. Lois said she just wanted to find out more about Rick's vision and was tempted by the idea of having more freedom and power, but realised it was a mistake and wasn't going to go. But I know it was more than that, she would have betrayed us. She was heavily cloaking."

Fuck it. I was scared as to what Markus would do to her. She'll go to our court but I bet he'll push for the maximum sentence. We didn't need anything that could encourage protests or even dissent. The death penalty has always been controversial in our community.

Markus was keen to send in Ned. Maybe a bit too keen. I wondered if he felt it was a way for Ned to prove himself to us, especially when he refused to send back up with him. It had made sense to me to have a safety measure in place, but Markus insisted that a tracker on his phone and him keeping contact with us was enough. He didn't want to arouse any suspicion and risk losing Zaphire. That did make sense too; Ned on his own would look legitimate as he was on the invite list. So, I let it go, pleased enough to have Markus back my plan.

CHAPTER 45
Eliza

Soft knocking woke me from my slumber. Irena walked in purposefully and seemingly wide awake at 7am. She decidedly opened the curtains and threw open a window. The sun came streaming in with the promise of a beautifully warm summer's day ahead.

"It's rank in here!" she exclaimed whilst waving her hands in front of face. We both heard a groan appear from underneath a duvet mountain on the sofa.

"My head," Daniel mumbled, clearly still in pain.

"What on earth did you two get up to last night?" Irena quizzed whilst scanning the room for evidence of alcohol and such. Of course there was none. His headache the sole result of me bashing him over the head with a lamp. "Rick arranged you a full make-over today. Grab a quick shower but don't bother about washing your hair. He's booked you a fashion and hair stylist and they will take care of everything. Apparently he has a special hairdresser chair and sink and everything!"

Irena seemed rather excited by the whole thing. Me less so. Couldn't think of anything worse in fact. I just wanted today to be over with. However, I had to snap out of it and play my part. At least Irena attributed my lack of enthusiasm to the 'heavy night' she thought Daniel and I had experienced. She even whispered in my ear before she left to give her the secret to hiding the alcohol scent so well, which made me smile a little.

I got up and fixed Daniel a cup of coffee and some painkillers. He sat up but looked groggy. I hoped he wasn't concussed. He hadn't been sick, but he should really have his head seen to, just in case. However, it would have to wait. I would keep a close eye on him myself, which wasn't going to be difficult as he was going to be by my side for most of the day. He'd taken control of his phone again after we agreed our deal, and checked any communication I had with Zack. I managed to warn Zack that our conversation was monitored, but only after he'd sent me the message telling me Ned was coming to the convention to find out anything he could and just in case I needed help.

It was dangerous Daniel knowing this, but I was convinced I could still trust him to uphold his end of the deal until Zaphy was free. Then my time would be up. I sighed deeply, earning a wary glance from Daniel. He hadn't spoken a word to me yet. I wasn't surprised to be honest. I decided to jump in the shower and fully throw myself into the theatre of today.

"I'm speechless," Rick managed to squeak upon entering my room. Did I even spot his eyes tearing up slightly? I have to say, despite everything, I felt like a goddess. Ava and Harley had worked their magic on me, and managed to sweep me up in their enthusiasm so I even momentarily forgot all my worries. I twirled like a princess.

"You look gorgeous and strong. Ready to be by my side and be introduced to my followers." Rick brimmed with pride.

Now I felt like a warrior queen, ready to go to battle. His words and pride did something to me. I wanted to be by his side and earn it, I didn't want to let him down. I craved him to be proud of me again. These were not feelings I wanted to admit to. Could not admit to.

"Is Zaphire going to join us today?" I asked innocently, bringing myself back down to earth. Rick cloaked immediately.

"I don't think it's a wise move, so I decided against it," he said reservedly. I didn't confront him about the

285

cloaking for the moment.

"Don't you think it would show our strength?" I pressed a bit more.

"That's what I initially thought. But now I think it may be a bit too provocative," he mused.

"I'd like to see her, please," I demanded. It was worth trying.

"Soon Lizzy, but not today. We need to focus."

Rick was desperate to get away from the subject of Zaphire, but I wasn't quite done yet.

"Where is she now? Is she okay?"

"She's nearby. She's fine."

No amount of cloaking covered that lie. He was nervous.

"What's up, dad? Please tell me what is going on."

I tested him to see if he trusted me enough to divulge his treatment of her. Apparently not.

"Leave it, Eliza. We will talk later. Let's go or we'll be late."

I didn't push any further. He'd used my full name.

"Daniel, you need to get changed. You're a mess. You look like you have a hangover but you don't smell like it. What's going on? Are you ill?" Rick asked in a slightly annoyed tone. He wasn't aware Daniel hadn't left my side in the last twenty four hours. Irena hadn't bothered him with my snooping around incident. But he had a good look at Daniel now and I could see he was going to grill him. He could smell his presence all over me and the room, despite the windows being wide open all morning. I jumped in.

"Yes, hurry up Daniel. Go get changed, I'm with dad. I'll see you there," all the whilst ushering him out the room. Daniel's eyes were dark with warning, but he couldn't really do anything but get changed, so he reluctantly sped off to do just that.

The mansion that served as Rick's headquarters was magnificent. It had an old fashioned grandeur about it, which could have been intimidating, but upon entering felt comfortable at once. The interior designer had managed to successfully marry the old with the new, blending it into a warm but functional space. The meeting hall was done up with soft lighting and impeccably laid out tables, covered with a variety of white flowers. Unlike me, Zaphire would fully appreciate the beauty of it. A pang of longing seared through my whole body, making me shiver. I missed her so much. I had to shove those feelings to the back of my mind as quickly as I could before they might take over. I was scared if I let them in, I would completely lose control.

People started to fill up the place, and as there were plenty of ordinary people (I could not bring myself to call them Dullards) mixing in with the Sensorians, a plethora of vibes, sounds and smells were hit my senses. Awe, nerves, excitement and anticipation overpowered all other outputs. It was going to be a tiring day, coping with all of these and constantly having to cloak. I don't know why my father was so keen to live amongst them all. Only the medication I used to be on made it just about bearable.

I felt nervous. I didn't like being the centre of attention, but that was exactly what I was. I could feel everyone's eyes on me. Then I felt my dad's reassuring hand on my shoulder and my VH kicked in. Seeing the room through my father's eyes was different. He might have looked relaxed on the outside but he had eyes on everything and everyone that was in that room. He focussed on particular people and noted who was talking to whom. He spotted two men having a rather heated discussion and I knew he was listening in right now. I did too. A few seconds in, it was apparent that it was something personal and nothing to do with the cause, so he moved on, turning his attentions to me briefly.

"Are you ready for this?"

I shrugged.

"As ready as I can be, I suppose."

He took that as a yes. He rubbed my shoulder and moved off to do some more surveying. The moment of his speech was getting nearer and my heart rate sped up. Daniel, despite his anger, took my hand, squeezed it and gave me a little smile. My nerves must have been so obvious. He was such a good guy.

I spotted Ned mixing with some girls on the other side of the room. He caught my eye and signalled for me to come over. I was just about to go and say hello to him but suddenly the atmosphere in the room changed. Anticipation was at record levels when Angelique made her way to the microphone and announced for everyone to take their seats. There were those that had a place at the tables, presumably the important members, predominantly Sensorians. I saw Ned at one of them, right amongst some high ranking police officials and politicians. Then lots of people in the rows of seats at the back. There must have been over two hundred people in total. I moved to the head table and sat down next to my father. My throat dry and heart racing. He stood up and got ready to take the stage.

"Fellow Sensorians and Followers, thank you all for coming to this gathering at such short notice. Things are moving quickly at the moment and I wanted to keep you all updated. As alluded to in your invitation, I have two important announcements to make.

But first, let us remind ourselves what we are striving for. Let's never lose sight of our end goal: A just society for all, where crime will be eradicated. Where money does not determine whether you get justice and where criminals don't have more rights than victims.

Us Sensorians have lived long enough in the shadows of the existing society; working hard to get justice where it's needed, using our gift to help the police find evidence, but it's always been hidden and unrecognised. That's how we used to fulfil our destiny, hiding and serving the ordinary people. But it's not enough. Criminals get away, fraud and corruption rule, and I can't sit back any longer and let that happen.

It's time to step up, come out of the shadows and take over. It is our responsibility as Sensorians. I believe that's why we have been put on this earth. Not to be serving communities, but to be ruling them. Leading the ordinary people into a Fair and Just Society for all".

Rick paused to allow the people to burst into a resounding applause and hoots of support. He lifted his hand to signal calm and within seconds it was dead silent again. He commanded a huge amount of respect amongst his followers and any newcomers fell in line pretty quickly. I noticed he carefully avoided calling ordinary people Dullards, not to alienate any of them.

"It's not going to be easy to make this happen and unpleasant and unpopular decisions will have to be made along the way. Decisions that I previously may never have considered or even would have condemned. But my previous leaders, first Valentino and then Markus, were not wrong when they taught me that consequences need to be followed through to maintain leadership and keep course towards a common goal. Our goals are just different.

When I was younger I once broke away from my community because I was angry about how my friend was treated when he had to pay the ultimate price for his betrayal. But now I realise it was what had to be done to maintain the status quo of our community at the time. I recently realised it was the status quo that I disagreed with, our goals needed to change. So I decided to break away once again, as I couldn't live any longer in the Sensorian community where our true potential was stifled.

I, and all of us, need to live life to the full and to be able to do that, a new society needs to be created and that is what we are striving for. A society where Sensorians can fulfil their purpose on this earth and everyone will benefit, Sensorians and ordinary people alike. Only criminals and liars will lose out. It will simply be impossible for them to escape justice."

It scared me that he seemed to have made peace with Valentino's decision to eliminate his friend Tom. He was basically saying he would not hesitate to do the same. I seemed to be only one of a few with reservations, the majority of people were nodding and cheering vehemently in agreement and the atmosphere was getting close to frenzied. He was incredibly clever at focussing on the benefits of this new society he envisaged, and playing down the violence he clearly was willing to use to achieve it. People, both Sensorians and ordinary, were buying it. It did not bode well.

"It's time I got to the point as to why we have all

gathered today."

He glanced over to me and I knew my time to shine was getting near. My heart was beating so hard, it felt like it was going to explode. A fine sheen of sweat started to cover my face and body. *Breathe, for crying out loud!* I started visualising the sea.

"*Our leadership has been greatly boosted by the addition of no other than my own daughter. Please raise your glass to welcome Eliza Mankuzaj into our community. Come and join me up here Eliza."*

There was no option than to brave the crowds. I smiled and stood up, raised my glass to everyone, which was met with a raucous applause. I joined my father on stage and felt ever so grateful for my makeover, being under the scrutiny of hundreds of people.

"*The second announcement I can make is that, thanks to Eliza, we have a huge bargaining tool which made it possible to persuade Markus to let me into his compound to deliver our vision. He has given us Carte Blanche in recruiting new Sensorians to join us without repercussions for them or us. Eliza captured Zaphire, his daughter, and we have guaranteed her safe return upon him honouring the deal we made. Let's all raise a glass again in thanks to Eliza, for whom it must have been a difficult decision to hand over her former friend. But she did, for the greater good and to show her loyalty to us.*

To Eliza everyone."

Hundred of voices united when they toasted my name with reverence. It was the oddest experience I'd ever had. It felt surreal. I felt like a complete fraud.

CHAPTER 46
Zack

It had gone quiet. Ned had been giving us updates every ten minutes, but we hadn't heard anything for the last hour. I didn't like it one fucking bit, but we had to assume he was just in no position to text us and that he would do so as soon as he could. I started to doubt my recommendation to send him in, but I convinced myself it had been the best course to take to arouse the least suspicion. However, what he hadn't told us, and we subsequently found out from Lois, was that the invitation had come with a stark warning. Anyone coming with the aim to infiltrate or betray would be met with severe punishment when uncovered. We should have sent some back up with him. I feared Markus' decision not to, could end up stabbing us in the back.

"It'll be fine mate. We made the right decision."

I could always count on Brody for some reassurance. I felt a little useless, just sitting waiting around for messages from Ned or Eliza, but it was the only thing we could do at the moment. The last message from Eliza was rather cryptic and I couldn't be sure who'd actually sent it, as Eliza had said the phone was compromised. It hadn't read like Eliza's messages but it seemed to ask to confirm Ned's attendance, which was odd as I had already told Eli. I asked for clarification, but that never came.

In the mean time Markus was busy getting a team ready to deal with Rick for when arrives at ours the day after and deciding which people to send to free Zaphire. He'd already let me know Brody and I were part of the team, but neither of us would be leading. Frank, Michael and Rob, the VH expert, were most likely to be in charge and Laura was bound to come here and host the meeting Rick had requested. Markus didn't want me anywhere near Rick and he had made the right decision. I would have found it difficult to control the red mist in his presence. He may be Eliza's father, but all I wanted was revenge for his treatment of Zaphire. I wanted to fucking deck him one.

The plan was to leave for the North in the morning by private jet. I sincerely hoped we would know a bit more about Zaphire's exact location by then. We would need quite a few more people, if we had to go into several different locations. Not ideal.

"Let's ask for a break," I suggested.

I desperately needed to blow off some steam.

"Fancy a box?"

Brody was already on his feet. He didn't like all this hanging around either.

"I'll avoid your face," he sniggered. I wasn't in the mood for joking about that yet so ignored it, to Brody's amusement.

Markus gave us permission and sent someone to watch the phone so we could relax for an hour. It was good to clear my mind and I could literally feel the endorphins flood my system. If only I had known this was probably the last time I'd feel this good for a while, I would have savoured it a bit longer. Things were about to take a turn for the worse and nothing had prepared us for the message we were about to get.

CHAPTER 47
Eliza

"They love you my sweets," Rick whispered in my ear. His mind wandered though, as he picked up some disturbance in the room and he quickly went to check it out. I tried to find it too and my body jolted. Ned and Daniel had squared up against each other, and two guards were already at their side, trying to escort them quietly out of the room. I focussed on their conversation and just managed to hear Daniel demanding that Ned leave the event. Ned was shaking his head vehemently, telling Daniel to leave him the fuck alone. The guard took Daniel by the arm and tried to guide him away from Ned, but Daniel resisted and was then manhandled roughly. Ned tried to calm things down, but by then Rick was already there and managed to persuade Daniel to go with him. I breathed a sigh of relief as Ned tried to make himself scarce. However, I'd relaxed too soon as I saw Daniel starting to gesture wildly and pointing at Ned and within seconds the guards got to him. Ned calculated his chances; he resisted, got away and was caught again within seconds. He was escorted out so swiftly, most people already had gone back to their conversations, though I did notice a few raised eyebrows and confused expressions. I feared the worst. Did Daniel confront Ned? Did he threaten to expose him? Had he told Rick already? I needed to find out what had happened, but I was cornered by several admiring Sensorians and followers and they were bombarding me with questions. I couldn't get away.

Not long after I got my wish, but not quite how I would have liked it. Irena strode over with a grim look on her face.

"Come with me. Now," she said uncompromisingly.

I knew it was serious. I really hoped my cover wasn't blown. If Rick had interrogated Daniel, all was lost. There was no way Daniel could lie to him. All Rick had to do was ask the right questions. I felt sick.

I had to run to keep up with Irena's purposeful stride, her legs being so much longer than mine. My heart beat faster with every stride. She took me to the basement of the building, to a corridor lined with doors to what I assumed were rooms. The gloomy, sterile atmosphere was in stark contrast with the rest of the building and it filled me with a heavy sense of foreboding. We stood in front of room number 101 and even before she knocked I felt distress emanating from the room. I needed to shield. Cloak and shield with all my might if there was any chance of remaining undiscovered.

The door opened. My knees buckled. My stomach churned but I managed to walk in, hopefully looking in control. I was not prepared for what I saw next.

Ned, stripped naked and handcuffed, facing the left hand wall. Zaphire. My sweet, brave Zaphy, still deprived of her senses, sat, handcuffed, on the floor facing the corner on the right hand side of the room. In the middle, lay Daniel, passed out on the floor in recovery position. Rick stood over him, staring at me. Two guards stood on either side of Ned and Zaph, all with their guns out. *What the hell happened in the fifteen minutes or so since Ned and Daniel were hauled out of the room upstairs!* I could do nothing but stare. My mouth wide open.

Rick spoke first.

"We've heard some serious allegations, Eliza."

He was interrupted by two men that looked like paramedics rushing into the room. They quickly put Daniel on a stretcher and left with Irena in tow. They must work for Rick as they didn't bat an eyelid over the sorrowful sight of Ned and Zaphy.

"Wh...what the hell h..happened here?" I managed to stutter, in utter shock.

"Daniel accused Ned of being a spy. We got confirmation of that pretty quickly," throwing a disdainful glance at Ned. "But before Daniel, err, passed out, he claimed you were in contact with Zack," Rick accused.

"What!" I managed to sound incredulous. "Why did he pass out?" I deflected, to be met with an awkward silence and a little snort from Ned, which was immediately punished with a hard smack to the back of his head by the guard.

"I punched him."

Rick shrugged his shoulders in an apologetic way.

"You knocked him out!" I shouted, shaking my head in feigned disbelief. "Now we can't get to the bottom of this!" I shouted with mock despair. I sighed, still shaking my head. "What else did he say?"

I desperately needed to find out what Rick knew. He seemed to be put out slightly by my outburst.

"Nothing to start with. But he was holding back. I could tell. I pressurised and then he claimed you knew about Ned infiltrating. That's when I punched him. He said he had proof, just before he passed out."

The damned phone. However, it didn't look like Rick had the phone. *Where was the frigging phone?* I shook my head in answer to the accusation.

"It's nonsense. He can't have any proof because it's not true," I bit back.

"He wasn't lying, Lizzy. I would have been able to tell. That's why I lost it with him. I don't want it to be true. But what I do know for sure is that Ned was here under false pretences, he couldn't hide his guilt from me. He was warned about it in the letter and now he will suffer the consequences. For the other matter, well, we'll have to wait until I can interrogate Daniel further as to what else he knows."

My father looked genuinely upset and not quite willing to give up on me. I had to persuade him to believe me. And hope to God that Daniel would stay unconsciousness for some time longer.

"Dad, Daniel must just have drawn the wrong conclusions. He wouldn't be lying if he really believed I did what he accused me of. But I swear, on my mum's life, that I knew nothing about this. Trust me," I pleaded, cloaking hard.

Rick just stood there, intensely staring at me. Reading me. I couldn't read him very well at all. So much for not being able to hide your emotions from your closest relatives. I just hoped I was doing as excellent a job as him, hiding mine. I kept my mind blank, willing myself to believe my own story. Then, I noticed a little chink in his armour; his love for me. It made him make decisions he would normally never do. Reckless ones. He'd made up his mind.

"I'll give you the benefit of the doubt. You emit very confusing signals. You're cloaking. I can't decide. But I want to show you that I'm willing to trust you."

Irena was back in the room and I could feel her surprise at his decision. Rick was known to be an ultra careful man, making decisions only after hours of deliberation and looking at all angles. This was out of character for him, and Irena knew it. She was wise to keep her mouth shut though. I could tell he knew he was taking a massive risk and didn't want to be confronted over it.

"Thank you. I'm sure I'll be able to explain whatever Daniel thinks I have done."

Suddenly I felt a sharp pain, right in my gut. It was Zaphire's hate, hitting me like a tonne of bricks. *Shield Eliza. Ignore.* I managed to block it out, with difficulty.

Rick smiled ruefully. He had felt Zaphire's out-pour as well.

"That leaves Ned to deal with. We have to send a

strong message to Zack and Markus. We had a deal and they tried to undermine it. That cannot happen again. Agree?"

He looked directly into my eyes and I met his eyes with determination.

"Yes. I agree. We need to show we shouldn't be messed with."

I noticed Ned out of the corner of my eyes, shivering and terrified. I didn't realise what I had just agreed to sentence him to.

"Take him next door and deal with him," Rick ordered the guards, who eagerly complied, lifting Ned up under the arms and dragging him out. It chilled me to the bone, but I turned and followed my father out, leaving Zaphire a seething, desperate mess. A little bit of me died inside that moment and I couldn't show any of it.

CHAPTER 48
Zack

The message came in physical form. It came at 2.17am. Loud banging on my door woke me up rudely and I cursed so much, I swear the air turned blue. I shoved some clothes on and went to see what the urgency was, finding Markus and Michael already downstairs racing to the front door. I jumped the stairs and joined them just as they went outside. Stretched out on the floor lay a naked man. Facing upwards and completely covered in bruises and blood. His face barely recognisable but we all knew who it was. Ned. I threw up. Michael was already at his side, checking his pulse. Markus phoned 999, urgently making our location known. An ambulance arrived in under five minutes, and all that time I was rooted to the spot. Immobilised. In shock. I had been right to worry about Ned's loss of contact with us. This was my fucking fault. I heard an animal howl. No. It was me.

Then, a sharp pain spread across my face. Markus had slapped me. I looked at him, not comprehending.

"Come inside son," I think he said. I followed him like a lamb.

Several sweet cups of tea later, with the knowledge that Ned was still alive, but in a critical condition in intensive care, we sat in Markus' office trying to process what had happened. Ned's mother had gone to be with him, putting her grudge against him aside. His father still stubbornly denied him his forgiveness. *Harsh*. It reminded me of Eliza's indignation over this.

There was a note. It warned us in no uncertain terms not to try and undermine our deal a second time, or we would not see Zaphire alive again .

"Obviously we need to take this threat seriously. So far, we have gravely underestimated how far Rick is willing to go to achieve his goal. But I still want to stick to our original plan to detain him whilst he's in our compound, and we'll attempt to rescue Zaphire," Markus opened.

Laura and Frank had joined us. They had arrived back in the compound late last night. Laura wasn't convinced. Neither was I. I needed to hear from Eliza first before I would willingly agree to carry on with our plan. Frank and Michael agreed with Markus.

"What if Eliza's cover is blown? She won't be able to give us any more information as to the whereabouts of Zaphire. It will be a huge risk as at the moment we're only guessing where she could be held," I objected.

"Let's not speculate. As far as we know Rick still doesn't know about Eliza's collaboration with us. We'll know soon enough. For now we carry on preparing our rescue mission. Everyone get some sleep and we'll reconvene at 8:00am sharp tomorrow."

I was happy to retreat to my room, but sleep was out of the question. Ned's life was hanging in the balance and for all we knew Zaphire and Eliza's weren't safe either. I was scared what Markus might do to Eliza, if he found out about her betrayal. What if she needed rescuing as well? She had told me to concentrate on getting Zaphire out, but with the recent violence I was getting increasingly worried. Everyone I cared about was in danger and I blamed myself. I should have fought harder for Ned's safety and I started to doubt my decision to let Eliza go it alone.

I must have dropped off into a fitful sleep because my alarm woke me in a dishevelled sweaty state on the sofa. My neck ached and my face felt tender. I must remind myself not to get on the receiving end of Markus' hands or fists again. Not that I could help the last one. The fucking horrific scene I witnessed yesterday kept forcing its ugly way back onto my cornea. I shook my head violently in an attempt to rid myself from it, but it wouldn't budge and neither would the sickening feeling that accompanied the image.

My door opened. I became aware I'd ignored the knocking. Brody stepped in. His face distraught.

"I heard." He came over and for a moment wasn't sure what to do, but he stepped up and gave me a hug. "He'll pull through," he mumbled half heartedly.

Brody knew I blamed myself and was trying to be supportive, but even he was struggling to be positive.

I still hadn't heard from Eliza, and Rick was coming to our compound today. The meeting was scheduled to start at two o'clock in the afternoon which gave us barely enough time to pull this off. This could all go horribly wrong and I knew I would not be able to live with myself if something happened to Zaphire.

"Bro. You need to snap out of your fucking doomsday scenario now. Focus. Don't give up without a fight. That's not like you."

Brody was right. We fucking had to pull it off. Whatever the fuck it would take.

CHAPTER 49
Eliza

I followed Rick in a daze. I had to focus and forget the scenes I just witnessed. I needed to find that bloody phone. Daniel must have dropped it in the scuffle. I didn't get a chance though as Rick escorted me to my room and told me to get some rest. He locked the door on me. *Bollocks*. Naturally I had an extremely bad night's sleep. I dreaded the moment the door would open in the morning and find out that Rick knew. That Daniel had woken up and told him everything.

I woke up as I heard footsteps approach. It was Irena. *Was that good?* Her face didn't give much away but it wasn't hostile. I could hardly breathe, I was so nervous. I envisaged the sea and waves to calm myself down somewhat. She looked at me slightly peculiarly. I should be more careful.

"Rick wants to see you, before he travels down to Markus' compound," she informed me blankly. I think she was cloaking her distrust for me. She didn't want to upset Rick.

She escorted me to his room where he was sat

behind his desk when we entered. He got up and moved over to give me a hug. It took me by surprise, but I melted into it. I loved the familiar smell and it took me right back to when I was an infant. I remembered how he always made me feel safe and loved. I allowed myself to feel like that for a few seconds, revelled in it. I knew it wasn't going to last. He sighed. Readying himself to talk.

"Daniel regained consciousness."

I felt him observe me closely. I couldn't help slightly stiffening and my heartbeat rose significantly but I quickly answered, to disguise my signals to be coming from relief, rather than fear.

"Oh good. We can clear this whole mess up then, thank God."

He paused a few seconds before he answered.

"He can't remember a thing."

Again I was under close scrutiny. I wasn't surprised he had memory loss. He'd been knocked out twice in close succession. I was relieved but had to show disappointment. I'm not sure how well I succeeded.

"Ah. So what happens now? Do they know when he'll remember?"

"Not sure. It will have to wait. I think the wisest course of action for me is to have you closely guarded today, apologies for being cautious. I want to trust you, but I have to be sensible and until I can get to the bottom of this it's safest for everyone."

I sighed. But I understood. It would have been reckless to just leave me to my own devices.

"I get it, dad. You go to the meeting today and make sure you give your best speech yet. We will have time to sort this misunderstanding out afterwards."

"I hope so Lizzy," he nodded.

"I love you dad."

I meant it. Twisted and wrong as his ideas and actions were, he was my father, a part of me and who I was.

"I love you too," he whispered and kissed my head softly.

"Promise you will let Zaphire go afterwards? It was horrible seeing her in that state yesterday."

I couldn't help sounding pained.

"I'm sorry you had to see that. We will keep our end of the deal if they keep theirs. Don't worry."

I knew he would. He wasn't cloaking. Whether he would get the option to keep his word was a different matter. If not, Zaphire would be freed anyway if everything went to plan. It reminded me of the importance of getting that phone. Not only because it was the proof I didn't want them to find, but also it was the only realistic chance of contacting Zack.

"Bye, Lizzy."

He turned around once more before he left, his arm moved as if he was going to wave, but thought better of it. He'd given Irena instructions to be my minder. I had a job on my hands. It was 8:30am and I had to give Zack the location of Zaph, otherwise they would be searching for her blindly, with only a small chance of success. And if they were found out, Rick would know they had undermined the deal once again and Zaphire would be doomed to rot away somewhere we would never find her.

I had to wait for Rick to be on that plane, scheduled to leave at 10:00am, to execute my hastily put together plan. For now, I could only sit and wait, so decided to force myself to eat some breakfast.

*

It was 10:15am. I knew Zack would be shitting it by now, having received no further information from me. I had to get out of my room. I checked the door. Still locked. I could hear Irena was outside anyway. I checked the windows. The little one opened. Could I even get through that? And then what? My room was on the first floor. I could break my neck, falling out of that. My eighteenth birthday was coming up and I had no intention to die before then. I sat back onto my bed.

Could I trick Irena to come into my room? She had orders not to, but I had noticed before that she was no stranger to bending the rules slightly. It was worth a try. I had my tights ready in my hands and I positioned myself right behind the door.

"Irena?"

No answer.

"Irena? I know you're there," I tried again.

I heard her shuffle and felt her tense up.

"Come on, Irena. I'm bored. Aren't you?" I persisted.

Still no answer.

"Irena, come play a game or something. It'll be a long day otherwise," I kept at it.

"Please?" I now whined.

"Irena, please?" I felt her resolve dwindle.

"Just for a bit? What harm can it do? It'll break the monotony," I carried on.

I was winning. It wouldn't be long now.

I heard the key unlock the door. I got ready to

pounce. I only had one chance. The door opened and Irena cautiously entered. I pulled the door open and yanked her in. I took a swing at her legs, completely unbalancing her, turned her around and jumped on top, grappling for her arms to keep her under control. The element of surprise gave me an advantage, but she was passed that now and she fought back with all her might. I wound the tights round her hands as quickly and securely as I could and pushed her arms up. With my knee in her back, she had nowhere to go. I stuffed a pair of pants in her mouth to stop her from yelling out. She was absolutely fuming. Her rage was crippling me and I had to concentrate not to lose the upper hand. She may be bound and gagged but I didn't think it would last long if I left her to it. I needed more. I pulled her across the floor and stuck her in my clothes cupboard. I hauled my desk in front of it. She was kicking like crazy. I turned my TV on loud to try and cover up some of the noise. I didn't think I had long. I had to find that phone. Maybe not so much for hiding the evidence, that horse had bolted as soon as I overpowered Irena, but for giving Zack the location of Zaphire.

I opened the door and peeked into the corridor.

Nothing. I crept out and hurried along, trying to remember where the big hall was. I had to cross the main entrance area. I pulled my hoody over my head and tried to walk confidently along. There were a few people there but no one paid me any attention. I spotted the doors to the room where the convention was held yesterday. *Shit.* Angelique stood right by the entrance. I retreated. I didn't want her to sense me. I hurried into the toilets and waited five minutes or so. I tried again, carefully moving towards the hall, my senses on high alert. I didn't detect her, so I carried on. I managed to slip into the hall and closed the door behind me. A few of the staff were still cleaning the place. I hoped to God that no one had found the phone and handed it in. I went to the area where Ned and Daniel had their argument. Nothing obvious stood out as to where the phone could have been. My senses stood on edge. Someone was approaching. I turned in the opposite direction to the source and started to walk off.

"Hey, Miss. Are you looking for this?" a soft voice called.

I turned around. One of the cleaning girls strode purposefully towards me with a stretched out arm. In her hand was the mobile. Rick didn't know it was a phone Daniel had been talking about, so I guess no one had thought to ask the staff to look out for it.

"I found it just a few minutes ago, it had slipped under the plant pots. You're lucky a little bit poked out, otherwise I would never have found it," she said, very pleased with herself.

"That's fantastic. Thank you so much," I said, trying to sound friendly but without looking directly into her eyes. My heart throbbed so loudly, I was sure even a non-Sensorian could hear it. I grabbed the phone out of her hand. Nodded once more and made my way out of the room as quickly as I could without breaking out into a run. I sped back to the toilets. They seemed to be the safest place to hang out.

I rang Zack, willing him to pick up. I didn't have to worry, he was on it after the first ring.

"Yes?"

His voice sounded stressed, eager for information.

"Got to be quick. Don't know how long I have. She's in the basement of Rick's Head quarters. Room 101. Armed guards." I managed to say but got distracted. I heard hurried footsteps, urgent voices approached fast. I broke off contact and listened carefully. It was Irena. *Shit!* That was bloody quick. I looked around me. There was nowhere to go or hide and she was following my scent. I chucked the phone in the toilet, covered it with paper and hoped for the best as I pressed the flush. I hopped to the other cubicle after pressing the flush again and stuffing more paper in. Pulled down my trousers and sat down, just in time before Irena and guards burst in.

"The bitch is in the cubicle on the right," Irena shouted. She was furious. My door burst open and the guards hauled me up and handcuffed me. My trousers still down my ankles, they stood me in front of Irena.

"Make her decent," she snarled at one of the guards, who roughly tried to hoist up my pants and jeans. The tight trousers presented a problem and the guard cursed, not being able to get a grip on it. I couldn't help but let out a snort of laughter at the ridiculousness of the situation. It earned me a slap from the frustrated guard. He finally succeeded. Even Irena rolled her eyes.

"What have you done?" she growled exasperated.

I took a breath to answer. Could I claim a momentary lapse of sanity? But she held her hand up.

"Don't say a thing. Take her to the basement. I'll search the area. Don't alert Rick yet. He needs to

317

concentrate on his event."

I wished heaven and earth for that phone to have flushed. At least it would buy us some time. I knew they wanted to make doubly sure what they were accusing me off, before informing Rick. No one wanted to be responsible for fake news.

I prepared myself for the brutal interrogation I was going to face. I had to stay strong mentally to be able to create enough confusion about what my intentions were and what I'd been up to. At least, until they were absolutely sure I'd done something wrong, they wouldn't hurt me too much. I hoped....

CHAPTER 50
Zack

This was it. The *message* we had been waiting for so desperately, confirming where Zaphire was being held. I was relieved to have received the call, but it sounded like Eliza was in trouble.

"Sir," I addressed Michael. "I'm worried Eliza's cover has been blown. Do we need to get her out of there too?"

"We've discussed that scenario with Markus, and we decided the mission needs to focus on getting Zaphire out. It is too complicated for diversions. If it turns out that Eliza needs our help, we do have the option to use Jessica as a bargaining tool, so we can deal with that after the mission."

It felt wrong leaving Eliza there if she was in trouble. Michael picked up on my misgivings.

"That's an order. Is that understood, Zack?" he asked sternly.

"Yes, Sir." I submitted. I couldn't really see a way to liberate both either. *Fuck*. We didn't even know where Eli was.

The timing of our move was a difficult one. We had

to act quickly in case they found out information was leaked to us about her whereabouts, as they might move her. We also had to be sure Rick was in our compound. However, we were still on our way and hadn't even met up with the whole team to double check our strategy.

There were ten of us, six men and two women going into the building and two staying behind in the van. Tristan was our driver and Archie would stay with him to deal with the communications. Vivian had stayed behind with Laura and Markus to ensure the capture of Rick. Frank was the overall leader with Michael and Rob as deputies. Brody and I were the youngest, but both of us did have a lot of experience. Our normal missions were never this complicated though, and we normally have the upper hand. That certainly wasn't the case in this mission. Going up against rival Sensorians was not something that happened often.

We knew very little about the building. We were practically going in blind. Archie, our computer expert had already looked into plans of the building, but they were hard to find. He had cobbled together a sketchy map of it with bits of info he'd found on the internet and that's all we had to go on.

They had guns, so we needed to weapon up. Brody and I were given special permission to carry for this mission, but neither of us were confident users as we didn't have a licence yet. Frank told us it was only for our own protection in an emergency. We should be covered by them. I fucking hoped so. I could hardly remember how to use the fucking thing. There was no shoot to kill policy, but I wasn't sure if I were even fucking able to shoot to maim. It would be complete pot luck on where I would hit anyone.

Our main ace was Rob, who had to be our eyes, using the people in the building by Vision Hacking them remotely. It would at least give us a much better chance to avoid being seen by people and dealing with those that may have caught a glimpse. A dose of luck would help too. I wasn't happy with the low odds of this mission succeeding. We were so underprepared. Not how we liked to conduct our business.

It was 11:30am. We still had no confirmation on Rick's whereabouts. The tension and adrenaline in the air was stifling, not to mention the restrictive bullet proof vests making us overheat and grouchy. But we had to stay put. There were too many Sensorians around to risk our scents being picked up by one. We had sprayed ourselves repeatedly with disguising spray, but there were ten of us so it was hard to cover it all up. We couldn't shield and cloak the whole time to the max as that would exhaust us before we even started our rescue mission, so we just had to endure it.

12:30pm. Finally, Rick had been sighted near our compound. It wouldn't be long now till we got the green light. Twenty-five minutes later our mission went live.

After having applied a fresh batch of spray, we hopped out of the van in twos and threes, not to look too conspicuous. Archie had fitted all of us with earphones and mics so we could communicate at all times. When we got to Rick's headquarters Phaedra and Saleem went to the front door to create a distraction whilst the rest of us went round to the back of the building. There should be a window we could easily enter through. We got the all clear from Archie who had managed to interfere with the signal of their security system, which would hopefully give us at least a few minutes unseen access, until they manage to bypass Archie's interference.

We heard Phaedra and Saleem creating some consternation at the front door, we didn't need our earphones for that. It sounded like a lover's brawl played out in front of the people who'd opened the door for them, with Phaedra hysterically screeching for help. We could hear them trying to calm things down. I picked up the scents of several people including at least one Sensorian. Good. That kept a few out of the way. Hopefully a couple of the guards would go and suss out what was going on. We had to get a fucking move on.

Rob scouted the area through the eyes of several unsuspecting Dullards. The coast was clear. Frank broke the glass of the window. He did it so expertly and quietly, I hardly noticed it. That was a skill I wanted to learn! The six of us crawled through the opening and it looked like it had brought us right where we needed to be. If the map was correct, we had to get out of this room, turn left, go to the end of the corridor where there should be a door leading to the basement. Adrenaline pumped through our bodies, I could feel and smell it. The spray wasn't strong enough to hide it. Fuck it.

Speed was of the essence. We had to act before

our scent was picked up. Rob was up front and opened the door. Next minute he hauled a man inside. Michael jumped on him and injected him with Thiopental. It knocked him out after about ten seconds and he was shoved aside. He should stay out for at least ten minutes. Rob said the guy was on his own as he hadn't seen anyone else through his eyes. We filed through the door after the all clear was given, but Frank and Sonia stayed behind to keep our way out guarded. It was up to Michael, me, Brody and Rob to find and liberate Zaphire. We ran as silently as we could to the door at the back of the corridor. We got there no problem. I hoped the security system was still down, because the place was fucking covered with cameras. The steep stairs led us to the basement which opened out into a corridor lined with doors. I briefly picked up Eliza's delicious scent, though it was laced with fear and despair. I felt she was near and in need of help, but we had our orders to get Zaphire out, first and foremost. We couldn't risk the whole operation. So, even though it made me feel sick leaving her here, I pushed it to the back of my mind. I had to concentrate on the task in hand.

Michael stopped dead and backed up.

"Guards," he whispered.

There was nowhere to hide. We couldn't approach them without being seen. *Fuck*.

Rob VH-ed the guards.

"It's just the two of them," he confirmed

"We need to lure them out. Both won't come but if we can get one of them to come over, we can use him as a shield," Michael decided.

"Cameras are still out," we heard in our earpiece.

We didn't need to do anything to lure the guard, because he was on his way already. A Sensorian; his scent unknown to us. We looked at each other, slightly panicked. He would sure pick up our scents soon and alert the other guard. Michael gave Brody and me the signal. We were the fastest and strongest. We didn't have a choice but to go for it. We stormed through the door. Raced towards the guard who immediately reached for his gun. It took us only seconds to overpower him, but the other guard was already on his way. He fired his gun in the air as a warning. But we were hiding behind our captive. We hoped that was enough to stop him from firing directly at us. Rob and Michael joined us. All careful to be in line with each other.

"Drop your gun!" Michael shouted at the other

guard. He was still pointing it at us but with his other hand he was trying to reach his radio. Frank shot his hand.

The guard screamed out in pain, dropped his weapon and fell to his knees. The noise and the guard's outburst hurt every fibre in my body. I had to concentrate on shielding or I would collapse with him. By the look on everyone's grim faces, we were all suffering the same. We hurried to room 101, kicked the door open, guns at the ready. The guard in the room was prepared. He shot instantly. Michael got hit, but the bullet luckily only skimmed his arm. Rob shot back, making the guard have to take cover. Brody and I ran in to get Zaphire. She was sat on the floor, bound, blindfolded and gagged. I hauled her over my shoulder and ran. Rob behind me, leaving Brody and Michael to deal with the guard.

"Cameras are live," Archie's calm voice informed us, totally at odds with the situation we were in. *Fuck!* This was bad.

We ran up the basement stairs. I sensed people running towards our area. They were minutes away. Michael and Brody caught up with us. Shots were being fired. I heard Michael cry out in pain again, but he was still moving. We burst out into the corridor and all four weapon carriers were shooting to create cover. Frank and Sonia tried to keep the corridor free for us to run. Brody got his weapon out too and was randomly shooting away into the corridor. I just fucking ran, blindly. Hoping for the best. We got to the room. Brody squeezed himself through the window. I shoved Zaphire through whilst he pulled. We had no time to deal with her restraints. I felt her frustration boil. I heard Brody's gun fire again, Rob struggled through the opening and helped Brody fend off the guards outside. Rob screamed. He was shot in the leg as bullets were flying everywhere. We ran out through the back garden, jumped the fence as best as we could. Practically pulling Rob and throwing Zaphire over it. The van was waiting, sliding doors open. We all bundled in, but Michael and Sonia weren't there. I couldn't see them anywhere. We didn't have time to go back.

"Go! Drive!" Frank shouted at our driver Tristan, and we sped off.

CHAPTER 51
Eliza

Bloody hell. Mayhem. Gun shots, shouting, an onslaught of smells, vibes and sounds. I could sense Irena wanted to go out there and help but was torn between that and making sure I didn't escape. She chose me. I felt and smelled Zack's presence in every fibre of my body. So near and yet so far. I picked out his running gait, so familiar to me after the hours and hours of fitness training we had done together. I desperately wanted them to knock down my door too, room 103, as they'd done to Zaphire's. I wanted to scream for help, but Irena had gagged me before I'd even thought about uttering a sound.

They were retreating now. I think they had Zaphire, I could smell her too. It was over so quickly, it almost felt like it hadn't happened. But the cries of pain and frustration were left hanging in the air. It certainly had happened. Irena was dying to go out there. She finally managed to get someone to mind me and she rushed out, but I felt her frustration finding the corridor and room empty. Shots were still being fired, a little further away. Possibly outside. In the far distance I heard police sirens. How were they going to explain this away?

I doubted I was going to find out. The sour faced guard refused to engage with me. All I could do was wait. I felt utterly useless.

Within the hour Irena was back. The hair in my neck stood on end with what I heard and smelled next. The scent of Michael penetrated my nostrils. It wasn't a good smell. He was in pain and scared. There was another vaguely familiar smell too, equally rank. They must have captured two Sensorians from our team. *Shit.* I heard them being locked away in the adjacent rooms. All of us separated. All this to capture Rick, and now they had different bargaining chips to get Rick out if Markus had even succeeded in detaining him. A feeling of hopelessness engulfed me. If after all this Rick still got to walk away from it all, we might have just as well waited for Rick to return Zaphy, without all the pain and risk of loss of life. It was a complete balls up. Also, there would be no way for me to talk myself out of this. Irena's grim face told me as much. I was done for.

"Rick will be heartbroken," she started. "He really thought you had joined him. You two would have made a great team. He loves you, you know."

She paused and circled around me. Stopped right

in front of me, face inches away from mine.

"How does it feel to have betrayed your own father, knowing it was all for nothing?" she spat out.

It felt frustrating. I felt like giving up. I couldn't speak as I was still gagged and to be honest, I didn't think Irena was in the slightest bit interested in what I had to say anyway. Irena enjoyed her little power play.

"We got Markus' message. Markus captured Rick moments after Zaphire was freed. I knew you had to be involved somehow and it has just been confirmed after beating the shit out of Sonia. I thought about sparing her, but I knew Michael would never speak. You gave them Zaphire's location and you have been in contact all along." Her disdain and hate for me were tangible. I think if it was up to her, I would be dead by now. "Lucky for you, Jean-Pierre is second in command and he's decided to offer Markus a deal. You and Michael are the lucky ones. Poor Sonia will be the messenger."

She actually smiled. I knew Irena was tough, but I hadn't seen this sadistic side of her. It made me feel cold to the core. She wasn't finished yet.

"After this is all over, you'll wish you'd never been born. You'll never fit in anywhere. You will never be completely trusted by anyone. You'll be all alone for the rest of your life. You have ruined your only chance of a successful life here, where you would have been respected and loved. I almost feel sorry for you," she sneered.

I decided to tune out from that moment. I simply blocked her out. I did not want to think about what she'd said, scared that I would agree with her. Instead I honed in on the sea. The calming, rolling waves. I was only vaguely aware of being tied up and blind folded. A sack was put over my head. I welcomed it.

CHAPTER 52
Zack

When we finally untied Zaphire, she cried with relief. Apart from a few bruises she was physically fine. Mentally she was a mess. But Zaphire was still in there. She'd get over it. I knew. I hugged her tightly and I never wanted to let go of her again. All I wanted to do is take her home and take care of her, but we were still in the middle of the mission. We'd informed Markus who immediately arrested Rick. He hadn't even started his speech yet. However, we knew we might not be in the strong position we imagined we would be in. Having to leave Michael and Sonia behind was a nightmare. We didn't know if they got away or what. They hadn't contacted us so that didn't bode too well. But it could be explained. They might not be in a position to contact us if they were hiding out somewhere.

Our hopes were dashed fairly soon though. When we got back to our compound an ashen faced Markus welcomed us back. His face momentarily lit up when he saw Zaphire and held her in his arms, but it was soon replaced by darkness again. He informed us Jean-Pierre had been in contact with the message they had captured Michael, Sonia and Eliza. *Fuck.* And I'd been right about Eliza needing help too. She'd been found out.

I glanced over at my sister, who looked exhausted. I wanted to take her to her room and put her in bed, make sure she was okay. But thankfully Laura took over, lovingly taking her in her arms. Just as well, because Markus had no intention of releasing me. We were all summoned to the meeting room.

Markus silently showed us the video that was sent. I understood Markus' dark mood instantly. We were all shocked to the core. We just witnessed one of our own being shot in cold blood. Sonia was dead.

We stood in silence. No one knew what to say. We all worked hard to cloak as our own feelings were already hard enough to deal with, without having to take on each others pain. Phaedra cracked in the end. Sonia had been her friend and work colleague for years. She let out her pain which hit us hard. Frank took her aside and escorted her outside the room to calm down. His shield must be as hard as steel.

"As you can see, the situation has escalated rapidly. Their demands are to be met immediately as I don't want any more casualties. We have got to cut our losses and start anew. We have to release Rick, but the mission has not been futile. We will hunt his followers down and break up the syndicate. We know who are involved. We will have seriously slowed down their progress which will give us time to attack again when we can. Don't give up. Don't feel it was all for nothing. We had to take the risk and it didn't pay off this time. We know what a ruthless man and organisation we're dealing with now, so no more mistakes. No more actions initiated off your own back."

With that he poignantly stared in my direction.

"We have to work together on this. But at least we have given ourselves some time to re-group. We may not succeed in breaking up his organisation for good, but we have made a huge dent in it, and will continue to do so."

He paused to let it all sink in.

"What's the arrangement?" Frank asked, who'd rejoined us after having dealt with Phaedra's emotional breakdown.

"They will release Michael and Eliza as soon as we have returned Rick and Jessica to their head quarters," Markus replied matter of factly. My heart rate spiked.

"You can't just hand over that fucking bitch too," I

interjected, letting my vengeful feelings rule my mouth.

"We will do exactly what they demand, Zack. Mind your language," Markus bit back. "We need to keep calm now and wait for further instructions," he warned and dismissed us to reconvene when needed.

I slipped away to see how Phaedra was coping. I found her in our Room of Tranquillity. I worked with her before, when I was still training. She was about five years my senior and I hadn't paid much attention to her before. But she stirred something in me. She intrigued me. She was sitting on one of the benches, and as I approached she moved up a bit to make some space for me. I sat down next to her silently for a moment. She didn't need to speak for me to know what she felt. I put my arm around her and she leant into my embrace, resting her head on my shoulder. We must have sat there for about half an hour, before my phone pinged. It was Zaphire. She needed me.

"I'll come and find you later Phaedra. Look after yourself, okay?" I whispered gently in her ear. She looked up and nodded.

"Thanks for being there for me Zack. It means a lot to me," she said quietly with so much vulnerability it made my heart melt a little.

"Hey, Zaph. You look somewhat better," I tried cheering my forlorn looking sister up a bit.

"Yeah, who are you kidding?" she replied sarcastically. Good. That meant she was getting on top of things. "Laura wouldn't tell me anything. Fill me in brother. What's happening," she demanded.

I thought for a second, but no one had given me any orders not to say anything so I gave her the full update. She was shocked with Sonia's fate but her fury spiked when I mentioned Eliza's name. I hadn't quite expected the level of hatred Zaph was carrying for her.

"Why do we even want her back here? She cannot be trusted!" she hissed venomously.

"She has always been on our side, Zaphire. We just couldn't let anyone know," I tried to calm her down.

"What do you mean 'we', Zack? Did you know all along?" she asked scathingly. "You need to tell me everything. It doesn't make sense!"

She sounded furious and lost at the same time. So, I told her everything, from the moment Eliza told me she'd decided to go undercover to try and infiltrate her father's organisation and win his trust. How she decided no one was to know, including Zaphire, to keep all reactions natural and not raise any suspicions.

"Why didn't she trust me?" Zaphire couldn't help letting out a sob, born out of frustration, anger and sadness.

"It wasn't about trust Zaphy. It was about making the mission work. Giving it the best chance to succeed. If it helps, not to include you in the plan was the hardest decision she ever had to make. She did it partly to protect you, though she would never admit to that. However, it was essential that no one knew," I tried to explain.

"Apart from you," she said bitterly.

"Apart from me," I whispered.

CHAPTER 53
Eliza

I couldn't breathe. Not just because of the gag, but my body had gone into some kind of spasm. They forced us to watch Sonia's execution. I closed my eyes, but it didn't help. Michael and I both felt Sonia's anguish and desperation. I wanted to scream. They didn't need to do this to get what they needed. Right up to the moment they pulled the trigger I believed they wouldn't go through with it. That it was just an elaborate show to scare us. How wrong was I. I opened my eyes just at the wrong time. Blood sprayed from Sonia's head. Irena was stony faced and Jean-Pierre had no expression at all. The guards seem to enjoy their role. It was sickening.

Finally, I was able to get some air. It must have been an automatic response of my body, forcing oxygen into my system. I wished it hadn't. I wished I'd passed out. Michael and I were taken back to our separate cells again. I sat down, numb. No idea what was going to happen next.

Bile rose to my mouth, the gag making it impossible to be sick. One of the guards released it.

Swore and threw me a cloth. I couldn't do much with it as my hands were still bound. It was gross.

Michael didn't seem to be faring much better. I could feel his pain through the wall. He was wounded and I doubted anyone had checked it out, or cleaned it up. It would get infected soon and then they wouldn't have to shoot him.

I had no idea how long I was in that cell. Time seemed to have no meaning. It could only have been hours, but it felt like days. Every time I closed my eyes, the haunting picture of Sonia's face just before the bullet hit appeared. Then the blood. The brain. I tried to shake my head to rid myself of it, but it was stuck there. Her desperate eyes staring me in the face. I still couldn't quite believe it actually happened and I suddenly panicked when I thought about Ned. What if he met the same fate! No. They wouldn't have gone ahead with the mission if Ned had been shot in cold blood. I needed to stay calm. No point winding myself up even further. I was driving myself mad. The room smelled disgusting. I felt disgusting. When was this ordeal going to end? If it was going to be much longer I wasn't even sure if I'd care anymore.

Hurried footsteps approached. I could make out at least ten people. Something serious was about to happen. I wasn't sure if I could take anymore, but obviously I had no choice. Irena opened the door and visibly recoiled, unable to cloak and clearly surprised by the state me and my room were in. She recovered quickly and ordered the guards to escort me out. I heard Michael being hauled out of his cell, unable to walk for himself. I was gagged again. We were marched out of the basement. Michael was dragged up the stairs, then pushed along. He collapsed. There was a lot of swearing at him, but I knew if Michael could walk, he would. He was in a bad way. I wanted to tell them. Shout at them. But all I could do was mumble and squeak. That damned gag.

I sensed Jean-Pierre and Angelique were near. I was knocked on the back of my legs, which made me buckle and kneel. A heap of human mess was thrown next to me. Michael. Were they going to shoot us? Right here? Was this how my life would end? Not even reaching adulthood? I thought about mum. The thought of her grief broke me and I collapsed into a heap too.

"Look at you. All pathetic on the floor. How different

could this have been if only you had chosen our side. What a waste."

Angelique spoke with disdain, but I detected a smidgen of pity or regret. Jean-Pierre took charge, but to what end I still wasn't sure. I was close to not giving a shit. He untied me.

"Help him up. Listen to our instructions. We have a gun trained on the both of you. If you try anything, we will shoot to kill," he warned us. With Sonia's fate still fresh in my memory I was absolutely sure they would.

CHAPTER 54
Zack

The call had come. We were to deliver Rick and Jessica to their Headquarters. For some perverse fucking reason Markus had put me in charge of Jessica. Once again pushing me to face up to my emotions and deal with things professionally. Even in this situation, he was still training me.

"Oh, this must be killing you Zack," she goaded. She just couldn't help herself. Her fucking smug face almost sent me over the edge, but I kept my cool. I did manage to inflict a little pain tightening her restraints just that bit too much. Probably not what Markus wanted, but it made feel better.

"Shut the fuck up. You are not to talk," I growled at her.

"Or what Zack?" she sneered dismissively, still as arrogant as ever. I gave into my urges and backhanded her in the face.

"Anything else, Miss?"

My turn to sneer, but earning me a warning glare from Markus. I didn't care at that moment. He wasn't one to talk anyway.

Blood trickled slowly from her nose. She looked

pathetic and I decided to try and rise above her taunts, feeling less smug about giving into my anger.

Rick looked groggy. He must have been administered some kind of sedative. Both captives were buckled in and then injected with Thiopental. That should make for a quiet flight. It would give me time to gain control over my emotions again too.

We arrived bang on time. Our van parked at the end of their drive.

The sun beamed down on us. It was like a scene from a film. Jean-Pierre and a woman stood at the other end of the drive. Six guards with guns stood along side the two interim leaders and behind I could just make out the sorry looking figures of Eliza and Michael.

My heart dropped and skipped a beat at the same time. She looked a mess, but I still couldn't help my instant desires surfacing. I needed her. In my arms. Safe. *Fucking Focus.*

Frank, Saleem and Tristan drew their weapons when we poured out of the van. I didn't trust myself so I left mine in its holster. I had to make sure Jessica was behaving herself anyway, so I had my hands full when I roughly manhandled her to where I wanted her to stand. Rob guided Rick out, who had fully come out of his state of sedation now. Rob took no chances and had his gun pointed at Rick's head. Rick must have realised at that moment his daughter had betrayed him. Up until then he hadn't known for sure, but seeing her there made it all too clear. His pain was immeasurable. It dug deep into everyone's core. It fucking hurt like hell, even with trying to shield it. I felt Eliza's reaction too. It crushed her.

"Walk up ten meters and then turn back, leaving Jessica and Rick. Michael and Eliza will do the same." Jean-Pierre shouted.

We obeyed, making sure Michael and Eliza walked up too. They did, if you could call it walking. A guard either side. Michael leant heavily on Eliza, who nearly buckled under his weight. Rick looked old, broken, his eyes cast down, clearly avoiding Eliza's desperate efforts to catch his eye. Hers were full of apology and hurt.

We stood facing each other. Three meters apart. We had to turn around and move back to our original position. Michael and Eliza's guards did the same. The tension was excruciating.

"Now, the four of you, walk past each other. No

contact, eyes down. A step a second. I will be counting. One...two... three...." Jean-Pierre barked.

They all moved at the pace Jean-Pierre indicated whilst he kept counting. It took nineteen steps to cover the distance.

"Now, go! I'll give you five minutes before we open fire." Jean Pierre shouted, uncompromisingly.

We quickly bundled them in the car and sped off.

Fucking hell. They stank. Vomit, puss, sweat, urine, excrement, you name it. It was all there, hanging pungent in the air. But the relief was palpable too. We wrapped them in blankets as both were shivering, despite the warmth outside. Michael was in a bad way. We rushed him to the private hospital we used for the rare occasions one of us got hurt on a mission. They didn't ask questions. They took the money and treated whoever needed treatment.

Ned had been transferred to the same hospital. He was still in a coma. He had come out of it, but they induced it again to give his body and brain more time to recover. Whilst they looked over Eliza I nipped over to see him. Ned's mum was sat by his bedside. I put a hand on her shoulder and she grabbed it with both hands. He was a sorry sight. Every part of his body that was visible was covered in bruises and cuts. *Fuck.* They really had done him over badly. Anger bubbled up inside me, and before it spilled over, I hurried out of the room.

CHAPTER 55
Zaphire

Despite Zack's heartfelt explanation of Eliza's actions I couldn't forgive her. I blamed everything on her. Ned's suffering, Sonia's death, Rick's release, Zack's involvement, it all led back to her decision to go to her father, without the proper back up. However much she was right about gaining his trust and not raising any suspicions, she had made the wrong decision. But most of all, I hated that she hadn't trusted me to be involved. I just couldn't get over it.

I was so happy to see Sam when she arrived back at our compound. We fell into each other's arms, Sam's tears stained my shirt. She nodded full of understanding over my feelings regarding Eliza.

"I tell you, at one point I was ready to kill her if I had to," I told her, remembering my vengeful feelings towards her from the moment she captured me. "I still don't know how she deceived Rick. Maybe somewhere inside herself she agreed with him," I said a little spitefully.

"Remember she did help us find you and she did betray her father for us, even though we aren't her family. It must have been hard," Sam called me out. I sighed.

"My brain knows, Sam. I just can't help feeling this way at the moment."

They were back from the trade we were forced to make. Well, everyone apart from Michael. He needed to stay in hospital to make sure his body coped with fighting the infection. The doctors seemed confident though. The wounds weren't that bad, they just had suffered from lack of cleanliness.

I spotted Eliza. She wore an odd combination of clothes they probably had cobbled together and her hair was all bedraggled, but she was clean. Her face told a thousand stories and none of them particularly pleasant. The little seed of hate in the pit of my stomach started to grow again. I couldn't handle it. I couldn't handle her. She had betrayed and hurt me too much. I turned around and walked off. I caught Zack's face out of the corner of my eye and to say he wasn't happy with me would be an understatement. His eyebrows practically rose above his head with indignation. His eyes threw daggers. What did he expect anyway? That I was going to fall into her arms and forgive and forget instantly? Well. That just wasn't going to happen and the sooner he got used to that, the better. I did not want to have another argument with my brother about Eliza.

CHAPTER 56
Eliza

I was physically and emotionally exhausted. Zaphire's reaction hurt. I should have expected it but in my muddled state of mind I had created an alternate universe where Zaphire understood and had forgiven me. I imagined falling into her arms and carrying on as before. It didn't happen. Not surprisingly.

Zack took me to my room to get changed and make myself look decent. I'd had a shower in the hospital, but still felt dirty. Zack hadn't left my side since the moment we got to the van. He made me feel safe.

"What day is it?" I shouted from the bathroom, realising I had actually lost count on how many days had gone by.

"Tuesday," Zack answered dutifully but with a slight question mark hanging in the air.

"Happy birthday to me," I mumbled. I had turned eighteen today. This is not how I'd imagined my milestone birthday to be like. I wasn't one for a huge fuss, but this was the complete opposite. Zack knocked on the door whilst slowly opening it.

"Is it okay for me to come in?" he asked gently. I nodded. I was just doing my hair. He turned me to face him and kissed me softly on my forehead. I had to block my sometimes involuntary VH. I didn't want to see my pathetic self through his eyes

"Happy Birthday, Tiger." He'd heard me of course. "We'll get your mum over before the end of the day," he assured me, already on his phone to make it happen. "Are you nearly ready? Markus wants the team to assemble in the meeting room in ten minutes."

I nodded, but all I wanted to do was crawl on the sofa with a blanket and hot chocolate. Maybe later. Instead I had to muster all the energy that I had left in my body to face Markus. I wasn't sure if I could cope with a grilling.

"Don't worry. He said it wasn't going to be an official debrief. He just wanted to say a few words."

Zack always knew exactly what I felt. Sometimes a blessing. Sometimes a curse. Today it was just what I needed.

Markus stood tall, imposing in his black suit. The man always made me feel like a little girl. Even though I didn't always agree with his leadership style, I couldn't deny he was a true leader. Someone you wanted to be proud of you. I understood what Zack craved from him. Thanks to me, he wasn't going to get much of that in the near future. I practically forced him to go behind

Markus' back. I was in no doubt there would be consequences to be endured.

Everyone who had been involved in the mission was there, apart from Michael and Ned, and Sonia of course. The thought of her death made me feel instantly sick. Her eyes, the blood, the images all forced themselves back into my psyche again. I felt Zack's hand on the small of my back, steadying me. But also awakening naughty little sparks inside me. *Stop it.* How could I.

Grief was etched on everyone's faces. Most of us had never had to deal with a mission that had gone so badly wrong. It was a reality check for each and every one of us. Phaedra sidled up to Zack, looking for his support. Zaphire was hiding in the back of the room, behind Sam, busily avoiding eye contact with me. Brody was just behind us. Strong as ever. Even Frank looked gloomy. Laura stood next to Markus. Her face an enigma, but what shone through was her determination and resilience. She was remarkable. Markus wrung his hands before he spoke, Laura's hand subtly touched his back to show her support.

"I asked to see you all today, not to analyse our

mission, but to say thank you. We all need some time to digest the events of the past few days. All of us have gone through an ordeal and I want to make sure you know how much we appreciate the effort that took and the toll that it has taken. We have decided that out of respect for Sonia, we declare three days of mourning till her funeral on Thursday. I have put a different team on monitoring Rick for the moment and they are also tasked with locating and dealing with everyone on the list that Eliza gave us access to. But I don't want you to worry about any of this. It's all under control. I want you to take these three days and use them to grieve and recuperate. Give yourself a little break, you deserve it and moreover need it. I've scheduled the official debrief for Friday. Be ready for it."

He dismissed us all with a short nod. I noticed Laura giving his hand a little squeeze. We all mumbled a 'thank you Sir' before we left the room.

Markus' words felt like a veiled warning. We were given a delay of 'execution', but it was coming. And we should be prepared. For now though we could breathe a little easier and deal with our emotions first. Looking at everyone, it was needed.

"What do you reckon?" I asked Zack when we were

safely back into our room, referring to Markus' speech.

"I think you need to get some sleep. Your mum is on her way and arriving in a couple of hours. Then we should celebrate your birthday," Zack answered, totally ignoring my question.

"I don't know...," I hesitated. "It doesn't feel right, you know?" I questioned.

"We'll see," Zack said with a little smile playing around his lips. Hell, I had missed him.

*

I hated to admit it, but Zack was right. He'd arranged a nice dinner at a local authentic Italian restaurant with my mum, Sam and Brody and to my surprise Bella too. I couldn't believe it, and my joy must have been infectious as Zack's face was beaming. It had been a long time since I'd seen anything resembling happiness showing on his face. Zaphire wasn't there and it stung, but I made myself focus on the positive and it worked. For the time being.

I'm not sure what my mum knew about my 'adventures' over the last few days, but I suspected Markus had given her a very clean version of events, not to worry or involve her too much. She didn't look overly worried and was extremely happy to see me, so whatever story Markus had spun her had worked. Moreover, I was happy she lived in relative ignorance. It had started to become too easy to lie.

We had fun. Everyone did their best to put their grief and worries aside for the evening and we were all grateful for the opportunity to do so. I started to appreciate my gift again, fully taking in all the stimuli on offer. The food and smells were gorgeous and the feelings of joy, exhilarating. I'd almost forgotten what it felt like. We opened a champagne bottle and a couple more followed suit pretty fast.

"Are you even allowed some?" I teased Zack, as he had told me earlier that Markus grounded him and his sister and banned them from alcohol indefinitely.

"I've broken all the rules now, may as well break this one too," he joked shrugging his shoulders.

I couldn't help furtively staring at him all evening. He was so bloody sexy. I felt guilty but I couldn't help myself. My feelings for Zaphire were strong as ever, but my attraction to Zack hadn't gone away. And he was here and hard to ignore.

At the end of the evening I was definitely tipsy. We all said our goodbyes. Mum was staying in a spare room and Bella came to my room. It was like old times and I let myself believe for a moment that all was good.

CHAPTER 57
Zack

She was fucking killing me. With her beautiful eyes staring at me all night, secretly of course, as if that was even possible. The girl needed to fucking back off. I didn't need her to give me bloody encouragement or hope, because I would not be able to stop myself. And I would ruin everything. It was never going to work. She didn't love me. She loved Zaphire. I was just a fucking object of lust to her and I shouldn't forget that. It was hopeless. I should focus my attentions to Phaedra. In fact, I decided to go and see her. Probably wasn't the best idea as I had been drinking, but fuck it. I needed to move on.

Phaedra lived in one of the apartments on the second floor. Highly sought after by the young singletons in our community. I hopped rooms, wherever I was needed really, but I also still had my room in Markus and Laura's flat, but I aspired to live in one of these sexy pads.

I knocked on her door, my bit of Dutch courage spurring me on. I wasn't quite sure what she would make of my late night visit. She opened the door, looking rather dishevelled. She wasn't quick enough to hide her embarrassment as her cheeks went bright red. Her blond sleek hair was in stark contrast with Eli's messy dark bob. *Fuck. Stop comparing.*

"Hey, it's you?" she said a little bemused.

"Yeah. Just wondering how you were holding up?"

"Not great, but thanks. Do you... err...wanna come in for a bit?" she asked hesitantly.

I accepted, against my better judgement. Anyway, I wouldn't let anything happen I vowed. But she was nice and really easy to be around. And some might say she was stunning. Actually, we had a great time together, drinking some more wine, we chatted deep into the night and we both felt relaxed in each other's company. So, all good intentions aside, she was after comfort and who was I to deny her. Of course we ended up in bed together. But she was taking as much advantage of me as I was of her and fuck, it felt good.

The next morning I didn't feel too good though. A combination of two things. Too much wine after having been dry for ages and feeling a little bit of regret about my activities last night. However, waking up next to Phaedra was cozy. She had such a quietly confident manner about her which was so relaxing to be around.

She was good for me. She seemed to like my company too, and it felt nice. No extreme feelings playing havoc with my brain and senses. I began to like this feeling and I wanted to experience more of it.

"Want some breakfast?" I asked her gently. She was still sleepy, even though it was 11 o'clock. We had been rather active last night, and it wasn't just me who was to blame! She'd been insatiable.

"Yes please," she mumbled pleasantly surprised.

It was amazing to wake up with no obligations for today. Of course I wanted to check up with Eliza and Zaphire, but I knew they were being looked after by Alice and Laura. Bella was still around too, though she would be going home soon. We didn't like her to be here for too long, because we had to hide our gift around her. She was already suspicious about the story I'd made up to get her to sign the confidentiality papers. Some Sensorians were furious about my rather reckless spur of the moment action to invite her, but the look of complete surprise and happiness on Eli's face made it all worth it. I was already in so much trouble, it didn't really matter anyway. Alice could stay longer of course, no problem.

"Are you okay... about last night?" I asked her over

our plate of scrambled eggs, looking for signs to tell me otherwise. There were none. She just nodded. She was so damned uncomplicated. I wasn't used to that. Breakfast tasted good, despite my slightly dodgy stomach.

"Are you?" she countered. I couldn't help showing a glimmer of guilt, even though I had enjoyed myself. She raised her eyebrows slightly. "We don't have to repeat it," she tried helping me out. She didn't sound pissed off at all.

"No, I...erh...would want to. It's not that...," I stammered awkwardly. She smiled.

"Let's just see what happens. We're both in fragile states. No strings attached okay?" she offered. *Was this woman for fucking real?*

"Yeah. That sounds good."

I kissed her. She was a good kisser. She tasted fresh with a little hint of sweet. Very different from Eli who was more of a honeysuckle mixed with patchouli kinda girl. *Stop comparing!* I admonished myself again.

I briefly thought about lifting Phaedra up and throwing her on the bed for another round. It was tempting. My dick certainly wanted it. Instead I took a shower.

I left Phaedra to it to go and find Brody, but instead I bumped into Eliza. Instant electricity coursed through my body when I laid eyes on her. What the fuck was going on with me. Why couldn't I control my bloody feelings. I cloaked as quickly as I could, but she must have picked up some vibes as she looked coyly away. I walked past quickly, ignoring her and even though I heard her call my name I kept walking. I would have to deal with it later. But not now. I felt her confusion burrowing its way into my heart.

I spent the rest of the day with Brody. We visited Ned, but he was still in his induced coma. Just seeing him, lying so helplessly and battered, fired up the guilt I felt for the state he was in again. Brody tried to distract me from myself torture and managed to draw me away from Ned's bedside.

"Do you want to hear some good news?" he asked upbeat.

I nodded, shrugging my shoulders.

"Markus has suspended fitness tests for those who are involved actively with a mission. It looks like your ploy worked with this one," he laughed. "And it looks like you got away with instigating it too," he added, punching me on the arm.

I smiled. A victory, even as little as that, did the soul some good.

We checked on Michael next, who was looking a lot better than yesterday. He would be out fairly soon. We also paid our respect to Sonia's parents, who were grief stricken, but busily arranging her funeral with Frank's help. I managed to avoid women for the rest of the day, apart from a brief visit to Zaphire, who was miserable as fuck, so I left her to wallow. But by the evening I decided to bite the bullet and see Eli. She would be wondering what the hell was up with me. To be honest I hadn't even fucking worked it out myself.

CHAPTER 58
Eliza

A knock on my door sent my heart beating a little faster. *Was it Zaphire?* But, it was Zack who poked his head in. He pissed me off earlier and he knew it, judging by his sheepish expression. My mum made her excuses and left the two of us to talk. Despite not being a Sensorian, she had good intuition.

He sat himself down. Typical Zack; not waiting for an invite. The sort of thing I hated and loved about him at the same time.

"Thank you for arranging the dinner yesterday. That was really sweet," I said, deciding to push my annoyance about earlier to the back of my mind.

"I'm glad you enjoyed it. I think everybody did."

I kept quiet because I knew there was more to come.

"I actually came over to apologize for ignoring you earlier. I don't know what came over me."

He paused to gauge my reaction.

"That's a first. An actual apology."

I couldn't help myself. I had to make him squirm a little. I didn't get the chance very often.

"Yeah okay. I deserve that. But we do have to talk,"

he started but then waited again. He didn't really want to talk at all.

"What about?" I asked innocently, but I knew exactly what this was about. I just didn't want to make it easy for him. I don't know why, but I sort of enjoyed seeing him struggle with his feelings a bit. I was being a bitch. He sighed.

"I stayed the night at Phaedra's last night," he blurted out.

Ouch. I didn't see that one coming. He noticed I was perplexed. I wasn't cloaking at all. He carried on.

"It's all a bit arse about face, Eliza. I'm struggling with my feelings for you. Phaedra and me...well, it's sort of easy and it made me feel good."

"I bet it did," I snorted a little unfairly. "Does she know you're using her?" *God where was this coming from?*

Zack looked a little put out.

"No, it's not fucking like that. I actually really like her and I have to move on. You clearly are still in love with Zaphire. That's not going to change any time soon and I don't want to be your fucking in between bit until you clear your beef with Zaphy!" he answered vehemently.

I felt a little ashamed as he was trying to open up to me and all I could do was slam him down. The good thing about being a Sensorian was that I didn't need to tell him this. He already knew how I felt. Normally he would make me spell it out, to make sure he was correct, but he left it today. Instead, he moved closer to me and gave me a hug.

"I'm sorry Zack," I sighed, melting into his warm strong body. "I don't even know what I feel anymore. It's not fair on you, I know, but I think I love you as well as Zaphire and I don't know what to do. I trust you and feel completely myself when I'm with you," I confessed.

"I can't be second best, Eli. We can't be with each other. So we need to agree to ignore each other's urges and desires, because they will keep popping up. We just have to accept that. Can you do that?" he pleaded.

"I will try," I sighed giving in, and hoped to God I could actually do it. I wished I could be with them both, but it looked more like I wasn't going to have either of them.

"Okay. Let's move on. How do you feel about the situation with your father?" he started, all matter of factly. *How did he do that?*

"I don't really want to talk about that Zack. It's too painful," I admitted.

He observed me for a while, not saying anything. He bit his lips and slightly sucked his cheeks in, like he so often did when he wasn't happy with something I said or did. He folded his arms. It looked like he wasn't going to let me defer talking about it. But then he sighed.

"Okay. Leave it for tonight. It's too fucking much. I'll come back tomorrow. We have to talk about it before the debrief. You need a couple of days to talk and think it over before we get grilled over this. It's not going to be easy," he said gruffly and abruptly left, leaving the door wide open.

It left me feeling drained. I was incredibly relieved to have mum here. I'm not sure I would have coped without her. But Zack was right. I had to address my feelings over my broken relationship with my father. I had stuffed it so deep inside that I could almost pretend it hadn't happened. I had to face up to it before the debrief in two days time.

CHAPTER 59
Zack

I was in a mood yesterday evening, having left Eli in a hurry for fear of saying or doing something I might regret. I wanted to help her prepare, but she clearly wasn't ready for it. I went to see Phaedra and she had managed to tease me out of my dark place ending up with me staying over yet another night.

This morning, Eliza and I had our talk. It was hard for her, but she had been totally honest and open with me. She struggled to reconcile the feeling of wanting her dad to be proud of her and having to betray him because she doesn't condone his actions. Her head knew she had made the right decision, but her heart ached for a different outcome. She had been tempted with the respect and adulation she was promised working alongside her father, but she knew she wouldn't be able to live like that. She did not agree with Rick's world vision and his methods to achieve them. That, she was a hundred percent sure of and I knew she was telling the truth. I trusted her implicitly. I urged her to explain it exactly like that at the debrief.

Our three days of respite were coming to an end.

The funeral had been a heartbreaking affair and not something I ever wanted to experience again. Phaedra managed to stay strong for Sonia's parents' and sister's sake, but I could tell she hurt like hell. I tried to be there for her. I think she appreciated it. She asked me to come over later that night again and I said yes. I was glad I did. I knew the next day was going to be fucking hard for me and I was in no doubt we would have to suffer the consequences for our actions. Phaedra and I made the most of it. Sex was a great distraction.

We both lay on our backs afterwards. Each sunk into our own thoughts. Phaedra broke the silence first.

"You really are in love with her, aren't you?"

I looked at her, wondering where that had come from. I kept silent. I didn't have to say anything.

"Don't worry. I don't mind. I'm in love with Tristan and have been for years. He sees me as just a friend and pines after your sister too."

"Fuck me. Damned Zaphire," I sighed despondently, feeling Phaedra's pain. "We're both fucking doomed," I concluded.

"I cried myself to sleep for months on end when I realised," she sighed. "Have you cried over her?" she asked, genuinely interested. No goading.

"I haven't properly cried since I was thirteen."

It was a painful memory. Phaedra wouldn't let it go though. She gently stroked my hand that rested on her stomach, whilst probing a little deeper.

"Why? What happened?"

"Markus taught me crying is never a solution. It made me fail a task in the Dark Room. I lost focus and it had dire consequences. Or at least I thought it had. It was the worst feeling I had ever felt and I vowed never to let that happen again," I said bitterly.

"Not everything has to be a solution. A good cry can make you feel better," Phaedra tried.

I didn't want to talk about it anymore. I turned towards her and caressed her face.

"Shall I make you forget about Tristan and Zaphire for a few moments?" I whispered in her ear. She giggled as she pulled me on top of her. "I guess that's a yes," I mumbled, silencing her giggles with my mouth.

*

"Are you ready for this?" Eliza asked me the next morning just before entering the meeting room. She gave me a funny look, just for a millisecond, but I spotted it. She could probably smell Phaedra on me.

"No idea," I sighed. It was going to be fucking hard.

The whole team was there, even Michael. Phaedra caught my eye and winked. She said she would back me whatever, but she didn't know the whole story. I couldn't be totally sure she would respect me the same after this.

As per usual, Markus started the meeting off. We didn't expect what he did next though.

"Frank is going to lead this debrief. I'm too emotionally involved and can't guarantee I won't lose my temper. I don't want a repeat of last time."

Everyone looked at the still present bruise on my face and nose. I wanted to fucking hide. I hadn't told Eliza nor Zaphire, and I could literally feel their eyes burn into me. Markus was still bloody seething. This did not look promising, but as always, Markus proved he was a good leader, recognising he might not act rationally and therefore he had deferred to Frank.

"Thank you Markus. I shall proceed then. We need to look at the mission to see what we can learn from it. To start though I'd like to stress again that it was not a complete failure and I'd like to congratulate everyone on their efforts. We're currently decimating Rick's followers and have sent out a strong message throughout the Sensorian communities across the world not to consider joining forces with him. We have reiterated the dangers of being exposed, which could lead to our gifts being abused, and putting us all in danger. The need for secrecy about our existence is paramount to our well-being and even our survival. Our number one rule is as important as ever. Sooner or later we'll deal with Rick as appropriate to our laws, and everyone involved with him will meet the same fate."

Frank paused a moment to let this sink in.

I thought about Lois. This was going to be controversial and bound to create unrest. She had always been well liked and respected, especially by the younger generation. I knew when the time came to act on this I would have to bring this up and probably risk another disagreement with the leadership. I was not a fervent supporter of the death sentence, but the punishment was entrenched in our community and accepted as necessary. By most, but not all.

My focus was drawn back to Frank, who had raised his voice slightly, having noticed my momentary inattention.

"The mission started however, in an unusual, and

dare I say it, illegitimate manner. For those who are not familiar with the events; Eliza and Zack decided to do this on their own, without permission or guidance from the leadership. Zaphire went to investigate, again without the leadership's knowledge and they managed to drag Sam and Brody in as accomplices. This cannot ever happen again. I know all of you will try and defend your decisions, but the leadership has decided that if this ever was to occur again, the people responsible will be stripped of all their responsibilities and will never work on any mission again. And on top of that they would get a hefty prison sentence. We have to nip this in the bud. I hope you all agree a community like ours cannot be undermined like this."

Frank stared at all of us one by one for what seemed like hours. Emotions were running high in the room. I tried to block them all out. I didn't want to get rattled. I knew we would get the opportunity to respond and I had to keep my fucking act together for that moment.

"I want to let you know that each and every one of you are going to have weekly counselling sessions to help you through any trauma sustained. And it'll be obligatory," he paused for a moment. "Stop rolling your eyes Zack and Sam," Frank admonished us wearily. Nothing escaped the man's attention. "But before we deal with the offenders, I want to focus on finding out what we could do differently practically, if we find ourselves in a similar situation again. All go in groups of three and discuss," Frank ordered.

Phaedra sidled to my side and joined Archie and me. I spotted Zaphire move to Sam and Saleem, as far away from Eliza as possible, who ended up with Brody and Rob. We worked for about an hour and a half and at the end we actually had come up with some sensible conclusions. The other groups had some different views and an interesting discussion evolved from it. This felt good. It was constructive and we learned some valuable lessons. I kind of wished this session wouldn't finish as I wasn't looking forward to the next phase. It was inevitable though and it was about to start. We were allowed to get some coffee and told to get back in ten minutes. Nerves reared their ugly little heads.

CHAPTER 60
Eliza

I was physically shaking now. I wasn't sure if I could get my point across to all these people. It had been hard the other day with Zack, but he managed to guide me through it. He wouldn't be able to do that today. I was on my own. Frank's explanation on how the leadership viewed our action was crystal clear, and looking from their viewpoint, wholly understandable. It was my turn to speak. I hope I didn't make it worse for me or anyone else. I was called to step forward and explain myself. I took a deep breath to regain control over my trembling body.

"When I first thought of my plan, it made perfect sense to me. I was getting frustrated with the lack of progress and I couldn't see how else to get my father to trust me enough to let me be in his inner circle. My father is quite the genius in working out what people want and extremely hard to fool, so I thought if he picked up any suspicious reaction or move from our Sensorian Community, he wouldn't take the risk."

I was on a roll and explained all my inner struggles like I had done to Zack. The atmosphere hadn't turned hostile which spurred me on to lay everything out in the open. It was a relief to be able to be so truthful about my actions and feelings, even though it made me sound like a liability at times, or even untrustworthy. I hoped my actions spoke louder than my thoughts and would convince everyone where my loyalties were. I belonged here and I wanted to be a fully operational member of this community. If they let me.

Frank nodded.

"Any questions anyone?" he asked.

There was a bit of a pause, like there always is in these situations, but I felt the room was full of questions. No one wanted to be the first one.

"How do we know we can trust you? If you were able to deceive your father, you must be an expert at cloaking and in redirecting questions so it looks like you're not lying. How do we know you're not doing that to us, right now?" Zaphire piped up.

Her fiery eyes pierced through me. It was the first time she had looked at me properly, but with so much venom I wished she hadn't looked at me at all. The tension mounted in the room.

"Don't let your personal issues interfere, sis. It's

clear she...," growled Zack in my defence until Frank interrupted decisively.

"Zack. Be quiet. Zaphire asked a valid question. Let Eliza answer it."

"Oh for fuck's sake...," Zack grumbled, barely able to look at Zaphire.

"What was that Zacharya?" Frank asked menacingly, eyebrows raised.

"Nothing Sir. Sorry Sir," Zack quickly apologised, narrowly remembering now was not the time to annoy anyone.

I took another deep breath before I answered.

"I understand why you find it difficult to trust me Zaphire. I'm so sorry for having captured you. At the time it seemed like it was the only option I had, to maintain my cover. I hadn't foreseen you would be used as a pawn by Rick or that he would hurt you. It was a spur of the moment action and I'll always regret it. However, I have always only had one aim whilst I was with my father; to take him and his organisation down. I'm totally and absolutely loyal to our Sensorian Community and its beliefs and values. I can't say anything else to convince you or anyone else who struggle to trust me."

I tried to catch Zaphire's eye during my little speech, but she stubbornly looked down to the floor. She was cloaking to the max and I couldn't work out if what I'd said had made any impact on her. Zack had moved closer to me, grabbed my hand and gave it a little squeeze. I knew he felt for me and he found it hard not to help me fight my battle. A warm feeling spread across my whole body. He noticed, and promptly let go of my hand. I hated this.

"Thank you Miss Mankuzay. We'll take your explanation into account when we decide how to deal with you," Frank dismissed me, leaving me feeling a little bemused. It looked like I had to wait a little longer to find out what my fate would be.

"Zaphire. Step forward please," Frank ordered. "The leadership was extremely disappointed with your decision to break your promise to Markus and Laura. You were grounded and they gave you the benefit of the doubt to let you go and see Laura. You betrayed their trust by going off to find Eliza, by yourself."

"What the hell were you thinking?!" Markus butted in, not able to contain himself any longer. He was fuming and I was glad Frank was there to calm things down.

"Markus, Sir. Let me handle this, as agreed," Frank interjected sternly.

"Do you have anything to say Zaphire?"

"Not much, Sir. I wanted to find out for myself what was going on with Eliza. I paid the price for my selfish action."

"We agree with you. It was a poorly thought out, childish action. You have no excuse for your behaviour, other than being immature. We're going to remember that in any future mission you are involved with. You'll go back to basic training as you are clearly not ready for responsibility and you need to be closely monitored, like a child," Frank condemned. "And that's the same for Sam, who should have resisted your request for help and reported you to Laura."

Ouch. That was embarrassing. I could feel Zaphire's shame flood the room, not able to cloak it. Sam shuffled shyly out of the way, wanting to hide as well. She declined to speak up for herself when given the opportunity.

"Zaphire, you won't be punished any further than that. You've had to endure your imprisonment by Jean-Pierre and had time to regret your impulsive actions.

Sam, you will go into isolation for two weeks to think about your actions."

As always they were so damned fair. Though I'm sure Zaphire would rather have had a stiff talking to and isolation than the humiliation she just had to endure. It did make me a bit worried they hadn't told me my punishment. I got the feeling that was not good news.

CHAPTER 61
Zack

Fuck. Was I glad it was Frank leading this meeting! The outcome would be the same, but it was bound to be much less painful without Markus' temper flaring. I already felt exhausted dealing with all the emotions banded about in the room and the effort it took to shield from it. That's why they left me to last, I'm sure. I felt sorry for Brody, who really wasn't to blame for any of this. He'd just been a good friend. I hoped they would be lenient on him. After they spoke to him and he had his say, which wasn't much, it finally was my turn to step forward. Markus' stare was unbearable. It was anger and disappointment rolled into one. I tried to ignore it as much as I could.

"Zacharya. I don't quite know where to start with you. Most of the time your decision making is impeccable and it's always a pleasure to work with you on a mission. You are loyal, clever, reliable and hard working, and you always have everyone's back. So this is hard. We can't ignore your blatant insubordination on this mission, which has led to the tragic death of Sonia, Ned's coma, Rob and Michael's injuries, Zaphire's kidnapping and ultimately the forced release of Rick. That is not a pretty list, is it Zack?"

"No Sir."

I hung my head and lowered my eyes. This was indeed a disaster. I knew I'd fucked up monumentally. I sensed Eliza stirring behind me. I hoped she would keep quiet and not make this any worse for herself or me. But no. Of course she didn't fucking keep quiet. It was Eliza after all.

"Sir, may I please speak?" her voice a little more shy than normal.

Frank allowed her.

"I know Zack was ultimately responsible for me. That was his task. But and this is a big but, I didn't give him a choice. I would have done it with or without his help. He could have told you what I was planning, but I would have denied it. I would have ended up in that cell one way or the other, and word would have come out. He decided to help me as the lesser of two evils. To protect me. And the plan worked to start with. I just hadn't foreseen what happened with Zaphire and by then we were so far into we couldn't turn back. I hope you can take this into consideration. Thank you for letting me speak, Sir."

Damn. She had learned a lot. A couple of months

ago, she would never have spoken to our leaders the way she did now. I afforded her a little smile. I didn't think her defence of my actions was going to change any of their minds, but it was sweet and well meant.

Frank glanced over at Markus and Laura. I got the feeling Markus wanted severe punishment, but Frank and Laura were leaning towards a more sensible consequence.

"Thank you Eliza. We're aware of your manipulation skills. It has just shown us we have given you all too much responsibility too soon. We're partly to blame. The problem is that we have difficult times ahead. Rick will resurface at some point and there's a real danger that too many ordinary people are on to us. Many are aware of our gift at the moment and it will be hard to quash all rumours about us. Our community needs to be as tight as ever, with everyone obeying our rules. Having our most promising Sensorian breaking those rules left, right and centre is not conducive to this. As a consequence to your actions Zack, you'll have to earn back our trust before you can resume your role as a trainer and mission leader."

It was like being punched in the stomach. I had expected it, but it still fucking hurt. Was I even allowed to say anything in my defence? The others had been given the opportunity to express themselves. I was going to risk it. Couldn't fucking get any worse anyway.

"Sir, may I have permission to speak?"

Frank gave me the nod, but if people had heckles, Markus' definitely stood on end. I had to be ever so fucking careful.

"Markus, Sir, and the rest of the leadership and team, I just wanted to say how deeply sorry I am for my actions and the dreadful things that have happened as a result of those. I realise how much I have disappointed you, Markus and Laura. You're right, I made the wrong decision this time, but it wasn't a decision I took lightly. I truly believed it was for the good of the mission. Mission comes first is our motto after all. So, maybe wrongly, I put the mission before being truthful to you. It killed me to do so. I've never been in such a dilemma before. But I made that decision. I took the responsibility and I'm proud of that, no matter what. The aim of the mission was to bring Rick's organisation down and capture him. We have nearly achieved one of the aims, and I ask you not to forget that. I still believe that we wouldn't have been able to do that if Eliza hadn't managed to infiltrate the way she did. Things don't always go as planned and I will bear the consequences, but I refuse to be accused of not being trustworthy or irresponsible. I take my responsibilities extremely seriously and will always put our community and the mission first, whatever the consequences and you know you can rely on that."

Okay, I'd said my piece. Now I waited for the fallout.

Markus asked to speak. Frank allowed him, but with a heavy warning to keep it calm. *Fuck*. I hoped he listened.

"Zack. You have so much potential and you know that," Markus started but paused. I could feel the tension mount. I looked at Frank, who was entirely focussed on Markus. Willing him to remain calm. "But you can also be bloody stubborn and an arrogant dick."

"Language," Frank interjected. Markus took a deep breath.

"You need to realise you're still young and contrary to what you believe, you don't know everything. You can't go behind your superior's back. I just don't understand how you don't get that! In any other job, your arse would be out on the street by now."

He paused for a moment. I kept quiet.

"I'm going to ask you a question now and you have to answer truthfully. We'll all know if you cloak, so don't. What your answer is will determine what consequences you will face. Do you understand?"

"Yes Sir," I knew what was coming and I knew I was going to fail it. Disappoint Markus again.

"Knowing what you know now, would you have taken the same course of action?"

He fired the question at me like a bullet. His eyes distant.

I took my time to answer.

"Hindsight is a beautiful thing. I think it's an unfair question Sir," I tried to deflect.

Markus took a long slow breath.

"Zack. I'm just so disappointed and bloody angry right now. I don't feel I can trust you anymore. Don't shield. I want you to feel this and remember it," he warned.

His anguish burnt. My eyes watered.

"You can trust me to be loyal Sir," I whispered. My throat felt tight.

"Take over please Frank," he growled.

"What Markus wants to know is, if this situation or similar happened again, would you tell the leadership," Frank clarified, demanding a real answer.

"I honestly don't know if I would Sir," I answered truthfully, condemning myself to the worst case scenario punishment. I felt fucking sick.

CHAPTER 62
Zaphire

My brother was indeed a stubborn arrogant dick. Markus was absolutely right. But how I admired Zack for it. This time anyway. He was right, he probably would do exactly the same again if he thought it was the best way. He's a leader and makes decisions, popular or not. They will always be at loggerheads over this. I sneaked a little peak at Eliza. She looked apprehensive. She also had admiration in her eyes for my brother. The bitch.

"Fine. That settles it then. Over to you Markus," Frank grumbled. He wasn't happy with the situation at all. He probably had worked out some reasonable consequences for both Eliza and Zack, but Markus had insisted on asking this question and base the punishment on the outcome. It looked like Markus had pulled rank and was getting his way. Poor Zack. All because of Eliza and her stupid plan. Talking about arrogance. How that girl thought she was ready to do this after only a few months of knowing about her gift, I'll never know! Zack was a good trainer, but that was ridiculous, whatever Zack believed.

"I will start with Brody. Stand up." Markus ordered, who had taken over the meeting again.

Brody complied.

"You should've known better than to go along with Zack and turning a blind eye to his actions. I do admire your loyalty to your friend but that's not how this organisation works. You're going in isolation for one month plus back to basic training after."

"Yes Sir," Brody sighed.

Sam and I seemed to have got off lightly. At least both of us would be active soon, albeit as trainees. We would work ourselves out of that pretty quickly, I'm sure.

Next Zack was up. He stood stoically facing Markus. Hands behind his back. He was cloaking but I could still read him. He was pissed off but had resigned himself to whatever was coming his way.

"Beside the fact you are temporarily relieved from your duties as a trainer and mission leader until further notice, you will serve six months in isolation working on compliance to rules and anger management."

Six friggin' months! Half a bloody year. Zack's face gave nothing away, but that was harsh.

"Yes Sir," he answered without hesitation.

I hoped Eliza would get the same or worse. It

would mean I wouldn't have to deal with her, or my conflicting feelings for her. Of course my love for her hadn't been switched off like a light, I just felt so bitter and betrayed by her. I could never let her into my heart again. The longer she was put away, the better.

Eliza was up now. She looked nervous and shocked over Zack's punishment.

"Eliza. You will be serving a minimum of six months in isolation, working on compliance to rules. You will be allowed to work on your Visual Hacking. You will be given targets to work to, and your progress on those will determine whether your confinement ends in six months."

She looked mortified. Her legs nearly gave away. She couldn't speak and just nodded. Markus didn't let her get away with it and forced to answer properly. She choked it out. Tears ran over her cheeks, but she stood tall, having recovered after her initial wobble. I remembered how hard she found the month in isolation before and I knew she would find the next six months almost unbearable. Still, I was with Markus. I was satisfied. She needed to suffer. Zack displayed more emotion over her punishment than his own. It was so obvious he still loved this girl, despite his recent closeness to Phaedra. *How could he.*

Their isolation started straight away. No goodbyes allowed. Zack, Eliza, Sam and Brody were led away in silence. I felt a little pang of sympathy for Alice. I liked her a lot and she would take the six months separation hard. I actually felt empty and a little despondent myself. I loved my brother deeply and part of me was going to be locked away in there with him. It was our twentieth birthday in a few days and I wasn't going to celebrate that without him. How depressing.

I checked Markus and Laura. Laura actually wiped away a little tear. She was upset not to see Zack for so long. Markus on the other hand look grim but satisfied. He thought he had done the right thing. But I knew it wasn't going to make an iota of difference in Zack's future decisions.

Laura's feelings toward me were ambivalent. I knew she felt hurt because I had taken advantage of her protectiveness over me. She had defied Markus and let me come over and I had used it to go and find Eliza. There was no glossing over it and pretending it had just happened, that it had been without premeditation. I had some apologising to do. I hoped she'd forgive me soon.

A sudden change of atmosphere in the room caught my attention. Tristan had turned on his phone and let out a gasp. Everyone looked up at him immediately alarmed at the signals he was emitting. Whatever it was it wasn't good.

"Check your phone. Check the news," he managed to utter.

Everyone quickly switched their phones on. Gasps all over. Overwhelming stench filled the room.

Shit. I felt sick to the stomach. This was bad. Very bad.

ACKNOWLEDGEMENTS

I would like to start with thanking my husband Steve for his support and patience helping me with the computer side of things. A lot of patience was needed! He still hasn't read either book though, so it's my little revenge on him. The rest of the family have also been fantastic, and with this book in particular, my youngest daughter Hanneke, who very patiently (and eagerly) listened to me reading out loud to her, helping me identify potential pitfalls in grammar and use of language. Also thank you to Nienke who still helps me with promotion and the occasional advice and Bentley, who just lets me get on with it, with an occasional grunt if he happened to read something over my shoulder.

My little army of proof readers, Clare, Annemarie, Carol and Margot have been amazing and super encouraging. Without them the book would be a mess grammatically and spelling wise, plus the occasional gap in the plot! Thank you all so much!

The blurb was another chore which I couldn't have done without Clare, Annemarie, Margot and Denise. Multiple texts backwards and forwards were needed to get to the end result.

Last but not least a huge thank you to Miquel, who designed the awesome cover which, I believe, is even more beautifully weird than the first one! You can see more of his work on www.lumigo-film.com or on his Insta account @luismiquelgonzalez

AUTHOR PAGE

I hope you enjoyed the second book in The Sensorians Trilogy and that it lived up to your expectations!

I would be super grateful and honoured if you would take the time to leave a short (or long!) review on Amazon and GoodReads. It helps us Indie authors enormously.

I am currently working on book 3 and aiming to publish that by summer 2021. For up to date information visit my Insta account: Brigitte__books or my Facebook Account: Brigittewritesbooks.

Hope to hear from you soon!

Brigitte

Printed in Poland
by Amazon Fulfillment
Poland Sp. z o.o., Wrocław